Blood Ties
(Thalia Series, Book 3)

Kiraran

Ukiyoto Publishing

All global publishing rights are held by

Ukiyoto Publishing

Published in 2023

Content Copyright © Kiraran

ISBN 9789360160647

All rights reserved.

No part of this publication may be reproduced, transmitted, or stored in a retrieval system, in any form by any means, electronic, mechanical, photocopying, recording or otherwise, without the prior permission of the publisher.

The moral rights of the author have been asserted.

This is a work of fiction. Names, characters, businesses, places, events, locales, and incidents are either the products of the author's imagination or used in a fictitious manner. Any resemblance to actual persons, living or dead, or actual events is purely coincidental.

This book is sold subject to the condition that it shall not by way of trade or otherwise, be lent, resold, hired out or otherwise circulated, without the publisher's prior consent, in any form of binding or cover other than that in which it is published.

www.ukiyoto.com

Contents

A Handsome Visitor	1
Trouble in a Bottle	8
Define Babysitting	15
Puberty	19
What Party?	29
Escort	41
It's PRINCESS Rose	53
Belle of the Ball	58
Party Crasher	67
Connection	77
Escape Plan	82
History	88
Bloodline	93
Weapon Room	99
New Morning Routine	105
Liliana	111
Vision	116
Linked Dream	124
Chimera and Nagga	130
How to confess	135
Happily Ever After	143
Party Prep	150
Daniel	155
By The Shore	168
The Second Prince of the Sea	177
LADY Grace	183
Princess Mississippi Bloom Shakalaka	191
Calling of the Tamer	200

Aftermath	208
New King of Atla	214
Knights	222
Ghost of The Castle	233
Hazy Dream	239
Drunken Magic	248
Ouija Board	256
Enchantment	266
About the Author	*271*

A Handsome Visitor

I stay on my bed, staring at the ceiling. I have just awoken and desperately want to go back to sleep, but I couldn't. When I think about the reality that was brought to me the other day, I don't know how to go back.

I suppose I finally got some abilities, but at the expense of being a princess.

A real princess with actual royal blood. Who would have thought of that? For sure, it wasn't me. I would never have imagined that I would be someone relevant - not to mention that I come from a royal family.

No offense to my royal ancestors, but have they met me? I barely graduated from table etiquette! They can ask Prince Nate for an evaluation on that.

Thinking about food, my stomach suddenly growled.

I'm hungry. Now that is definitely a good reason to get out of bed this early.

I hurried and changed. As I did, I stepped on something and heard a whimper. It's Custard, whose tail I accidentally stepped on.

Custard is a little brown baby wolf. He looks as harmless as a puppy in this form, but when he is in his beast mode, he becomes this big, bad white demon wolf—as the twins like to call him. Also, he is my familiar that I bonded with.

"Sorry, Custard. I didn't see you there." I wince out of sympathy for my spirit partner. "What do you say we go down and get something to eat? Though I don't know what you eat. Can I get you some milk?" Custard's only response is a tilt of his head. "I take that as a yes. Come on, boy." I beckon him to follow, which Custard happily obliges as we make our way to the kitchen.

I ask one of the servants to make me some eggs for breakfast when we get to the kitchen so I can go get some milk from the storage area. After that, I searched for a bowl that Custard could use. I pour milk into the bowl and place it on the ground. Custard sniffs it for a bit before licking it clean.

"Wow, you sure love milk," I observe while watching the little wolf in fascination. I'd never had a pet before, but if getting warm and excited was the feeling of getting one, then I consider myself fortunate to have Custard.

I wonder if I should give it more milk?

"Well, look, brother. It's the princess." I have to fight a groan the moment I hear the twins making their approach.

"Hush, brother. Rose doesn't like being called a princess. You might bring out one of her *moods*."

"You mean her *beast mood?*" Dan says, and they both start laughing.

My veins are pulsing with rage at their joke. "Say, guys. Would you like some milk?" I ask nicely and raise the pitcher of milk I have in my hands.

"Of course!" Dan answers without hesitation.

"Wow. Who are you, and what did you do with the real Rose?" Ren looks at me skeptically at my sudden change of mood.

"Brother, brother, brother, Rose is now a *changed* woman. She's a real princess now, so it is only natural that she would become kind and gentle like a real princess." Dan places a hand on Ren's shoulder while he gestures the other one to where I am standing.

"You are absolutely right, brother. *Change* is good." Ren nods in agreement before turning to face me with a contented grin, along with his twin.

It took all of my willpower not to pour the milk over their heads as I grabbed two extra bowls, poured milk in them, and dropped them on the floor in front of the twins. I put on a self-satisfied smile at their perplexed gazes.

"Dig in," I say sweetly.

The twins look at the bowls at their feet before looking back at me. Dan closes his eyes and rubs the back of his neck before leaning close to his twin.

"She's mad," Dan whispers to his brother.

"I can see that!" Ren responds and elbows his twin for being too close to him.

"Princess, your breakfast is ready." While the twins were jabbing each other, one of the housekeepers informed me.

"Coming. Let's go, Custard." I shov the pitcher of milk into Ren's hands and rush past them. "Excuse me, boys. My breakfast is ready."

"Princess, no running in the palace!" They scream in unison, but I ignore them.

The maids place my food on the table, and Custard accompanies me by sitting on the empty seat next to me.

"That looks good." Nate comments behind me.

Oh, boy. So much for a peaceful breakfast.

"Hey," I greet him, trying my best to be civil.

"Hey, back. How are you?" Nate wonders and takes the other vacant seat at my other side.

"Doing good. I gave the twins milk in a bowl earlier." I unconsciously smirk as I recall the memory before cutting through the eggs on my plate.

Nate laughs. "Let me guess? They pissed you off?"

"Yep." I nod. "It's too early in the morning and I have no energy to deal with them at the moment."

Nate looks at the way I use my utensils and frowns. "Elbows down when you cut, Rose. You are a princess now. Better practice it properly."

And there it was again. A princess.

I didn't even bother to finish cutting my eggs. Instead, I place both utensils on the table as I got up.

"Hey, where are you going? You are not finished. It's bad manners to-"

"Lost my appetite. Come on, Custard." I head out of the dining area with Custard following behind me.

Seriously, they need to stop reminding me that I am a real princess. Can they give me a break from something? Or talk about other things besides me being a princess?! This day just keeps getting worse. I wish that they could just get the hint that I don't want to talk about it just yet.

I was about to walk through the door when it suddenly opened, and in walked a man dressed in fancy clothes, carrying a case of some sort.

I can't help but catch my breath when I look up at him.

"Hey, Rose. How are you? I heard the news and came here as fast as I—"

"Fred!" I squeal with glee, rushing forward to embrace him.

Finally, something good happens today.

I catch him off guard, and we nearly fall to the ground. Luckily, he is able to balance us. Fred laughs and pats my hair.

"I miss you too, Rose."

"What are you doing here?"

Fred is just about to answer when someone else speaks for him. "He's here because the queen called him. We need Prince Fred's help to know more about Tamer magic in order to help you." PRINCE Ace says, who has mysteriously sneak behind us. What a creep.

He is the most ungrateful, snobbish, rude, and spoiled bastard among the princes. He's an elf with some kind of weird mumbo jumbo magic that gives him the ability to see and communicate with animals and control plants.

"PRINCE Ace, nice to see you again," Fred waves in greeting.

"You too." Ace nods. I doubt that he feels the same way. I figure that he might just be saying that out of formality.

A servant suddenly comes into view, and Ace gestures for her to approach. "Please follow me while he takes your luggage to your previous room."

"Hey, we haven't talked yet. Come on! I haven't even introduced him to Custard." Beside me, Custard barks when his name is called.

"And now you have." Ace states while looking at my wolf with a frown. "There will be more talking later once we finish."

"Custard bite," It give the order as a joke, of course. But to Custard, I guess he assumes it as a command. He turns to Ace, but upon seeing the sharpness of the elf prince's gaze, Custard's ears flatten themselves on his head.

Impressive. Even a spirit wolf is afraid of the elf PRINCE. Who knows, maybe Custard sees that an evil spirit is possessing Ace, which explains his demonic mood all the time.

"Try it, you little devil, and you will become a literal spirit when I am done with you."

"But that may or may not kill me too." It is just an assumption that I have because of the bond. It hasn't been proven yet, and I haven't asked the queen if it is real.

"A double kill. Perfect." Ace seems like he is considering the thought, which frightens me enough to grab Custard and move him away from Ace.

"Freadiekins!" Just before I could retort, the twins came into view along with Nate.

"Fred, what are you doing here? I mean, it's great that you are here. I just want to know why." Dan asks, crossing his arms over his chest while looking at Fred with a raise brow.

Fred laughs at his expression. "I'm here because the queen asked if she could have my assistance doing a little research about Rose's records. Nothing more."

Call it weird, but I feel like Fred is assuring Dan of something.

"Good. That is very good, Prince Fred. Thank you." Dan grins, looking relieved.

Ren and I share a perplex look as we watch Fred and Dan exchanging words. "Am I missing something here?"

"Fred, why don't you go up first and rest. When you are ready, just look for the queen in the l-library." Ace stutters at the library part. He seems to be bothered by being forbidden from the library for a week, just as the twins are required to practice sword fighting, and Nate banned from talking to me even though he still does it secretly.

Maybe I should go and tell the queen about it later. That way, Nate's punishment will increase.

I smile at the thought. It would serve him right for disrupting my breakfast earlier.

"Oh, by the way, Prince Nate. The queen says she will give you one last warning for talking to girls. Especially Rose." Ace tells him as if he had read my mind at some point.

Nate's green eyes widen, and he fearfully looks around like he assumes the queen is spying on our group at this very moment. "How did—"

"Never underestimate the queen." Ace cuts him off. He looks at Fred and gives him a curt nod before leaving.

"Well then," Fred stretches his back. "I guess I should go rest. Rose, we'll talk more later, after I see the queen."

Is it a date? Is he asking me out on a date?

I can't help but smile silly at his offer. "Sure!" I didn't mean to, but I sound excited when I said it aloud.

Fred turns back and heads upstairs to his room, leaving me with Custard, Ren, Dan, and Nate.

"Well, that was nice. Hey, brother. What do you say we go out and practice — uhh — our sword fighting?" Ren turns to Dan.

"Do we have to?" Dan whines and slumps his body like a deflated balloon.

"Yeah, you do. *Never underestimate the queen.*" I say it, imitating Ace's voice and accent earlier.

Ren laughs and looks at me with his arms cross. "Yeah, yet you are not wearing the required heels for you." At that, I immediately stiffen.

"W-Well, I was hungry, and I....forgot. Plus, I let Custard chew on a few of them last night." I mumble the last part while avoiding eye contact.

Dan moves to my side and rests his arm on my shoulder. "Alright. We'll pretend we didn't hear that on one condition."

"What?" As I turn to him with a suspicious expression on my face, I slap his arm away. Something about this makes me feel uneasy.

I guess I probably should have kept the heel part to myself so they wouldn't have any sort of leverage on me.

"You need to watch us practice our sword fight. Wouldn't you want that, brother?"

Ren turns at Dan skeptically, probably having the same thought as me about his proposal. "Sure. That's okay, I guess."

"That settles it then. Let's go!" Before I can react, Dan is already pulling me out to the training grounds situated at the back of the castle.

Trouble in a Bottle

The whole morning went by with me watching the twins do their sword fight and Nate sitting a few spaces away from me to avoid a conversation.

As I watch the twins practice their fighting skills, I can't help but notice that Dan is purposely making himself lose to Ren, which Ren doesn't appreciate judging from the look of annoyance on his face.

"Don't you think Dan is taking this too much?" Nate says to Custard, which is his way of talking to me without exactly speaking with me. "Don't you think so, Custard?" Nate cooes and pets the little wolf, who is lying on his lap. Honestly, in such a short period of time, those two have become the best of friends, which is astounding considering their first impression with each other isn't that good.

"Uh-huh." I agree.

"That is it, Dan!" I jump a bit when Ren throws his sword on the ground in anger. "I don't know what your problem is, brother, but this has to stop *now*. Stop pretending to lose!"

"What did you say, brother? I can't hear you with all the bruises you gave me. Ow!" Dan acted up again and falls to the ground as if he's in pain.

"Stop it, Dan!"

"Stop what?" Dan blinked innocently at Ren, which only fueled his anger.

"If you won't fight seriously, then don't blame me if you lose an arm or two." Ren picks up his sword and brings it down to Dan, which Dan quickly parries.

"Hey, hey, hey. Watch my injuries. They are *tender*."

"If you have injuries, then you wouldn't be able to raise your sword."

"Hmm. You have a point there - Woah! And a rather *sharp one*." Dan quickly jumps to his feet and bounces back to avoid Ren's attack.

Ren grins. "You better run now, brother."

"Ohh, scary." Dan mocks and shakes his bum at Ren teasingly. "But you have to catch me first, brother!" And with that, Dan suddenly runs and jumps to the nearest window to get inside the castle.

"Dan, get back here!" Ren yells and follows Dan.

"I think we should go after them, Custard. Don't you agree?" Nate suggests.

"No, thanks. I rather stay here. Cardio isn't in my agenda — Eek! Nate, what the hell!?" I shriek just as Nate swoops me off of my feet. He carries Custard and I as he jumps in the window to pursue the twins.

"We could use the door like a *normal* person, but yeah, this works too." I am a little surprise by what had just happened. But considering that I live in a castle with supernatural princes, I was ashamed that I was even startled by it.

Ren charges his brother. Dan doesn't seem to falter as he makes farting gestures at Ren before he bolts up the stairs.

Of course, Ren follows, seething with rage at Dan's constant tease.

Before we pursue, Nate and I exchange glances. They make shambles wherever they go. The floor was littered with broken curtains, vases, and flower petals.

"The queen isn't going to be happy about this," Nate mutters.

I couldn't agree more with his statement and was already considering suggesting that we move as far away from the twins as possible.

The twins suddenly turned to a corner and got in a room where they continued to fight. Nate and I got in to see them jumping on a massive bed while slashing and stabbing each other.

"Stop running!" Ren growls.

"I'm not running. I am jumping!" Dan says with glee like he is enjoying being pursued.

"Hey, aren't we…" Nate trails off as he looks around the room.

I take a good look around us, or more specifically, the room we entered. Polished white floor, intricately designed red walls, a large bed against the far wall, and a piece of familiar luggage beside the bed I kept a close eye on. I suddenly remembered where I had seen it. Fred had brought it with him this morning. That can only mean one thing…

"We are in Fred's room," I say all too dreamily that made Nate give me a look.

"Great. The Princess is in her dreamland, which means you and I," he addresses himself and Custard. "need to drag those annoying brats out."

As soon as he said 'annoying brats', a vase came out of nowhere and hit his head. It shatters, and broken pieces rain down on his head.

I cover mouth with my hands, suppressing a gasp before I look at him worriedly, expecting blood on his hair, which seems kind of difficult since Nate's hair is already blood-red in color.

"N-Nate?" To my relief, Nate seems unharmed as he gently places Custard back on the ground and dusts the broken shards from his hair. Either he was unharmed because of his vampire blood or because he's simply just hard-headed.

I'm betting on both.

"Are you…?" I trail off when Nate looks directly at me. He gives me a sweet smile, but his eyes are already telling me stories on what he plans to do with the twins.

"Excuse me for a moment, Princess." He says before vanishing from my sight.

Nope, not vanishing, but running towards the twins at an incredible speed. The twins sees him charging and jumps out of the bed as they fought Nate, who looks murderous as he hit them with a pillow.

I know this is the time for me to intervene with them, but let's just say the picture of three handsome princes charging and ramming each other is such a sight to see. The scenery alone makes me want to drag a chair and eat popcorn as I watch them tearing each other apart.

~~It was fascinating.~~

I was suddenly broken from my trance when Ren, stupid Ren, opens Fred's bag and pulls out a bottle filled with blue liquid. "This looks nice."

That catches Nate's attention as he pushes Dan off of him to glare at Ren. "Rutledge, put that down!" That is all he can say since he doesn't know which twin is which.

"Nope," Ren grins and starts to play with the bottle in his hands. Nate grunts and charges Ren, but Ren has other ideas.

"Brother, catch!" Ren tosses the bottle to Dan, who easily jumps up and catches it in mid-air.

"Fangster, you were after this?" Dan teasingly shakes the bottle at Nate, which only infuriates him.

"Hey, you two put it back now!" It is now my turn to intervene as I march up to them.

"You heard the princess, brother. Put it back." Dan tosses the bottle to Ren.

"Me? You put it back." Ren tosses the bottle to Dan.

"Rose's orders."

"She asks you."

"But she prefers you."

And their throwing continues each time they say their lines.

"I DON'T CARE WHO PUTS IT BACK! JUST RETURN IT TO WHERE YOU GOT IT!" I yell.

"What's going on here?" We all stiffen up in response to the voice and focus our attention to the door. Fred and PRINCE Ace enter the room. Fred appears amused, whereas Ace appears annoyed. At that moment, all I could do was smile and wave like a fool as they approach.

"Hi." I greet them.

"Hey, Rose." At least Fred responded.

"Yo, Fred!" Dan yells and waves the bottle in the air. Fred was about to wave back until he saw the bottle in Dan's hand. "Sorry for touching your stuff. Here, catch!" And just like that, Dan tosses the bottle to Fred.

"Be careful with that!" Fred warns them.

Too late. Dan flings the bottle and causes it to strike the chandelier above our heads. Along with the shattered glasses, whatever liquid was in the bottle rained down on us after the bottle broke.

"Take cover!" When the bottle broke, Fred grabbed Custard and I to protect us from the glass and liquid falling on us.

The princes scream, and when the liquid hit Fred, I see him shudder. Due of my concern about what that weird liquid would do to us, I screamed as well.

Finally, it is all over. At first, I felt Fred's weight on me, then suddenly, all I was holding on to was his coat.

Or more like….his clothes…?

"Fred!?" I scream when I see his clothes on the floor. I look around the room to see that the others have also disappeared, except for their clothing, which is now on the floor.

In that moment, all I can hear is the rapid racing of my heart and the panic in my voice as I desperately call for them. "Fred! Ren! Nate! Dan! Ace! Where are you!?" I get up and circle around the room, my mind feeling empty as I do not know what to do.

"Guys, come out! This is not funny! Not funny at all!"

Still no answer.

Somehow, that liquid from the bottle…erased them. Flesh and all.

Now they are gone.

I'm starting to panic, but I quickly remind myself that I can't solve anything by sitting here.

"The queen." I suddenly blurt out. If anyone knows what happened to them and how to bring them back, it is the queen. I have to go to her and tell her what happened.

Custard barks at me. Or rather, at the pile of clothes that the princes left. "Yes, Custard. I know they are gone. You don't have to remind me." I sniffle and felt pain in my chest when I said it out loud. "B-But no worries, Custard. I'm sure the queens would know how to fix this. I hope." Custard just ignores me and continues to bark. He is even stuffing his nose in Fred's clothes.

"Hey, not fair, Custard. Show some respect. Even I—" Fred's clothes suddenly moves, which make me shriek. In a blink of an eye, I am already across the room. I think it is pretty obvious by now what kind of coward I am. "W-WHAT THE–"

Fingers emerged from Fred's clothes. Tiny fingers like the hands of a toddler. I observe when the strange thing shakes Fred's coat from its head. It's a…kid?

Curiously I move away from Custard to get a full view. Upon closer look, I notice something. This kid has blond hair and eyes as blue as the sky. It smile and reach out for me in recognition. "Wr-Wrose."

"What?"

"Wrose!" It says again.

"I really can't understand you with you baby talk, but let's just get one thing clear…I AM NOT YOUR MOTHER!" I point at the child, moving back a little and dragging Custard with me. I am not ready for such a responsibility yet.

"Wose!" It says again. To my surprise, I somehow understand him when I gaze into his eyes. I pause.

"Are you trying to say…Rose?"

"Y-Yes…" The kid smiles, and when he does, my heart skips a beat. I know that smile anywhere.

"Fred?!"

The kid nods shyly.

I gulp.

I may be stupid, but I am not that stupid to realize what I am about to face. "I-If you became a kid, then that means…" I trail off as my eyes wander and stare at the pile of clothes that the princes left.

"Oh, boy." I sigh.

As if on cue, the pile of clothes starts to shift until heads pops out of their expensive coats. I first noticed Nate looking like he had just woken up from a nap. Then came the twins, as they faced each other in wonder. The last one was PRINCE Ace trying to fit himself in his coat, but it seemed that it was too big for him.

Beside me, Custard let out a small whimper.

"Yeah, you are absolutely right, Custard," I mutter, feeling conflicted on what to feel at this very moment. "This is bad because I am never fond of children in the first place."

Define Babysitting

"Can you please bring me five pairs of trousers, t-shirts, and shoes fit for um…..say, 5-year-old kids?" I was in my room talking to a maid just outside my room. I left the door slightly open to talk to her without showcasing my room where the baby princes were.

"Yes, princess. As you wish." The maid wears a strange look on her face at my request, and I feel the urge to throw in some sort of excuse.

"I-It's my hobby! I….want to um…..dress my pillows and pretend that they are kids. You know. Practice for parenthood. Aha…ha…" I add a nervous laugh that ended in a choke. I am so embarrassed that I literally want to drown myself in my bathtub.

Fortunately, the maid didn't say anything more as she left to get me what I asked for. As soon as she's gone, I let out a sigh of relief and lock the door behind me.

After the princes became babies, I immediately rushed them into my room, wearing only their oversize T-shirts and polo shirts. Well, of course, Custard helped me since the twins seemed to find his tail fascinating and used it as bait for them to follow us. I figured that if anyone else saw the princes in this state, it would cause an uproar. If only I could get to the queen, maybe she knows how to turn the princes back to normal. Of course, I cannot do that with them wearing…well, something inappropriate.

"Gimme! That is my pillow I found." I see baby Nate pulling on one of my pillows that the twins are sitting on. His red hair is in a tangled mess as he fights with the twins.

"You left! You left! Therefore, it is ours." Baby Dan says, holding on to his big brother, baby Ren.

"Don't be mean to my brother, vampire, or I will hit you." Baby Ren puffs out his chest, trying to look menacing, but from my point of view, instead of a bear, he looks like a teddy bear.

Baby Fred is where I left him—sitting on a chair while his eyes look around in wonder. As for BABY Ace, he keeps on trying to open my balcony door by jumping up and down. Well, actually, he already managed to open my window and is now about to jump—*wait....!*

"HOLY CRAP, ACE!!" I leap to my feet and dash for the balcony, where baby Ace was about to jump. I grab him just as this little devil was about to kill himself and carried him back to my room. To keep Ace from committing any more suicidal missions, I lock the balcony door and place a chair in front of it to serve as a barricade.

When I look down, I notice Ace glaring at me. I would have glared back if he were his old self, but looking at him now, chubby cheeks and all, I can't help but think of what a cute kid he can be that I begin to laugh.

"Stop laughing at me. I am a *PWINCE!*" He pouts and crosses his arms over his chest.

"Yeah, sure you are, your highness. Now, would you please go and sit somewhere and behave?"

"NO. Not until you help turn us back." I ponder about his words for a moment. Turn him back into a jerk? Ha! Not a chance.

At least not yet, anyway.

I want to enjoy seeing them as kids because…

…well, cuteness is enough of a reason!

"I'll give you a cookie." I bribe. And just like any kid, I see his mouth quiver and shake.

"F-Fine." He blushes and goes to another sofa chair to sit.

I sigh in relief, thinking that the worst is over, but I am wrong. On the ground next to my bed, Nate is sobbing.

Oh boy. Now what?

I get up from my chair and rush to Nate's side. "Hey, what's wrong?" I ask in my most gentle voice even though what I really want to do is let out a scream in frustration.

Baby Nate points at the twins. "They won't give me my pillow! T-They w-won't even l-l-let me sit on the b-bed!" He hiccups as he cries.

Geez. I forgot how petty kids at this age can be…

"There, there." I pat baby Nate's back to comfort him when he suddenly hugs me for comfort. I look at the twins, both looking guilty as they sit on my bed. "Why don't you let Nate on the bed?"

"H-He's a vampire. A-And he was being mean to my brother." Ren mutters while playing with his fingers.

"Even so. Nate is your friend, so be nice to him. How would you feel if I did the same to you as you did to Nate?"

At this, Ren looks at me with his bottom lips quivering. "Y-You'll *hate* me?" Ren's eyes squint and start to fill with tears.

Uh oh...

Before I can stop him, Ren starts crying.

"R-Ren? Hey, stop. I won't hate you. Please don't cry." I move to Ren to comfort him while still carrying Nate.

"Y-You made my brother cry. Y-You hate him....after all I did to make you two happy!" Dan starts spouting nonsense and joins the two as they cry.

Great. I have three crying kids! Now I want to cry too. Even Custard tried desperately to block their cries by covering his ears. After this, I don't think that I will ever be ready into becoming a mother...

As I am sitting on the bed trying to calm the three kids, I feel someone pulling my skirt. I look down to see Fred about to cry as well.

"Fred? What's wrong?"

"I-I hate crying." He whimpered as tears rolled down his cheeks.

Someone help me. I have four crying kids!

I look at the spot where I last saw Ace only to find him sleeping despite all the noise. Well, at least the little devil is sleeping and not crying. It must be nice to have no care in the world. Sometimes I wish that I could have his personality.

"Tell my brother you love him!"

"Don't hate me!"

"Give me my pillow."

"Stop crying, everyone. Rose will be sad!"

I am starting to get a headache with all of this. "Guys, please calm down, or I'll be the one to cry!" I burst out, which is not something that you should do when in the presence of children.

Naturally, it was only a half-joke, but as soon as I said it, everyone stopped sobbing. The four children in front of me were all staring at me with wide, watery eyes that they were desperately trying to hold back.

"Don't cry, Rose. Don't cry."

"My brother and I will be sad."

"I would give you my pillow. Just don't cry."

"I hate crying. Especially if it's Rose."

Well, this is awkward yet so sweet. Even as kids, they still care. This is so very touching that I couldn't help but smile. They even tried to wipe away their tears so I wouldn't see them.

"Thanks, guys." I smile, feeling an immense amount of relief that the worse is over.

Now, I understand my mom's saying that all kids are angels. She was absolutely right!

We suddenly heard a crash when the flower vase sitting at a table beside Ace fell. He looks at the broken vase first, then at me, with no remorse for breaking it, before scoffing and going back to sleep.

The four princes and I gawked at him for a while before exchanging glances with one another.

I take it back. Mom was wrong. Not all kids are angels. Some of them are rotten demons, like the one sitting on the sofa chair before us.

Puberty

The clothes arrive, and I have no plans on dressing them They may be kids, but they really aren't—if that makes any sense. So what I did was hand them their clothing and leave so they could change on their own. Fred, Nate, and Ace seemed to be doing fine dressing independently, whereas the twins used them to slap each other's butts.

"Hey, quit playing, you two, and get dressed," I am getting a little bit annoyed because these two have a hard time listening to me.

"Aw. You are no fun." Ren pouts.

"We are going on a little adventure." I say in a sing-song voice. By adventure, I meant looking for the queen.

I know that I am tricking them, but hey, they're kids. They're gullible. Plus, it's for their own good.

The twins share a look of excitement and hurries to the bathroom to change. I turn to Custard. "Please watch them and make sure they don't slip and die."

Custard whines a bit but follows after the twins.

"Turn us back." I look down to see baby Ace glaring up at me once again.

So cute!

For good measure, I decided to tease him. "I.Don't. Wanna."

This irritates him, and he looks pretty amusing when he bares his teeth at me. "I'm a PWINCE! Do as you are told." He angrily stomps his little feet to the ground.

"Nope. Not when you can't properly say PRINCE." I giggle, hoping that Ace won't remember any of this when we turn them back into adults.

"Urgh!" I laugh as I place a hand on Baby Ace's head, stopping his advance while he threw punches in the air in an attempt to reach me. "When I turn back—"

I laugh again. "I could do this all day. Ow!" BABY Ace steps on my foot. The little devil! I glare at him. "That wasn't very nice." In response, he stuck his tongue out at me.

The nerve!

The door to my bathroom opens, and Ren and Dan come out along with Custard. Both were now properly dressed, but their hair was in a mess.

"Aw. Look at you two." I cooed and forgot about BABY Ace as I walked towards the two to fix their hair. Dan was pretty cooperative and grinned as I combed his hair with my fingers. On the other hand, Ren doesn't want me to touch his hair, but in the end, I was able to fix it after a lot of bribing on my part with cookies.

"Alright then. We shall now go on an adventure to find the queen. Who's with me?" All responded positively, except for Fred, who was staring at the door.

"Fred? What's wrong?" I ask.

Fred pointed at the open door and said, "PWINCE Ace just left the room."

I look at the open door, and my jaw drops. How did that little twerp open it?! "Fred, why didn't you say something?"

"You were busy taking care of the twins, and I thought that if I disturbed you while you were busy, you would get angry and think of me as a nuisance. Am I—are you upset with me?" He sounds a little afraid at this point, and it makes me wonder if this was Fred when he was a baby.

Come to think of it, the princes haven't beent acting like themselves for a while now. They act more like kids than adults. Nate would not cry that easily, Ren and Dan aren't that childish, Fred isn't this quiet, and PRINCE Ace would not get so worked up over me messing with him (trust me, we fight all the time).

Perhaps the effect of that strange liquid not only turned them into babies from the outside but also from the inside?

No, wait. Thinking about it, the minute they turned into babies, they were more like themselves. But after a few hours, they started acting like... babies! Maybe the longer they are in this state, the more likely they are to act like they did during their childhood.

"Ren? Dan? Do you guys know the proper way to introduce yourself to someone with a higher title?"

"Yep," Dan nods

"You put two fingers up your nose and make farting sounds with your lips." Ren goes first before Dan follows with,

"Then you run as fast as you can so you will not get scolded."

Okay, not bad. I'm pretty sure their adult version could think of something like that.

"Nate? Do you know what fork to use on a salad?"

"Um...the big spoon?"

"That's for serving. But close." I shrug and turn to Fred. "Fred, do you know how to waltz?"

"Mom says I have two left feet, so I can't right now until she hires Mckenly. He's a famous dance instructor."

Well, that is good.

"WHO AM I KIDDING! YOU GUYS ARE REALLY TURNING INTO BRATS THE LONGER YOU SAY IN THAT FORM!" I scream when I suddenly realize that this might be more dangerous than I thought. "Argh! We have to find BRATTY Ace. ASAP!!"

Ren's eyes sparkle with mischief. "I declare a race!" he says, pumping his small fist in the air, while Dan immediately supported his brother's idiocy. "Whoever finds Ace first wins!!" Then the twins bolted out of the door.

"Hey, wait up!" Nate follow, and so does Fred—not wanting to be left alone.

"Wait! Don't you guys dare!"I scream, almost hurling my slippers at their heads to jolt them into reality. Then again, they are kids, which is too cruel. "After them, Custard!" My wolf and I run out of my room only to find out that the idiots split into two teams; Ren and Dan going one way and Nate and Fred on the other.

Now I am torn about which way I should go.

"Go where Fred goes. Yes!" I decided to do a mini fist bump because it is an opportunity to spend time with Fred. Custard snorts next to me and gives me a stern look before pulling my skirt. "What?" I raise my brow at my wolf buddy. "You are more worried about the twins since they are imbeciles compared to Fred and Nate —" I pause as I ponder over my words. "Oh, right."

Ren and Dan are the most rowdiest kids that I have ever met. Who knows what sort of trouble they would get themselves into if I don't find them first?

I sigh in disappointment. Sometimes, I feel like Custard may be smarter than he looks. He's like my little guiding conscience.

"Come on, Custard." Against my will, we head off to where the twins ran.

***

Finding the twins was a piece of cake, thanks to Custard. He was able to sniff them out in the garden, where Dan seem to be picking flowers while Ren is just standing there talking to his brother.

"Brother, don't pick on the flowers. They'll wither and die."

"Some sacrifices are to be made, brother. You are giving this to Princess Rose."

"Why me?" Ren whines just as I crawl behind them for a sneak attack.

"Ah-ha! I caught you, you little buggers. One more stunt like that, and I'll take your wolf nose away." Since they are acting like kids, why shouldn't I treat them like children?

Their hands shot up to cover their noses when I mentioned taking them.

"As if you can!" Dan challenges me.

"Yeah. Noses are permanent!"

"Well, then I'll use magic!" I smile wickedly.

"You can't use magic!" They both scream at me, startling me at how bratty attitude. Geez. You can tell that these two were spoiled.

"You ask for it!" I crouch down, pinch their noses, make a popping noise, and pretend to hold their noses in my hand. "Got your wolf noses!" I wave my empty fist in the air.

"Our noses!"

"Give us back our noses!" Ren cries while Dan seems to be on the verge of choking—as usual, he is the dramatic one. I just hope that he won't be so dramatic enough that he will forget how to breathe.

"If you come with me, I'll return them." I smile like a shady dealer, which I should be ashamed of considering that I am talking to children.

"Never!"

"You can't boss us!" Dan says, seeming to recover from his dramatic display of distress earlier.

"I'll throw your noses out." I say in a deadpan voice to let them know that I am serious. My patience with children seems to be getting thinner by the second.

"Like we care!" They say it in unison.

Stubborn little brats.

"Alright then." I threw their invisible noses away like a pro baseball player. The twins run past me, screaming and crying as they try to find their missing noses, while I just stand at the side and watch them panic.

I started laughing when I saw them running around the garden like their lives depended on it.

"My nose! My wolf nose!" Ren cries, digging through dirt.

"I am no longer beautiful." Dan, well, he is just sulking in the garden and letting his brother do the job. If I didn't know any better, I would say that he simply gave up on life at that moment.

I started laughing even harder. Such gullible kids!

I may not want to admit it, but I feel like I am doing this as payback for their constant pestering of me when they are in their adult forms.

Custard nips at my leg, making my attention turn to him.

"What?" I ask. Custard gives me a look of disapproval as I continue to tease the kids. "Oh, alright. Fine." I grumble. "Yo, snot faces. Come back here, and I'll give you your noses back."

When they didn't come, I added, "If you don't, I'll feed them to Custard."

The twins jump to their feet and run hurriedly back to me. Both were still rubbing their noses and had wet eyes from crying.

"Now listen here. I will return them if you guys will follow me and not cause any more trouble. I will curse your noses and turn them into pig noses if you do. Are we clear?" Both nodded at my threat.

"Good. Here you go." I lean forward and make a popping sound as I *push* their noses back in place. "Let's go and look for Fred and Nate. Custard, can you transform into that giant wolf again? To, you know, carry these two knuckleheads on your back?"

Custard's reply is a short bark and a wag of its tail. I'm guessing that means yes.

"What do I have to do?" I ask and Custard starts eyeing my fingers as a response. I remember right away how he changed the first time he took a drop of my blood. "You need blood? Alright. Here." As a gesture, I stick out my index finger for my wolf. Next, Custard nips at my fingers, drawing blood.

After that, we waited.

And waited.

And…waited.

Nothing is happening.

"I think you're broken." I point out. Custard glares at me, seemingly offended by my comment. "Sorry." I quickly apologise. "Why are you not transforming?" Custard gives no reply but just stares at me as if it were all my fault.

I feel silly that I am the only one here talking. With a sigh, I shake my head.

"Well, you know what, let's mind it later. We need to find the others."

Fred and Nate were not hard to find—really. Just listen to the maids screaming, and you can see Nate crawling under their skirts while Fred is standing in a corner, asking Nate to stop.

"She's wearing blue! Hers is white! Hers is....oops she's wearing an *invisible* one." Nate all but announces the colors of their underwear.

Fred appears relieved as soon as he sees us. I felt at ease as well, until I feel someone getting under my skirt. After I scream, Ren runs after Nate and smacks him in the head with his baby fist.

"Can't say he doesn't deserve it," I mumble after I help Nate get back on his feet. He's crying and glaring at Ren at the same time—you know, the typical children rivalry look.

"I'll get y-y-you b-b-back for that, m-m-mutt!" Nate hiccup with teary eyes, glaring at Ren.

"Don't blame him for stoping you. You were very rude." I flick Nate's forehead.

"Ow! Rose, that hurts!" Nate protests.

"There, there, no one cares, so let's go and find PWINCE Ace." I wave away his cries. While I was babysitting Stella, my little sister back home, I was pretty sure that I wasn't this stressed.

Nate pouts and fiddles with his hands. "Can you carry me? My head hurts from where Ren hit it." I feel bad for Nate because he looks like he's in a lot of pain. Vampire or not, right now, he is a kid.

"Well, okay. Get some sleep, and then—AHH!" I scream when I feel where baby Nate's hands were. "YOU ARE WALKING, YOU HEAR ME?! WALKING YOU BOOB GRABBING PERVERTED CHILD! WHERE IS YOUR INNOCENCE?!"

So, now that I found the four kids, we were on the lookout for PWINCE Ace. Custard tracked him down at first, and we ended up in front of the library. I think that Custard's long pace means that Ace was trying to get into the library but couldn't because he was banned.

After what seemed like an eternity, Custard left, heading straight for the third floor, where we subsequently veered to the left and right. Then, we stopped and went left to the queen's office.

"You guys don't think the queen has seen him, right?" I turn to the kids, and they all shake their heads. "I think we should knock first. Should we knock?" I ask them again, and they all nod in response.

I gulp. "Here goes nothing." I took a deep breath and got ready to knock on the queen's study door, but before I could, the door opened on its own, revealing the queen herself. At her side is PWINCE Ace, hanging in the air like a kitten as the queen holds him up by the back of his shirt.

"Is he yours?" The queen asks.

"Your highness, please let me go. I am a PWINCE. I should not be treated this way." Ace says, looking lifeless as he turns from left to right with every small movement.

"W-Well, my queen. I-I don't..." I look at baby Ace and see him glaring daggers at me. I glare back, feeling a little furious that he has the audacity to give me such a look. "Well, I must say, I have never seen such an ugly child in my life! Is he yours, your majesty? Congratulations!" In the end, I decided to play it cool and pretend that I didn't know the abnormal child.

"No, he is not mine." The queen narrows her eyes and looks past me to where the other children are. "But maybe you would like to explain something to me?"

"Umm..."

"You did not give birth to them, right?"

"Your majesty!"

The queen starts laughing at my outburst. "Oh, I'm kidding!" She waves at me jokingly. "I think I know what's going on, but you have to give me more details. Well, any more details aside from the one PWINCE ACE gave me."

We were ushered into the Queen's office, where we began to explain how we had ended up in this situation. To cut a long story short, the queen was able to concoct a potion that reversed the effect of the one that turned them into children. Of course, we were all so eager to get back to normal that we overlooked one minor detail.

As soon as the princes drank the potion, they immediately grew back to their original size and age. While doing so, their clothes ripped and were barely holding on to their adult bodies.

"Eep!" While I still have the decency to cover my eyes, the queen, on the other hand, giggles.

"Oh my." She muses. If that wasn't even, she tried to take my hands off of my covered eyes. "Dear, don't be shy. Just look."

"Brother, what happened to our pants? Oh, nice abs, by the way."

"Thanks, brother. You too, great muscles, but um…I think we need new pairs of clothes." I hear Ren responding to Dan.

"Hey, is that Rose over there?" I hear Nate asking the others while I am trying to fight off the queen for attempting to corrupt my innocent eyes.

"Why is she crouching over there, covering her face? Is she in pain or something?"

I feel myself blush as I hear them scuffling around in the room with torn clothes, looking like seminude models.

"MOVE, QUEEN!" With a strong push, I manage to separate myself from the queen, but I become aware of a presence behind me. It's PRINCE (not PWINCE) Ace with a ripped t-shirt and pants like a lion tore into them.

"What are you doing?" He asks. If that wasn't enough, the rest of the gang came up beside him, modeling the same ripped outfits. Nate doesn't even have a shirt on.

"Rose? You look sick. Are you alright?" It was Fred. His shirt now looks like a necklace around his neck.

Being as sane as any girl out there, I manage to let out a laugh. "Boys grow up so fast."

Ace suddenly leans forward. His face is inches away from mine. "I told you, didn't I? When I grow back to my original age, you are going to regret it."

Well, that sentence alone brought me back to my senses. "Yeah, well, not today. CUSTARD, ATTACK!" I yell and throw Custard at his face. Custard wasn't prepared for it, and thankfully, neither is Ace.

With Ace distracted, I rush out of the room and race back upstairs. I can hear the princes calling my name. Hearing their adult voices instead of their cute baby calls made me tear up a bit as I ran.

Gosh. I miss their children's version already.

Why do they have to grow up so fast?

What Party?

"Based on our research, tamers use their blood to transform their beast. Why don't you try it, Rose?" Nate suggested as he led us to the training room for our breakfast. Since I am on Princess training again, I have to spend every morning with Nate to perfect my table manners.

"Nah. That is fake. I tried it yesterday, and it did not work." I recall how I gave Custard a bit of my blood to transform him into *'killer mode'*.

Nothing happened.

"Maybe something is wrong with your blood?" Nate suggests, opening the door for me.

"Or something is wrong with Custard. Am I right, boy?" I say in a mocking baby voice at Custard, who is walking by my side this whole time. His response is a low growl. "Or maybe it's your *attitude*," I add.

"*Or* maybe your dog doesn't want a pathetic master like you and is thinking of quitting to be your partner."

"Who—" I was about to say something rude when my eyes landed on the person who said it.

Well, go figure.

The space is designed to resemble a study room. I looked at Nate expectantly and asked him to explain himself. I was fairly certain that today was my scheduled training session with Nate and not PRINCE Ace.

"Sorry, Rose." He looks at me apologetically. "If I had said that you have a scheduled training with Ace—"

"Ehem!" Ace coughed.

"-PRINCE Ace," Nate correct himself. "I highly doubt that you would go voluntarily."

"Damn right you are," I turn to flee, but before I can take another step, Nate grabs my dress collar to stop me from escaping.

"Sorry, princess. Your family history is such a mess. Don't you want to know more about it?"

"Nope. Seriously, I don't care." It was a bit of a lie because I *do* want to know. I just don't know how to voice it out.

What's more, I don't want to take any lessons or studies with a certain PRINCE.

"You don't really have a choice here, Rose. As a princess you-"

"But I am not a princess. Technically, I don't have a kingdom anymore." I correct him, remembering something from the books that Ace explained to me a while ago.

Besides, being a princess is no fun! Maybe when I was a kid, I would enjoy the idea, but in actuality, there's a lot of work! Trust me, even when I was just pretending, there's already a lot of work to do and a lot of etiquette and manners to learn.

"—are required to. And besides, it won't be that bad."

I look back at Ace and then at Nate. I raised an eyebrow at the vampire prince, daring him to argue.

Not bad, my ass. As long as I am in the same room as Ace, it is going to be a disaster.

"No, I mean, you will not have a one-on-one lesson with PRINCE Ace." Nate corrects himself.

"Oh, so you are here too? Yippie." I pump my fist in the air sarcastically.

"Actually, I will be with you and Prince Ace." Suddenly, Fred enters the room and comes to stand beside Nate. His glowing appeal felt like a ray of blessing that filled me with warmth.

"Oh, hey, Fred. Good thing you are here. Rose, won't—"

"I am so ready for this class!" I immediately folded my hands in front of me like a proper lady while discreetly fixing my hair. "Are we going to start this lesson or what?"

At my sudden change of behavior, Nate glares at me.

Fred laughs. "I see that someone is eager to learn."

"Yup!" I chirp, not even bothering to hide my enthusiasm. There's just something about Fred that makes me want to learn anything as long as he's my tutor.

Nate snorts. "Yeah, right. A second ago, you were—"

"Oh, look at the time you're wasting, Nate. I think you should *leave **now**.* Buh-bye." I quickly get up and start to push Nate towards the door. Nate has his hands crossed the whole time and he is even pouting at me before I close the door behind him.

Today is my lesson with Fred, and no one will be able to stop me.

Oh yeah. RINCE Ace is here too. I guess I'll just pretend he's not here, since I can't kick him out like I did Nate.

Ace and Fred began briefing me on my ancestry as soon as we took our seats. I was initially intrigued, but as soon as Ace began to speak, I became bored. The spark wasn't there, and he spoke like he was forced to communicate with us.

"Rose, you come from a line of royal blood. The last royal blood—"

"Or so you thought." I cut Ace off by making a little joke to lighten the mood, but as usual, it just seems to annoy him.

"Yeah. Too bad it had to be *you.*" He says irritably. "Now, will you let me finish so you can finally know where you come from?"

"Nah. It's okay." I say with a shrug.

"Okay?" Ace scrutinizes me with his eyes. "Don't you want to know about your family history?"

"Nope."

"Or even being related to Queen Elizabeth?"

"Now that is definitely a no."

"Personally, I think your history is fascinating, seeing as our family was very close. My dad's ancestors and the late king of Gija, that is." Fred suddenly interrupts, looking at some papers that he had brought with him.

I sit upright, suddenly becoming interested in the topic. "Really?"

"Oh, now she's interested." Ace rolls his eyes.

If anything, Fred only laughs. "Well, according to some of the records, our families are trade partners. Our kingdom provides medicines and healing potions, while yours provides the ingredients needed for those potions."

"Oh, wow. Basically, our families are close. Is there talk about political marriage between the two families?"

Ace scoffed. "I thought you *weren't* interested?"

"Shut up, I'm listening on this *very important* subject," I shush him.

"Yeah." Fred nods, ignoring Ace and I's short bicker. "The late king of Gija and my great, great, great grandfather were childhood friends." Just hearing about it made my heart squeal with delight. And, for the first time since I learned about being a tamer, I'm curious about my background.

"Too bad you're not interested in knowing more. Let's call this a day so you can practice manners." Ace sets the documents on the table when he gets up.

"Oh, you are still here? Well, it doesn't matter. You can leave. Fred can tell me the rest. Bye-bye!" In my mind, I'm screaming with joy because I can finally have some alone time with Fred. But it all changes when I see Fred starting to follow Ace's lead in leaving. "Where are you going?"

Fred smiles sadly at me. "Rose? I don't think anyone has ever told you this, but I cannot teach you about your history as it is not my main job."

"What? Why?" I choke. My tone lace with disappointment.

Fred looks hesitantly at Ace. Ace returns his stare with more solemnity.

"Don't make me tell her. If I do, I won't do it nicely, and we'll end up fighting. And I can't promise I won't throw her out—Princess or not."

"What? What's happening?" I first glance at Ace, then at Fred..

Fred groans before grinning melancholy. "Rose, I won't be staying here to teach you anything. I am going back to my kingdom. I have responsibilities there. I'm really sorry."

The news was so shocking that I hit my head on the table to see if I was dreaming or not.

It turns out, I wasn't. And the impact hurt so bad that I suddenly passed out.

***

"*Fred, why would you leave again?*" *I ask as I run to keep up with Fred's pace.* "*Don't leave.*"

Fred didn't even look at me. "*Sorry, Rose. But I have to.*" *He says, looking troubled.*

"*Why? Is something bothering you? Do you have a problem? If you have, then, please tell me. Maybe I can help.*" *I insist.*

"*No, Rose. You can't. It is more of a personal matter. I can't...I can't subdue my feelings while I'm here. And besides, I cannot compete for another crown while I am already about to rule our kingdom.*"

"*Fred....*"

"*I'm sorry, Rose. It's not what you think it is. I have responsibilities too. Also....never mind.*" *He says.*

"*What is it, Fred? You can tell me.*"

"*It's nothing, Rose. My feelings....don't matter.*" *He shakes his head sadly.*

"*What feelings?*" *I ask.*

"*It's nothing.*"

"*Fred, you can tell me if it is bothering you so much.*"

Fred suddenly stops walking and turns to face me. "*I can't stand it, Rose!*" *He yells.* "*I hate it. I hate seeing you or any other prince in a single room! This..this sort of feeling...is this jealousy?!*"

"*F-Fred? Are you saying....*" *I feel myself blush a little. I don't want to be a little assuming, but maybe....ya know? A handsome and perfect guy like Fred comes to like me?* "*I love the princes, Rose! And I think you are becoming close to them. Too close for my comfort!*"

"....?" *I blink. My mind stops working as I badly try to run his words through my head.*

Did he just say what I think he said?

*"If I were born a girl, you would be nothing compared to my looks. Face it, honey, your only advantage is that you are a **girl**."*

"...!?!?!?!"

***

"GOD, NO!"

"Hey, hey!" Nate suddenly wakes me up from my disturbingly terrifying dream.

It was just a dream. Thank goodness.

I sigh in relief before looking back at Nate. "What?"

"You've have been stirring in your sleep. Is something wrong? Did you have a nightmare?"

I glare at him. "Oh, gee, I don't know, *NATHANIEL*. Is something wrong?" I return the question to him.

"Something about the way you speak my name seems weird." He points out.

I crossed my legs, arranged my skirt, and then sarcastically smile while placing both hands on my lap. "The answer to why I am in this mood might be that someone lied to me earlier, no?"

Nate looks into my eyes with his brilliant green eyes, trying to understand why I am so upset with him. He suddenly snaps his fingers like the idea finally reveals itself to him. "Is it because I lied to you this morning?"

"Ding ding ding! And the bloodsucker gets it right. Give him some blood orange!"

"I'm sorry, Rose."

"No. I will not accept your apology even if you give me those puppy eyes or beg for forgiveness on your knees." I quickly add the last part when Nate starts to get down on his knees. "*NATHANIEL*, I SAID QUIT IT!"

"Princess Rose," Hearing him call me princess make me flick his forehead, but he didn't seem to feel it as he continues. "I am deeply wounded that I may have offended you this morning by leaving you with another guy when you badly wanted to be with me."

"No, I don't." I deadpan immediately.

"Regardless of your denials, I am aware of your true feelings toward me. I understand your pain, but don't worry; I won't abandon you this time. As a result, I'd like to ask you a question. Please accept my sincere apologies and consider me as your devoted servant."

"Nathaniel."

"Yes?"

"Why are you kneeling and putting your hands together as if you are praying instead of apologizing?"

"To express my deepest feelings like a *virgin*."

"You crack! You just insulted me and the rest of the virgins reading this."

"Rose, fourth wall. That is against the rules."

"Sorry."

"And I am still a virgin, if you don't know."

"What?!" Alright. Now that confession catches my attention.

Nate starts laughing. "Just kidding! But who knows?"

I roll my eyes. Of course, he almost fooled me again. I should have seen it coming. "Damn, you are annoying," I push myself up. I see something from my peripheral vision, making my eyes widen with shock. "A COCKROACH!" I quickly jump back on the bed while pointing at the menace on my side table.

Nate follows where I point and sees the roach. At first, he just laughs at me before getting a book and slamming it to the spawn of the devil. But as soon as he lifts it up, the cockroach flies straight towards him.

Now, it's Nate's turn to scream and jump on my bed as well.

"What are you doing!? Kill it!" I yell, trying to push him out of my bed, but the vampire is hugging me, clearly terrified of the flying roach as well. "Get the book, and kill it, Nate!"

"Hell no! That thing is flying. No one told me that it would be flying!"

"You're a guy!"

"As of this very moment only, you can call me Nathalie." Nate, I mean Nathalie, and I scream and duck when the evil cockroach stars making its descent towards us. I am fully aware how Nate and I must look right now while we hug each other, scream like sissies, and wave one of our hands in the air to keep the vile insect away.

The door suddenly flings open, and the twins comes in time to see a badly misunderstood situation.

"I heard Rose screaming! Alright, you filthy vampire. What.did.you.do?!" Dan yells, waving a poorly carved stake in one hand. Ren is standing behind him, holding a basket of garlic that he's ready to throw at Nate.

"My garlics are ready." He says with as much determination as needed.

Dan's eyes shifts from me then to Nate, noting how we are hugging each other.

"OH, MY GODS! Nate, are you tring to seduce my sister-in-law!?"

"What?!" Nate and I looks at each other, wondering where they got that idea. Suddenly our gazes turns to each other to see that we're still hugging.

"..."

"..."

"Ah, no." I move away from Nate in order to dwindle the misunderstanding. "You see, there was a bug."

"A really nasty, flying bug." Nate adds before pointing at Dan. "Come to think of it, it kind of looks and acts like you—annoying."

"I don't believe you! First of all, I am handsome. Second, I know that you are just making up reasons so you can seduce her!" Dan continues screaming, and this time, he aims his anger at Custard, who caught the roach and killed it. "You were supposed to watch her and let no other guy get to her! Wolves stick together. Where is your loyalty!?" He march over to Custard and lifts him up by the scruff. "We were supposed to be a team! I trusted you, despite how you almost killed me, you little—Ow!" Custard suddenly bit Dan's nose.

I can't say he doesn't deserve it since he was mistreating him.

"Ha! He got your nose." I couldn't help but comment, remembering the time that I took their noses when they were turned to kids.

Dan drops Custard. Custard took that chance as he ran out of the room.

"Come back here!" Dan growls, running after him.

"Hey, Dan, you idiot. Come back here!" Of course, they would not be twins if Ren would not be running after Dan.

"You guys leave Custard alone!" I start to follow them since I fear what they might do to my cute little wolf.

"Rose, no runner in the hallway. The Queen will be furious." Nate shouts, and I can only assume he's running after us.

And again, it was a jolly day in the palace as four people with royal bloodlines ran around the castle, completely disregarding their etiquette. What's new?

"Come here so I can skin you alive!"

"Dan, we are already in trouble with the Queen. Please, stop breaking more rules!"

"TRY TO SKIN MY DEAR CUSTARD, DAN! JUST YOU TRY!" I scream in warning.

"Will everyone just stop running!?" At first, I hear Nate yelling behind me. Then suddenly, he appears next to me.

"Gotcha!" He manages to grab my wrist, but apparently, Custard made a U-turn and tackles Nate between the legs.

"Holy shi—"

"That's my boy!" I gleefully and pick up Custard when I see Dan running towards us. "Gotta go!"

"Dan, don't you dare try and run after Rose—" I hear Ren trying to warn his brother, but he only cut him off.

"Brother, I am really happy that you worry for her, but she has something that I want to kill right now, so move!" Rapid footsteps starts to come from behind me. I dash for the staircase, almost skipping a few steps and almost tripping on the hem of my dress. I'm not bragging, but running around in a dress has become so easy for me these days.

When I turn back, Nate is only a few steps behind me. As my last resort, I held Custard in front of his face.

"Custard, use scratch attack!" When Custard didn't do anything but stare, I grab one of his paws and use them to scratch Nate's nose.

Nothing to worry about since vampires heal fast…

"Ow! Damn it, Rose." Nate hisses.

"That's my boy!" I grin, hugging Custard and kissing his forehead.

Apparently, my spirit animal hates me and almost bit my nose off. "Eep!" I was so surprised that I didn't watch where I was going and trip on the last step of the stairs.

A soft and gentle voice laughs. "I see you guys are having fun as usual." Fred looks at us with amusement.

"Hey, Fred. Hand me that demon over there." Dan yelled behind me.

Either Fred didn't hear him, or he was too focused on reading my expression. "Um…Rose? Is something wrong?"

"Oh um….hey there, Fred. Uh…." I cough. "I-I am not handing Custard over, by the way."

"Yeah, I figured." He chuckles.

"Give me that wolf!" Fred and I were so busy talking that I didn't notice that Dan was already beside me. "I am going to butcher it!"

When Fred said Dan's name, he looked coldly at him for a brief moment. "Daniel."

Dan comes to a halt at the chilliness before it vanishes.

"Show off." I hear Dan mumble behind me.

Fred places his hand on top of my head. "Be careful when running up the stairs. It's lucky that you did not fall back."

"Prince Frederick." There's a voice behind him. Ace marches up towards us. He pauses for a bit, wondering why all of us were gathered in one place. When his eyes fixes on Fred's hand on my head, he looks away. "I was informed that everything is set for your departure."

"I guess I'll get going then." Fred starts to walk away.

"Wait, what? You are leaving today?"

Fred nods. "Yeah. Unfortunately. I was supposed to leave tomorrow morning, but I guess someone out there hates me. There was a report this morning about illegal magic practice. I need to go back and deal with it."

"Oh…" I am not going to lie. I am a bit disappointed to hear him leave so soon.

"Hey, don't worry, Rose. It won't be long until I visit again."

"Of course. Just a visit." Fred laughs when he hears my disappointment. I look up at him. "So when are you going to *visit* again?"

"At the party two weeks from now." He informs me.

"Huh? Party?" It might be my imagination, but I see Prince Ace, Nate, Ren, and Dan flinch. "What party?"

"The one where you are intro—" Fred pauses, staring at something behind me. Immediately, his expression turns awkward. "Er…I am guessing I am not supposed to mention it yet. Ha ha ha…."

Fred doesn't appear to be speaking to me. He seems to be conversing with the people at my back. When I turn around, the rest of the princes were there, making strange gestures.

Nate is trying to zip his lips, Ren is crossing his arms, Ace is shaking his head, and Dan is giving him the finger and gliding it through his neck. They immediately stopped what they were doing and turned away when they noticed me looking.

Dorks.

I return my gaze to Fred. "What do you mean about a party—"

I was about to ask, but Fred is already running for the door and waving at me in a hurry. It is no mystery that he is trying to run away before I can ask him anything.

"Good luck, Rose! I promise to be cheering for you." And with that, he is out the door.

Well, so much for trying to get some answers out of him. Maybe I should try my luck with the others.

As soon as Fred left, I turn around to address the rest of the princes. "Hey, guys. What did he—"

When I turned, the area was clear, save for their receding footsteps that echoed upstairs. I did a 360-degree turn to see if there was anyone I could ask.

There was none. Damn it! Only Custard and I were the ones left in the area.

Escort

Everyone was avoiding me as I marched my way to the queen's study—or whatever you call it. The princes were nowhere to be found, probably hiding from me as I stormed off.

Once I reach the queen's study, I did not bother to knock. Instead, I kick the door open, yelling, "WHAT PARTY!?"

To my surprise, I see all the traitorous princes there.

Dan jumps off the couch and accidentally spilled his tea on Ren's lap. Ren let out a girly screech while Nate quickly hides behind the curtains. As for Ace, he casually turns his back to me.

So this is where they ran off to!

"Dear, we have that round thing on doors called a doorknob—the one you just broke." The queen says while sipping her tea.

"WHAT PARTY!?" I demanded. I can't help but notice the prince's flinching at my question.

The queen almost chokes on her tea. "Goodness." She quickly composes herself. "Straight to the point, I see." Then, turning to the princes, she crosses her arms. "Alright, tell me right now. Who is the snitch here?"

"It was Fred." They all reply in unison.

"What. Party." I repeat, carefully this time so she'd answer me.

"Um.." The queen looks uncomfortable telling me and tries to make eye contact with the princes for help. Unfortunately for her, they were looking anywhere but the both of us after they answered her earlier question. My aunt turns to me with a very nervous expression. "Y-You see, dear. It was supposed to be a surprise. You know, a descendant of the people of Gija, not to mention of royalty, could not go on unannounced." The queen stands up and heads in front of her desk. "This is great news for all of the kingdoms. It means that Tordis had not won the war with Gija. You are my niece, and I want to introduce you as a true princess properly."

Go figure. After knowing the Queen for a while now, I should have guessed that she would pull this kind of stunt.

Still, I hate it when someone does something behind my back, especially when it involves me.

"How long were you keeping this party from me?"

"My dear, it does not matter—"

"How long?" I ask again.

The queen sighs. "The king and I planned this the day after realizing that you're a descendant from King Varon."

"What about them? How long have they known?" I gesture towards the princes.

"Dear, don't blame them. I told them not to tell you. They were only doing what I asked them to do. Well, except Prince Frederick, who is kind of a blabbermouth if you ask me." The queen mutters the last part with a hint of anger.

"How long?" I repeat the question. I stare into the eyes of the queen, making it clear that I would not stop until she answer me.

"The king and I planned the whole event the day after. Let's say, about six…days?"

It was almost a week then. They were trying to plan a party for me without me knowing. And not just any party, for that matter. It was to tell the whole kingdom that I am a princess of a ruined kingdom.

I take a deep breath before letting it out. It would be best to stay calm. "You mean to tell me that all this time, all the training that I was doing since I got back, was so that we could have another party and none of you bothered to tell me about it?"

"Rose, we—" Nate starts to say, but I cut him off by showing him the palm of my hand.

"When is this party set?"

"About two weeks from now," Ren answers, looking guilty.

"What if I don't want to have a party?"

"Dear, it's—"

"Cancel it," I am aware that I must be unreasonable, but now that I know that I have a royal bloodline, the last thing that I want to do is flaunt it.

"We can't just cancel it. Word that—" Dan starts.

"By order of Princess Rosalie Amber Stan, a descendant of late king Varon and queen Diera Izani Lanis," I add, which shocked everyone in the room. I may not look or act like it, but I do listen to Ace's lessons from time to time. I know that even when I do not have a kingdom to rule, I still have some authority as the hostess for the party that they plan for me.

Nate peers out from behind the curtains, and Ace gives me a startled look.

"Good heavens!" The Queen looked like she is going to have a heart attack.

I clench my fist. "I am allowed to have authority over the party, right? Since I am a princess, I have am allowed to do so. I can call it off if the ball is mine to celebrate. Your laws will be severely impacted if you engage the party without my permission." I turn to face PRINCE Ace at this point. "Am I right, PRINCE Ace?"

By then, everyone is looking at Ace and awaiting his confirmation. I can't tell what he is thinking because his expression remains stoic. "She's right." He sighs, looking defeated.

All of my lessons, I suppose, have paid off and have been put to good use. I breathe a sigh of relief.

"So, there you have it." I walk out of the room. I was so enraged that when I left, I didn't bother to look at their reactions.

***

After storming out, I decided to pay Cloud a visit at the stables. I recently discovered that grooming your pets can help you relax and unwind.

"Guess what, Cloud," I mumble. "Your previous owner, well, not really your previous owner, decided to conspire against me in order to keep a secret." I've also recently discovered that talking to your pets can be beneficial.

"A ball." I scoff. "Do they have to make a big deal of things? I mean, I am just a descendant of the previous king and queen of Gija, a land where they control dead animals." I say the last part rather dramatically as I wave the hand holding the brush in the air.

Custard did not appreciate my last comment because he growls at me. Tamer or not, he still scares me. He can be such a temperamental wolf at times. I guess it's kind of my fault for insulted animal spirits. It's my bad.

"Oops. Sorry." I laugh nervously. "Want me to brush your fur next?"

The little wolf exhaled an exasperated sigh. "Okay…I'll take that as a n—"

"Rose, don't do it!" I, Custard, and Cloud jump when Ren suddenly burst into the room looking panicked. He starts to run towards me and grabs me by the shoulder. "Don't run away again. It's dangerous out there. I know you are upset, but it would be better to talk it out rather than run away."

There was a long pause as I try to interpret what this idiot was saying.

"You…" I leer at him while prying his hands off my shoulders. "…think I'm trying to run away?" I force a smile.

And then there is the long pause as he consider the brush I am holding along with Cloud's missing reins and saddle. Ren lets out a nervous chuckle. "…You….weren't?"

"I wasn't." I cross my arms over my chest because I'm mad that he thought I might run away again. I mean, yeah, I would like to, but if I were to go somewhere, it would be back home to my family.

"Ohh…." Ren blushes and starts laughing awkwardly. "Well…I thought like last time that…you know."

Just to humor him, I laugh along with him. Soon, we both start laughing.

"Oh, you jerk," I say, chuckling while shaking my head at him.

"Sorry." He bows fearfully when he notices that my voice has become dangerously serious.

I shoved Cloud's grooming brush at him, dismissing my anger with a shake of my head.

"Make sure to brush Cloud's mane. I want it soft and clean when I get back."

Ren accepts the brush and mutters. "Crap. She's mad."

As I walk past him and out of the stables, I notice his twin, Dan leaning on the door like he was spying. When he sees me, he immediately jerks back.

"Hi, princess. I wasn't spying on you two or anything. In fact, I was not the one who told my brother to run after you just in case you'd run away again just to get you two alone. Another fact, I was just standing guard and not planning on locking you *both* in the stables." He rambles on and on, but I wasn't hearing any of it, nor did I bother listening to him.

Sometimes, Dan's pranks can be a little overbearing, but I have gotten used to them. Unfortunately for him, I am just not in the mood.

I sigh loudly, and just as I am about to calm down, Nate comes running toward us. "Rose, I heard you were trying to run away again. Is that true?" Then, he sees me with Dan. His expression changes to relief. "Good job stopping her, Dan."

When I look back at Dan, he's making gestures at Nate to shut up with his middle finger.

"You know what?" I throw my hands in the air. "I've had it! I am not running away, alright? I'll be in my room if anyone wants to look for me!" I push past Nate and began running with Custard following right behind me.

I was thinking of returning to my room, but I decided to take a break in the garden pavilion. I need to take a breath. I feel like I am so stressed even though I didn't do much today.

When I started lying down on the bench like a dead person, Custard gives me a strange look.

"Leave me alone to die, Custard." Gosh. I can't decide if I love this realm or hate it.

"Well, I hope that you do."

I let out a tired groan when I realize which prince I have to deal with next. "Oh, I'll die alright," I say without turning to look at PRINCE Ace. "But only if you die first."

Ace scoffs, leaning on the supports of the pavilion. "Well, nice knowing you then. Elves live longer than humans."

"Well, in case you've forgotten, PRINCE Ace, I am not entirely human, to begin with." I smirk. "And also, if you think that I'm going to run away like the rest of the princes, you can rest assured that I won't. I've learned my lesson the verybhard way."

"I know."

"Well, that's weird. Why are you here then?"

"You may not have wanted to run away before, but after being provoked by those idiots, well…who knows what you'll do."

"OH MY GOSH!!" I yell so loudly that PRINCE Ace almost slip off the balcony. I get into a sitting position so I can properly argue and scold. "I am not going to run away, alright?! I just want to relax and calm my nerves, but you guys keep on showing up, making it impossible for me to calm down. I am upset right now, and I want to be alone!"

I have had it. I guess staying at any other place other than my room is going to give me a headache!

I get up and start to head towards the castle. When I walk past Ace, he suddenly grabs my arm. "Hey!"

"Come with me." He says sternly. If I weren't angry right now, my legs would probably stop working out of fear. I mean, come on. I screamed at the PRINCE of darkness. I could only think of one reason why he would want me to come with him.

He's probably going to kill me.

My suspicions heightens when PRINCE Ace starts dragging me towards the forest.

Oh, boy. He will kill me and *then* bury my body in the dirt like a decent person.

Well, I hope he will at least put a tombstone on my grave.

"I will not kill you, even though I want to." He says.

"Oh, so now you're a mind reader?"

"Unless you're an animal, then I can." He responds, pertaining to his ability.

"Touché." I don't want to say it out loud, but I am happy that I still get to live for today. "Where are you taking me?"

We stop right then, and he turns around to look at me. He sighs. "In the Earth books, I read that when characters feel upset, they have to talk to someone."

I stare at him, unblinking. "Meaning?"

"Express your feelings through words, obviously."

"And you are willing to listen?" This must be a trap.

"I'll try." I can tell that he is forcing himself to say those lines.

I stare at PRINCE Ace for a few seconds while tapping a finger to my chin like I am considering his offer.

"Let me think. NO. Bye!" I quickly turn back, and bolted. Unfortunately, I didn't get far when Ace suddenly grabs the collar of my dress. "OW! Do you know how expenssive this dress is!? I don't, but it could be a rental!"

"*Talk.*" He insist.

"I have no desire to talk! Let me go, you jerk."

"I am trying to help."

"Help yourself! This is not helping. Helping is helping someone who wants to be helped!"

"So you don't want my help?"

"No!"

"Alright, you may go and keep your *feelings*." He says and then lets me go.

Fun fact about us girls: we're in denial of a lot of things. And even if we say something, it actually means the opposite.

"So that's it? You are not even going to insist or even try to persuade me?"

"What?" Now PRINCE Ace looks really confused. "I did, but you told me that you don't want my help."

"You could at least try harder!"

"Well, do you want my *help*?"

I cross my arms over my chest. "Well, now that you ask me, I don't want to."

It must be my imagination, but I feel like I see a vein pop in Ace's forehead. I can just imagine him planning my demise in his head. "GOODBYE."

I should have kept my mouth shut, but I felt so petty that I get to tease him. "Fine. It's not like you're going to listen anyway. Plus, you dragged me out here to talk when you don't even bother exerting effort."

PRINCE Ace stops dead in his tracks, moving back to stand a few inches from me. "I'll show you effort." Before I can guess—or think about running—thick vines starts wrapping around my waist and hauls me up from the ground. I scream.

"Oh, my Gawd! Ace, what are you doing!?" I yell at him. "Put me down!"

"Talk." He orders. "If you want me to let you go and we can call it a day."

I guess I shouldn't have pushes him this far. I was just enjoying the fact that I was winning against him for the first time.

I claw at the vines in an attempt to tear them off of me. No such luck since the vines were too thick. "You jerk! You could just ask me to talk."

"I. *Did.*" He shoots me a glare. "And it seems that it was futile to ask you politely."

"Let me go!" My feet kick the air. I even throw my shoes in an attempt to hit him right in the face.

"Are you going to talk now?"

"NO!"

"Fine." He raises one hand in the air. The vines starts to move again when they lift me higher from the ground. "How about now?" He ask again.

"You will regret that," I growl and look at Custard. "Attack him, boy!"

To my surprise, Custard springs into action and jumps at him. As Custard leaps for the attack, but Ace simply grabs him with one hand, stopping his advances. Custard whimpers when Ace gives him an icy glare. "You know that spirits can't do much harm without their tamers, right?" Ace gives me a sideway glance.

I look away, blushing. "I knew that."

Before I know it, I am being lifted higher from the ground. Curses leaves me mouth of out fright.

"You can talk, or I'll leave you there to rot forever." He says while still holding Custard. I didn't answer him, and he grew more irritated. "Fine then. See you when you're dead." With that, he starts to head back to the castle.

I begin to panic. If the other princes were in his place, I would know that they were making empty threats, but this is Ace that we are talking about. He doesn't have any empathy.

"Okay, fine! Fine!" I scream. "I hate parties, alright? Especially when I am about to be introduced to being a descendant of a dead kingdom. It is all so new, and everything is going too fast." I yell in frustration, fighting off my embarrassment. It was as if everything I was holding on to spilled out. "The idea that I wasn't normal and that I am not entirely human. It feels like my life is a joke, and you guys don't even bother to understand how I feel about all of these changes! Ren, Nate, Dan, Fred, you, the king, and the queen. You're all making decisions for me without even asking if I'm fine with it.Dragging me into this world, forcing me to stay, and now turning me into a princess!? What a load of crap!" I feel the sides of my cheeks wet from the angry tears streaming down my face. I can see Ace staring at me with a blank and emotionless face below.

A few seconds later, I see him closing his eyes. The vines start to slowly lower me down onto the ground.

Ace approaches me as soon as my foot touches the ground. He kneels and places the shoes that I had thrown at him right in front of my feet. I furiously wipe my tears.

"I'm sorry."

That made me jerk up and stare at him. "What?"

"I'm sorry if we never consider your feelings." He looks so genuine as he said it. He even looks away, as if he feels bad about everything.

There is a long pause, and it's getting really awkward. I bet we were both surprised by what had just happened.

Ace apologized for something.

Gosh, I must be in another dimension.

"Let's go." He starts heading back once he places Custard back on the ground.

With mixed emotions, I silently follow him.

"I'm sorry." He says again. He repeats himself. This time I raise an eyebrow, unsure what he is apologizing for this time.

Then, I came to a realization.

Ace was not completely silent the entire time because he cared about me. He was being quiet because he is struggling to contain his laughter.

"I'm sorry, but I have no regrets about putting you in that tree. You look pitiful, and I believe you got what you deserved because you irritated me." He cocks his head and smirks. "And this is just a suggestion from me: go to the party with the queen. After all, you're not going to be here indefinitely. For a change, just enjoy your time in this world. It is not my problem if you don't like it." He shrugs and resumes walking before saying, "Oh, and keep a 50-pace distance between you and me. I don't want anyone else to know I'm with you." With that, Ace starts heading back to the castle.

I stand there for a good three minutes before storming back into the castle with a very hot head.

To think I thought we were starting to become friends or that he was actually a nice person!

"That son of a—"

"Rose!" I wasn't able to finish my sentence since Dan comes running up to me. "Thank you! Thank you."

I gave him a confused look. "Okay. For what exactly are you thanking me?" At this point, I was beginning to have trust issues.

"PRINCE Ace just spoke with the queen, and he told her that you agreed to carry on with the party! Now, the queen is sending invites to all of the kingdoms!" Dan beams at me happily.

My jaw drops to the floor.

"HE.DID.WHAT!?!?!" I scream so loudly that I fear my voice could be heard all the way to Tordis. That sneaky bastard. "I never said that!" I protest. "Cancel it! Cancel everything!"

"B-But, Rose, the invites are already sent. If we take it back now, just imagine what the people of Thalia will think."

I stare at Dan, horrified, before I breathlessly try to calm myself. "This can't be happening!" I channel all my anger towards Ace. As of the moment, I don't think I would mind having the party as long as I can get back at Ace.

I need revenge!

"Oh, by the way, Rose. Have you decided on your escort?" Dan asks me sweetly while batting his eyes.

"Not now, Dan," I wave away his question while I think of some way on how I am going to get back at that jerk.

"But you have to decide now." He whines.

If there's one thing that the twins differ in some things, Dan is *more* annoying than Ren. And knowing him, he won't stop bugging me until I answer him. I don't want to be bothered because I am too busy thinking of a way to get even with a certain prince.

"Geez, I don't know, Dan. Why don't you be my escort?"

"I can't!" He answers hastily. "I'm...uh...I am going to have a stomachache on that day!"

I give him a weird look. "You predicted that you are going to have a stomachache?"

"Well, yeah. It's a wolf thing." He frowns as if realizing that what he said was stupid. "Anyway, I can't be your escort if I am not well. After all, being an escort is not easy. We have to follow you around and do whatever you ask us to."

The last part certainly caught my attention. "Come again?"

"We have to do as you say, like servants for a night." Dan beams at me. "Just like Ren back then when he was your escort. I mean, wasn't Ren a great escort? Perhaps—"

"Brilliant!" A ray of hope shines in front of me, and I am taking it! I rub my hands together like an evil villain.

"Rose, are you alright?" Dan looks at me with concern.

"I am great, Dan.!" I jump and give Dan a quick hug to thank him for giving me the idea. "Thanks to you!" I turn, running back to the castle, and leave a confused Dan behind me.

"You're welcome…?" Dan yells, utterly confuse about what just happened.

Now all I have to do is go to the Queen and tell her the good news.

Yes, there will be a party.

Yes, I will be there.

And PRINCE Ace will be my ~~dog~~ escort.

Oh, this is going to be fun. I smile like a maniac as I thought of how pissed off Ace would be. I'll be sure that I will be giving him unlimited tasks on that *very* special day.

And the best part?

There's nothing that he can do about it.

It's PRINCESS Rose

"No. Absolutely not!" PRINCE Ace protests the moment I announce to the queen my conditions for continuing the ball. One thing is for sure: He was not happy about it.

On the other hand, I am sitting cross-legged while I enjoy watching his troubled face. I beam brightly at the queen.

"Hey, you want a ball? You got one. As long as PRINCE Ace is my *escort*, that is." I give Ace a smug look and wiggle my eyebrows. I turn to look at the maid and call her over. "Tea please."

"What kind of tea, princess?"

"One that tastes like victory. Darjeeling." The maid bows and disappears to fetch me my drink.

Ace is giving me a murderous look, which suggests that if he could kill me right now, he would. "You and I both know that you are only doing this out of spite!"

"Good heavens, what do you mean?" I give him a weary look before smirking at him as soon as my tea arrives. "Well, that is not for you to decide now, is it?" I chuckle, sipping my tea with my pinky up. "Wow. Refreshing."

The queen looks like she is considering leaving the room, upon sensing how intense the atmosphere has become. "Are you sure that you want PRINCE Ace? What about the other princes as your escort like Prince Ren?"

At the mention of Ren, the door suddenly burst open with Dan barging in. "You are absolutely right, your majesty! My brother has proven to be a great partner and escort for Rose!" He suddenly announces.

The queen, Ace, and I stare at him in annoyance. "**Get out.**" All of us said it at the same time.

Dan laughs, looking taken aback by our outburst. "Well, it seems that I am not welcome here so....." He carefully retreats outside, though I am pretty sure that he's still eavesdropping

Once Dan left, I face the queen again. "Your majesty, the other princes are fine. But my condition is simple. Either Ace will be my escort or I will not show up at the ball even if you force me to." I pause and tap my chin. "Oh wait, you can't force me because technically I am a PRINCESS! And," I add. "You can't cancel now since you just sent out the invitations. Oh, my, my, my. What a predicament, right, PRINCE Ace?" I laugh like a crazy buffoon, knowing fully well that I have won this round.

Revenge. I just love it.

I bet Ace wants to break my neck right now because I have never seen him this angry. Well, except for the time that he and Ren fought off that giant snake.

The queen only gives Ace a pleading look. "PRINCE Ace, if you please be Rose's—"

"PRINCESS Rose." I correct her before I sip my tea.

"—PRINCESS Rose's escort, then we continue with the ball." The queen is clearly getting annoyed at my attitude, but she carries on to convince Ace.

If they have a problem with my attitude, I would remind them that they want me to be a princess, so I'm only acting like one.

A spoiled princess that is.

Ace glares at me for a few more seconds before he finally realizes that he has no other choice but to accept his fate. "Fine!" He says while gritting his teeth. "There better not be any games here." He threatens me.

"I will make no such promises." I answer, hiding my mischievous grin behind my cup.

***

"You chose PRINCE Ace as your escort?!" Nate looks at me in disbelief when I told him the story earlier. "Are you out of your mind?!"

"Nate, you and I both know that I already lost my mind the moment I was dragged into this world." I point out as we walk together.

Nate and I were headed for the door and towards the garden after my disclosure of my escort to the queen.

"Rose, this is Ace we are talking about. PRINCE Ace! With a capital P-R-I-N-C-E!"

I roll my eyes. Nate is overreacting—or maybe he isn't.

Well, maybe he is right to overreact.

"I know, I know. But hey, I got the PRINCE as a slave for one day, so I think it is worth it." I let out a maniac laugh and rub my hands together in excitement. My eyes then catches sight of Ren, who is also making his way to the door. I raise my voice and wave at him. "Yo, wolf boy. Done brushing Cloud?"

Ren only glances at me and nods his head once before jeading out. He is carrying his sword, so I assume that he is out to practice his sword fighting.

I turn to Nate. "Is it me, or does Ren seem a little angry?"

"Yeah, he does." Nate confirms.

"What do you think he's mad about?"

"I don't know. Did you do something to him? He kind of avoided your gaze earlier."

I thought of what happened when I made him brush Cloud. I remember getting angry at him before I stormed off.

"Uh-oh."

"What do you mean, uh oh?"

"I think that he *is* mad at me," I start biting my finger nails nervously. I like teasing the princes, but I don't want them to hate me or get mad at me—well, maybe except Ace. But for Ren, it was a big no-no. Ren is always there for me and seems to care a lot about my well-being. I can't afford to lose our friendship.

Nate nudges me. "Well, princess, what are you waiting for? Go and apologize." Nate says, pushing me forward. I lock eyes with Nate and give him a small smile as thanks.

That was all I needed to go after Ren.

I was right when I guessed that Ren was out practicing his sword fighting. He's swinging his sword in the air and fighting off invisible opponents.

"Hey, Ren," I call out, hoping that he won't ignore me.

"Hey." is his only response.

Yeah, I'm positive he's mad.

"So, Ren." I start. "I may just be imagining it but by any chance, are you mad at me or something?" I feel nervous. My lips and hands are already shaking.

I see Ren pause for a moment before striking the air again. "For what?"

Is it me, or does it sound more like a sentence than a question?

"Well, that is what I am here to ask."

Ren stops swinging and turns his back to me. "I don't know."

"You are mad at me, aren't you?"

"I said I don't know!" It's the first time that Ren has raised his voice at me. What's more, he continued to practice like I wasn't there at all.

I guess I deserve it.

"I'm sorry." Is all I manage to whisper. I don't know how to carry the conversation anymore so I start to turn around to leave. Maybe Ren just needs some time alone. I know that I would want to be alone when I am mad. At least I manage to say what I want to say.

"It's not your fault, Rose." I pause and turn back when Ren starts to speak. He stops swinging his sword and looks at the ground bashfully. "It's just…" Ren sighs. "I just…I heard that you picked an escort that is not me."

"You mean that I chose Ace as my escort?"

"Y-Yeah." I feel like my eyes are playing tricks on me, but he seems sad.

"Well, what about it?"

"I don't know. I just thought that since we're close that you would, I don't know, have me as your escort again." I feel really terrible because Ren looks really disappointed. He cast his eyes downward and avoids my gaze. "I'm really not mad. I just feel a little embarrassed that I must have done something during the last ball that made you consider someone else to be your escort."

"Ohh." That is all I can think of as an awkward silence passes.

Ren finally breaks the silence. "You know what, forget about it. I'm just glad that the party can still continue and you will finally be welcomed to the royal family."

"Yeah." I rubbed my elbows while trying to formulate how I can tell Ren the real reason I pick Ace as my partner. "You know, if it makes you feel any better, I chose Ace as my escort to become my servant for the day. If it weren't for that, then I would have picked you."

Or Nate.

And I was actually close to picking Dan as well, because I know that he will sneak off in the middle of the party. If I am going to suffer, so should he!

To my surprise, Ren starts to laugh. "Wow, I can't believe that I did not even think of that." He chuckles. "I should have known that it would be weird that you would voluntarily pick him a your partner. I mean, I can understand you picking the others, but never him."

"The world might end first before I ask him to be my escort." I grin.

Ren smiles. "Rose, whatever decision you make, know that I will always be there for you, even when your plans might involve provoking the demon king." I want to look up and see what kind of expression he's making, but he suddenly turns his back to me. "I think that I have had enough training for today. I should head back first. See you at dinner, Rose."

Belle of the Ball

Days and weeks of training have passed, leaving me exhausted and temperamental. It's really horrible. Preparing for the ball last time was not that stressful compared to this. Even Nate and the twins are getting serious during our training. The only one who was a little laid back was Dan. The guy would crack jokes here and there and pull pranks on his brother when he least expected it.

The other PRINCE hates my guts so much that he would not allow me to doze off, even for a second. He would continue to drill information into my brain even though I was tired, which always resulted in us bickering and me leaving through the window once. It hadn't happened again since he basically put some sort of magic barrier on the window. Trust me, I dislocated my elbow trying to break it.

Yes, I am desperate to get away from him and our training. The guy is nuts!

Don't get me started with the final fittings of the dress. It was not as bad as the training, but the tailor really pissed me off. You see, when they were taking my measurements and handed them to the tailor, I never remembered his name, which is more of a tongue twister, but let us name him Bob.

Bob eyes the paper with my measurements. His brows furrow at something, and then he says, "With a bust like this, it would be hard to design a good enough gown for her."

If no one understood that, he was basically telling me that my bust is too small.

It took all my willpower not to grab his hair and scream, "WITH A (hush word) HAIR LIKE THIS, YOU ARE LUCKY ENOUGH TO HAVE A (hush word) JOB!!" Thankfully, I managed to keep my temper in check at that time.

"Princess Rose, it's time to get ready." The soft voices of the maids woke me up from my slumber.

I squint my eyes to see that inside my room, preparations are being made. My make-up and hair accessories were being prepared on my dresser while the tailors made a few adjustments to the dress I'll wear at the party, which is worn by a wired mannequin.

Right. Today is that dreadful day.

I groan and draw my blanket over my head like a protective shield. "Go away. As Princess, I command...." I doze off to sleep before I can finish.

I don't know how long I napped after that, but suddenly, I woke up dripping wet when cold water is poured on me.

"OH MY GOSH!" I bolt upright and throw the wet covers off of me. "WHO PUT ICE IN THERE!?" I demanded.

"Good morning, dear." The queen greets me with all smiles while holding a bucket. "They told me that you were being stubborn, so I decided to drop by."

I glare at her. "D-drop by, you mean drop some ICE!?" The queen did not answer but only gives me a menacing smile.

"Sarah, Gix, and Heira, please clean up this young lady. Make sure to scrub her from head to toe, brush her hair a hundred times before you curl it, and tie it. Give her a manicure and a facial before you wax her leg and armpit hair. Then, give her a lovely makeover. I want her heels to be a bit high since her escort is a bit tall. Oh, and can you get a box from my office? Those are her accessories. I believe they would go well with the dress. Oh, and about the speech—"

I cut her off. "Woah. What speech?" I stop shivering and focuse my attention on her.

"Your opening speech, dear." The queen raises her eyebrows at me. "Didn't PRINCE Ace tell you?"

PRINCE Ace. THAT BASTARD! I know fully well that it is not like him to forget anything as important as that. This could only mean one thing.

He purposely hid it from me!

"NO, he didn't!" I scream and bolt out of the room faster than I have ever gone out of bed before.

I suck at speeches. Heck, I can't even imagine speaking in front of a crowd, much less a crowd of magical royals.

Forget the speech.

Forget the party.

I am out of here!

I will hide in a bathroom until the day ends. There are at least a hundred bathrooms in this castle. I doubt they could find me in one of them.

I was just giving it a thought when I was picked up from the ground like a sack of potatoes.

"REN, REN, REN! I found your runaway bride." Dan screams excitedly, running in another direction to where I assume his twin would be.

"What the? Why are you carrying Rose? More importantly, why is she still in her pajamas?"

Wow, that's all? Not 'why is she soaking wet?'

"I just found her," Dan says, like someone saying they found a lost animal.

"Your highnesses." I glance up and too see that the maids are already there. "Princess Rose is trying to ditch the party."

I couldn't see the twins' faces, but I can hear them chuckling like they aren't the least bit surprise about it.

"It's not me!" I quickly defend myself. "It's all because a certain PRINCE purposely forgot to tell me that I was supposed to give a speech!" Dan places me back on the ground to give me a look.

Nope, it wasn't sympathy.

It was a mocking look.

"AHAHA!" The two cackle. "You got punked by PRINCE Ace!" Dan starts laughing hysterically.

I stomp on his foot with my bunny slippers. It seems like it has no effect because of the weight of it.

Ren taps me on the shoulder and offers me a white glove. I grab with before smacking Dan with it. Now, I am the one who laughs this time.

"I always wanted to try that again." I grin.

"Princess, we have to get going." The sound of the maids brought me back to reality, ending my temporary happiness of slapping someone with a glove.

I start to turn around and run, but Ren grabs the collar of my shirt. "Where do you think you are going?"

"Uhm...somewhere? Just until the party is over."

Ren snorts. "And you think I'd let you?" With one swift motion, he throws me on his shoulder, just like how Dan carried me a while ago. "You are going to the party, and that is final."

"You traitor! I will never forgive you." I proclaim.

"Lead the way, ladies," Ren says to the maids.

We start to move. Dan is following behind Ren, smirking teasingly at me at my current predicament. I raise an eyebrow at him, wondering what he wants. Whatever he wants. I am in no need for it today.

"Hey, Dan. Come closer so I can slap you again." Dan sneakily walks away while Ren has to deal with me alone.

Ren finally places me down when we reach my room. "Ladies, make sure to treat her well." Ren waves before walking away. The maids were dazed, and as soon as the door shut behind him, they snap back to reality.

"Prince Ren is a wonderful person." One of the maids sighs.

"Prince Ren is a wonderful person." I mock and make a gag sound as I sneakily make my way to my balcony.

Maybe I can somehow escape from there. I did it before, so maybe I can do it again.

I'm just a few steps away when my path is suddenly blocked. I look up and face Tanya. She's an elderly woman and is in charge of the maids. Also, she's wearing a really scary expression right now.

Princess or not, Tanya only follows the queen's orders and has no regard for me. "Where are you going, Princess?"

I let out a nervous laugh. "Um...ahaha....heaven? God is calling me, I think."

"Ladies, bring Princess Rose to the bathroom, and make sure you follow the queen's orders." Tanya's voice is booming with authority, snapping the ladies back to their tasks.

My futile attempts to flee came to an end with that. Against my will, I was dragged into the bathroom. I was stripped down to my underwear and thrown into the bathtub. The maids behaved like soldiers in the presence of Tanya, making no noise and cleaning me up. Tanya was staring me down with her hawk eyes, making me want to hide. I mean, dude, I'm completely naked! Can't she be a little gentler with me with those glares?

"So, Princess Rose. Do you understand the schedule for the ball?" This weird-looking vampire butler then asks me as I'm getting my hair done.

"I got everything except for the speech part. Can we just skip it?" I suggest.

"I am sorry, Princess, but skipping is not an option."

Then I would rather skip the stairs later. If I survive the fall, I'll just have to play dead.

The queen appears out of nowhere, twirling and dancing in her white gown—does she think that she's in some kind of fairytale drama or something?!

"Is my niece all set?" When she sees me, she gasps dramatically. Her eyes were glistening like a 5-year-old's when they see a toy that piques their interest. "Oh, my goodness, dear. You look lovely!"

"And you look younger despite your *age*." The queen slaps me on the back of the head for that.

"None of that sarcasm in the party." She warns me.

Finally, I was ready to leave the room after completing my preparations.

I hear a faint whimper to my side and turn to see Custard with a small bow around his neck.

"Aren't you just the cutest?" I draw in a breath, trying not to laugh because the corset is already squeezing enough air out of me. Despite the fact that Custard looks adorable, my little wolf companion dislikes his outfit. He scratches his neck again and again, rotating the bow completely around his neck. I snatched him into my arms, comforting him with a gentle pat on the head.

We exited my room and were led back to the preparation hall, where the other princes were waiting. The princes rose to their feet when I arrived, as a sign of respect for the 'princess,' as they call me. White and gold coats with long backs are worn by the twins. Their hair was still spiked, but it was styled in a neat manner. Because everything in them is styled similarly, they really do play the role of twins. Dan grins and elbows a gaping Ren, jolting him awake from his reverie. I give them a sneer.

Traitorous wolves. I should throw them in the dungeon. The question is, do we even have one?

Nate went all out, donning a maroon-colored coat with intricate beadwork. His cuffs are encircled with gold and silver details that contrast nicely with his coat's color. He doesn't wear a cape this time, most likely because he doesn't want me to step on it. Because he hadn't cut his hair in a long time, he had to tie it back into a half ponytail. He stated that he wanted a new look for the ball and that he would cut his hair only afterward.

"The night's biggest star has finally arrived." He nods, his gaze moving up and down in approval.

"You clean up well too, Nate." I try to return the compliment before I lean in and whisper to him. *"Get me out of here."*

"No." He whispers back.

Well, it was a good effort on my part.

Finally, ladies and gentlemen, I'd like to introduce my escort: The lord of darkness, king of bookworms, god of bad attitudes, and son of demons—PRINCE Ace.

He is the only one staring at me, as if I were some sort of pest that needs to be exterminated. His coat is black with white lines running down the length of his body. It gives him a muscular and powerful appearance. His hair is combed back, allowing his frowning eyes to be seen.

"What kind of *garbage* are you wearing?" That was the first thing that he said to me.

"Garbage!?" I question him. I'm dressed in a turquoise off-shoulder dress that hugs my waist tightly. Pink flowers and beads are used in the design. The skirt is cut high in the front and low in the back to show off my legs and shoes. I had my hair up in a braided bun with curls at the sides to draw attention to my face. When I last looked in the mirror, I thought I looked good as if I were a true princess, which I am.

How dare this thug right here think that he can just badmouth my dress like that?

"This is not garbage, you fool! Do you even know how much my aunt paid for this?" I sound boastful, but in reality, I really have no idea how much the dress costs. I just hope that it is an impressive amount of sum so I won't look like a fool.

"Yes, sorry for my mistake. Why is *a garbage* wearing that dress?"

"Hey, man." To my surprise, Ren comes to my defense, leering at Ace, which is something that he rarely does when he's angry. "Stop ruining the mood. She looks great in her dress. If you have nothing better to say, you should just keep your comments to yourself."

A brief silence falls between us until we are interrupted when we hear the introductory trumpets behind the door.

"It's about to begin. Rose, are you ready?" Nate asks.

I answer him with a shrug. Surprisingly, I feel a little better since Ren got mad at me for my part—or more like I was still trying to process what happened.

Taking that as a yes, Nate takes my hand and leads me to Ace's side before heading to the twins to take his position.

A gust of wind greeted us as soon as the doors parted, along with crystalline white lights illuminating the party in front of us. The guests who had been invited to the ball were standing below us on the stairs. There were so many people wearing flashy gowns and tuxedos that I became dizzy.

"Don't pass out in front of me. I despise having to carry pigs." When he offers me his arm, I glare back. "Just keep your cool and hold my arm. It's the same way we practiced. Don't make a blunder." Although it may appear to be a threat, his tone is anything but.

To calm myself, I loop my arm around his and take several deep breaths. For a brief moment, I feel relieve to have Ace by my side. It means I won't have to go through this ordeal by myself.

Ren, Nate, and Dan begins to descend the stairs in unison, looking fierce and regal while flashing dashing smiles at the guests. I couldn't blame a few princesses, duchesses, and ladies for staring at them as if trying to memorize their features because they all looked so good.

Soon, it was our cue to follow them.

Custard is pacing on the opposite side of the room, looking eager to join the other princes, but he knows he has to stay put.

I can do this. Not a big deal, right?

Ace takes the lead, and I carefully follow him down the stairs, forcing my chin up instead of down, just like we had practiced. We are almost at the bottom when I became tense after remembering the speech. Ace becomes aware of my distress.

We aren't even halfway through when I slip due to a slight cold on the tips of my toes. Clinging to Ace was the first thought that came to mind.

If I am going down, I might as well take someone with me.

At first, I thought Ace would push or swat me, but the exact opposite happened. He acted faster than I could have anticipated. Ace grabs my waist and jumps all the way down to the bottom. In mid-air, he was able to change his grip on me into a princess carry, allowing us to land safely.

By the time I open my eyes, everyone is staring at us. Nate, Dan, and Ren all look nervous as they switch their attention from the crowd to us. I look for Custard as well, but all I see is him running back to our room.

TRAITOR!

"U-um. I-It's a traditional Earthling greeting...?" I suggest with a smile. It is the only excuse I could come up with for my embarrassing fall. I could just feel PRINCE Ace warming up to slap me. I really thought that I was doomed, but that is, until the crowd began to cheer and applaud us.

Party Crasher

The crowd is still watching us while I have just come to realize something very important.

The speech.

"U-uh, I-I am Princess Rosalie, a tamer. It may be hard to beleive me right now since my spirit partner just ran away upstairs." I gesture behind me to where Custard ran off to. I nervously laugh when I am met with silence and a few more nervous looks from my aunt, the king, and the princes. "And this here is my slave—er, escort—PRINCE Ace, who is a nice dance partner and a nice person in an alternate universe." I look at Ace and see him breathing deeply. He's clearly mad about my lack of preparation for this.

Well, it's not my fault that I delivered a speech unprepared!

Well, I hope that he will continue to wear that look on his face so the other nobles would cower.

"That's really all I have to say so, have a good evening and enjoy the ball?" I say it lastly, just to end my suffering speech.

Fortunately, the crowd seems satisfied with my speech as they started to applaud, making me let out a sigh of relief.

Ace breathes deeply beside me. "If you do that again, I will pretend not to see you the next time you trip."

"Wow. What a gentleman." I fake a swoon.

As the party begins, we make our way toward the others. Now, I have to mingle with the guests, which is my least favorite part of the process.

"Nice save, Rose." Ren leans, trying to hold back a snicker.

"Please keep your voice low. We wouldn't want anyone to hear that." Nate buts in as we head for the group of girls gathered in one place, as per Nate's request.

As we got closer to the group, I adjusted my posture and attire to make myself appear more presentable—and princess-like. When one of the girls noticed us approaching, she alertd the others.

"Princess." A vampire lady curtsies as she greeted me. The other girls follow her gesture.

As a princess, I can only nod in acknowledgment to their greeting as I have a higher title than them.

"Good evening, Lady Jhosel." I greet her first, before turning to the others. "And to you, Lady Rica, Lady Eileen, Lady Savi, Lady Maria, Lady Tasche, and Lady Stacey." I recall their names from my lessons with Ace. I admit that I do find pride that I remember their names. To me, it's an accomplishment!

But just to make sure that I got everything right, I take a glance at Ace. Sure enough, he doesn't want to kill me, which means I got the names right.

Finally!

The girls are also taken aback, but they seem pleased that I know them. "We didn't expect you to recognize our names, your majesty. It's not meant to offend you in any way." Lady Savi asserts.

"We didn't expect her to know your names either." Ren jokes, earning a few light chuckles from the crowd.

I continue to chat with the other ladies. To be honest, I am surprised that I didn't find them boring. Though the topics, were about politics, I somehow find it interesting to listen to them, even though I have nothing to share. Still, it is interesting to learn about the politics from another realm.

Seeing the others eat makes my stomach grumble. I turn to PRINCE Ace, and glares at me in return

"I want the meat rolls." I tell him. I believe that it is time for him to do his part as my escort.

He let out a grumble before going to the buffet table to give me what I asked for. I didn't bother to hide my joy as he presented me with the meat rolls.

A sudden bell brought us all to attention, just as I am about to eat.

"Evening dance is about to begin." A butler announced.

Ah, shit.

PRINCE Ace stops me from eating and places the plate of meat roll on a nearby table.

"I'm sorry, PRINCESS, but we're about to begin the dance." He says, as if he feels amused by my expression of horror. He's already dragging me to the dance floor before I can say anything.

Dang him!

When I return my gaze to the group of ladies, I notice that the others have formed pairs. Ren's eyes seems to be trailing in our direction before inviting one of the ladies to the dance floor. Dan also seems to be looking at us before he invites Lady Tasche to a dance. Nate approaches the other group of girls and asks Lady Caroline, a witch, to join him as his partner.

Speaking of witches, maybe I should ask Lady Caroline about Prince Fred? I haven't seen the guy at all!

My eyes are still wandering, trying to search for the familiar figure I have been dying to meet all night.

"Prince Fred is discussing some matters with the queen right now. He will appear sooner or later." PRINCE Ace says.

"How did you—"

"You're too obvious."

Before I could ask more, it is already time to switch partners. Soon I am dancing with Dan.

"Well, hello there, princess. You are up for a dance with my brother next."

I raise an eyebrow at him. "I kind of know that, so it defeats the purpose of you giving me this information."

He grins. "Isn't this *exciting*!?" Looking behind me to where his brother is probably dancing with another girl.

"Why is everyone is so live—"

"OKAY, I DEMAND A SWITCH," Dan yells and immediately throws me to the side. Then, he runs over to Lady Faeya and literally *carries* her to the dance floor.

Yes. He was <u>*carrying a lady to the dance floor*</u>. Let the words sink in for a bit.

When Dan pushes me, I bump into Lady Amara.

"I-I-I'm sorry." I stutter and glare at Dan for the embarrassment the he puts me through. He and Lady Faeya both glance at me before they chuckle together as if having a secret conversation.

Luckily, Lady Amara is nice.

"Oh, Princess Rose!" She curtsies and looks back to Prince Ren with a kind smile. "Please dance with each other. My feet hurt and I can barely walk." I stare at her.

She's lying. She seems fine!

To his credit, Ren actually seems concerned and acts like a proper gentleman by offering her assistance. "Are you sure? Do you want me to escort you to the table?"

"Nope!" She declines the offer quickly, along with a shake of her head, sending her blue curls bouncing on her shoulder. "I can walk on my own. Please, have fun!"

"Alright. Have a good rest, Lady Amara." I know better than to comment about it and simply watch her fake limp off the dance floor.

I could have imagined it, but I think I see her and Dan exchanging a thumbs up.

"Would you like to dance?" Ren smiles and offers me his hand. As soon as our hands touch, I hear a squeal. I look back in Dan's direction, but he seems to be too busy dancing with his partner.

It must be my imagination.

Just as the switching of partners was about to commence, I saw Dan, Lady Faeya, and Lady Tasche pushing Lady Eileen towards Ace instead of Ren. Poor Lady Eileen has to endure Prince Ace's killer looks.

What exactly are they up to? Nothing ever goes right at these social gatherings, I swear.

"Is it me or are Dan and his new gang preventing other girls from dancing with you?" I whisper to Ren.

"Oh good; you also noticed it. I thought I was getting crazy." Ren looks both relieved and troubled.

"Excuse me. Mind if I cut in?" A girl suddenly asks. It's another duchess from a well-known family—Lady Maria.

Before Ren and I can agree, Dan cuts in and says, "Oh look. PRINCE Ace is available! Come right this way, pretty lady." Dan takes her hand and literally pushes her to Ace.

Ace, who was never a gentleman, surprisingly catches her. Lady Maria flushes a little before fixing herself. Without a word, Ace asks her for a dance out of courtesy to the young lady.

"What is up with your brother?" I start to get worried because it seems like he is plotting something.

"Why are you asking me? I'm just as confused as you." Ren shrugs his shoulders.

Two figures appear beside us, not a second too soon. A golden cuff held Prince Darem's long golden-brown hair in a ponytail. His older brother, Prince Eltur, stood beside him, his silver hair flowing neatly down his back. They are Elven royalty and Ace's older brothers.

"Oh, hello, Prince Renevier and Princess Rosalie." Darem greets me. Beside him, Prince Eltur brings along a petite lady. "Lady Amara here wants to have a dance with Prince Ren. Mind if she cuts in?"

"Regrettably, I—" Lady Amara, who appears distressed, begins to object before being shove into Ren's arms. Dan quickly appears out of nowhere, looking dissatisfied with the arrangement. When Prince Darem sees him approaching, he grabs his hands and pretends to smile.

"Ahhh, Prince Daniel. MIND IF WE HAVE A DANCE?"

"No! Fuc—" Dan's cursing is cut off when Prince Darem leads him away in a waltz. How he manages that throughout Dan's protest is beyond me. I also see Lady Tasche, Dan's scheming partner of the night, trying to rescue poor Prince Dan, but Prince Eltur takes her by surprise and includes her in the dance as well.

Well, that's something that you don't usually see in formal parties.

"My beautiful, Princess Rose." I jump in surprise when Nate whispers in my ear like a creep. Nate chuckles at my reaction. "Easy there. I don't bite. I just want a dance." He syas, offering me his hand.

"Well, don't mind if I do." I place my hand in his as I accept his request. Nate and I start to dance as the music changes to a more subtle tune. "It's nice of you to pick me up from that chaos over there."

Nate laughs and casts a sidelong glance at Prince Darem and Prince Dan, who are still dancing the waltz. "What can I say? When a lady is in distress, Nate is there to impress."

"How many times have you repeated those lines this evening?"

"Twelve times."

"Nice."

His stare suddenly softens, and his goofy grin is now gone. His mouth starts to move as if he wants to say something. "If only the girl I kissed in the lake was really you, it would have been worth drowning." He days dramatically.

"I WISH YOU **DID** DROWN!" I hear Dan yells in the background.

"Are you uttering a curse or something?" I joke. Nate looks like he has woken up from a trance. For a few seconds, his eyes dart fearfully towards Prince Ace, who is now dancing with another lady.

"Of course not. I am serious when I say you are the most beautiful creature I ever laid my eyes upon." I start to laugh after that. "Hey, why is Prince Ren dancing with Prince Darem?" He suddenly ask.

"Oh, that's not Ren. It's Dan. Ren is currently dancing with Lady Rizzi."

"The black-haired werewolf girl?"

"Yeah, that's the one."

"Ace looks busy." Nate took a glance at Ace, who is now partnered up with another poor lady. From the movement of Ace's lips, I would read his words.

Try to speak and I will trip you so hard you will put your shoes on your hands to walk.'

"I don't understand why so many girls want to dance with him this evening."

"Maybe they were curious and wanted to see why you chose PRINCE Ace to be your escort." Prince Fred suddenly interrupts us, appearing at our side. As always, the warlock prince was dressed to impress in a nice suit. There were no beads, but his suit seems to glitter in just the right spots. His blonde hair is pulled back on one side and left in a semi-messy style on the other.

I couldn't contain my joy upon seeing him and I start to grin from ear to ear.

"Prince Fred!"

Fred chuckles and gestures at Prince Ren and PRINCE Ace having new partners. "They have already changed partners. Mind if I cut in?"

Nate let out a loud sigh. "Great timing, Fred. Really great timing." By his tone, Nate seems displeased.

I don't know if he was faking it or not, but Fred just laughs. "Sorry, my friend. I got really busy and only had a few minutes before the queen calls me over again."

"I see," Nate grumbles "Well, I guess I leave her in your care for now." After saying this, he winks at me and kisses my hand. "Until the next ball, princess. I'll take a break from dancing for a while. I'm satisfied with my dance with Rose." He tells us and heads off to get himself a drink.

There will be no next ball if I can help it.

"You really have a huge impact on people. Do you know that?" As Fred waltzed us to a new song, he remarks suddenly. The feeling of being able to dance with him again feels so amazing. Our last dance in the maze was heartbreaking, and I never thought I would be able to waltz with him again. But look at us now, doing the waltz as if everything is fine. For a moment, I don't even care about anything else.

"What kind of impact?"

Fred shakes his head. "Nothing. Hey, you are getting good at dancing. Did you practice while I was gone? "

"Nah, I just had this really amazing dance teacher before."

"Oh, really?" Fred fakes shock. "Was he handsome?"

"No. He's hideous." I say bluntly. "Not only was he ugly, but he left without saying a proper goodbye. I say good riddance."

"Ouch?" Fred flinches. "You know, I also have a dance student who really sucks at dancing and calls me ugly when I am clearly not." After his comment, I step on his foot intentionally. It doesn't seem to bother him, and he just laughs it off.

"Be careful, Fred. You are starting to sound like Nate." I warn him.

"Well, in the least. My student, who really sucks at dancing is my little sunshine. I miss her dearly when I am away."

"I miss you too, Fred. We all do."

Fred smiles and pulls me into a hug.

"I think it is time for you to go back to your escort before he scares any more of our female visitors." He whispers, looking at Ace, who is glaring at every female who seems interested in dancing with him. "You really made a big mess here. You made him popular with the ladies by making him your escort. Now, every female wants to dance with him for good fortune."

"Is that how it works?" I raise a brow.

"You didn't know?"

"I only made him my escort for slavery."

Fred threw his head back and laughed.

"Only you can think of making a prince into a slave." He kisses my forehead before leading me to Ace. Meanwhile, I am too daze by the kiss to argue. "Seriously, go back to your escort before he snaps."

A moment later, I found myself in Ace's company; he seems so furious at me, I'm surprised he hasn't thrown me out of the window. *Yet.*

"Well, it's nice to see you having a good time." He mocks me.

"Well, of course. I am a PRINCESS and this party is for me." I reply smugly.

"Enjoy it while you think it's fun." He says. "You know, we should stop dancing and meet the leader of the other kingdoms to formally introduce you."

I stop smiling. "Is that your excuse for wanting to take a break from dancing?" I joke.

PRINCE Ace gives me a silent look, one where I question my time of death. I swallow nervously.

"U-um..yeah. S-Sounds like a-a p-plan. It's not like I am agreeing with you because I am scared of you or anything. Don't get the wrong idea." Ace's only response is to roll his eyes. He offers me his arm and leads me to where the Queen is talking to the leaders of the other kingdoms.

Just as we are approaching, Ace's head suddenly turns to my left. His eyes register a look of horror before he pulls me close to him.

"Get down!" He yells and moves me away to use his body as a shield when an ear-piercing crash occurs.

One of the windows in the ballroom shatters when a badly beaten tiger is thrown in.

"Sives!" Dan screams as he runs up to the tiger, who is beginning to revert back to human shape. His injuries are so severe that he never recovered enough to transform into a human and instead kept his tiger stripes and fangs when Dan found him. "Sives, what happened to you?" By now, almost all of the people in the ballroom are so quiet that we could hear Sives talking even from afar.

I hadn't even realized it, but the other princes now stood beside me, except for Dan. Sives's eyes scanned the room until they found mine.

"It's you." He says. After addressing me, everyone starts to look at me as well. "King Ferius wants you." He whispers.

I feel chills runningdown my body at his words.

Ferius? Who is that?

Sives looks desperate and when he addresses Dan. "King Ferius wants h-her, my prince. Don't let the rogue king have her." Sives whispers before he begins to choke in his own blood.

"Guards! Secure perimeters. Make sure whoever did this will pay!" Dan orders, looking really enraged. "Go find the bastard who did this!"

There's a roar in his voice when he uses his alpha genes to command every beastmen around us.

"Get her out of here!" The queen orders from the other side of the room. I did not realize the queen was referring to me until Ren nudges me.

"Come, Rose." He says. "Rose?" I couldn't move. I was frozen on the spot. I was being targeted by the rogue king for reasons I don't know. I am not trying to be stupid. I really want to leave, but my whole body stops moving the moment I hear the name. It's like the name has a magical effect on me that I cannot explain.

Unsafe.

I don't even know who that Ferius person is, but why is my blood running cold? Why am I so afraid? It feels like…I should know him.

"As long as we are here, no one is going to hurt you. Come on." Ace promises as Nate covers my vision with his coat.

Finally, I can feel my body moving again, allowing me to leave the ballroom while being escorted by the princes.

Still, my mind pegs one question as we start to leave—*who is Ferius?*

Connection

The party was a disaster. Everyone was in a panic as security measures were being taken.

    Someone did this to get to me. Ferius. Even just remembering the name makes my body shiver. Thinking about it, I can't believe that I have frozen like that. Usually, I would run at the first sign of danger, but at that time, it seems like I just stop functioning.

"Come on, Rose." Ren squeezes my hand, bringing me back to my senses.

"Get her to my office. It has wards, and only those who do not have an urge to kill can enter." The queen is suddenly at my side and places a hand on my cheeks. "You will be safe there. I will meet you once this is settled."

I don't know what she's planning to do by staying here. Why doesn't she come along? What is she going to do? Murder the culprit?

"You heard the queen. Let's go." Nate gently pushes my back and urges me to follow Ace. My heart is hammering in my chest so fast that I couldn't even hear the shrill of panic as we left the party.

We arrive at the queen's office, and I don't even feel the least bit safe. Ren opens the door and ushers me in.

"What the hell!" Immediately Nate and I turn to see PRINCE Ace and Ren strand outside the room.

"What are you guys doing? Get in here." Nate doesn't seem annoyed. He looks amuse as he watches the two princes standing outside with equally puzzled expressions.

Ren grunts and starts banging at an invisible wall by the door. "I want to, but as you can see, I cannot!" He starts punching the wall in agitation. On the other hand, PRINCE Ace rubs his temples as he watches Ren trying to break the invisible wall.

"Calm down. The more bloodlust you have, the more you can't get in." He explains to Ren. "I said stop that, you moron!" Ace snaps when Ren doesn't listen.

"The queen did say that those who have a killing intent cannot enter." Nate stares at the two. "Why do you guys have killing intent?"

"I want to kill whoever did this to our men. And to whoever is threatening Rose's life." Ren says and gives PRINCE Ace a look. "You also want to kill who's responsible for this, don't you?"

PRINCE Ace does not even look at him when he answers Ren's question. "I just want justice for the murder. That's all."

"Then, if you want justice, why can't you enter then?"

"Because I always choose violence." Ace says it like it is the most obvious answer that he has. He takes a couple of deep breaths before he effortlessly tries to get in. This time, he's successful, leaving Ren the only one standing outside the Queen's office.

"Damn, know it all." Ren huffs.

I start to head for the nearest couch and sit there in a daze. A hand starts to rest on my forehead, and I look up to see Nate.

"Geez, Rose. You're not a vampire, but you're as cold as we are when we're hungry."

I am in a daze. The amount of fear that I felt was incomparable. I can't understand why? I just heard the name of King Ferius, and my blood ran cold like it somehow recognized that name.

"Rose!" The queen suddenly barge into the office, carrying Custard with her. Custard happily jumps on my lap and start to nuzzling my neck. "Are you doing okay, my dear?" The queen gently touches my cheek. I numbly nod when I answer her. For some strange reason, I seem to have some difficulty formulating words. It must have been from the shock of what happened earlier. "You must keep your familiar with you. Always. He might not look reliable, but he will protect you."

"Why were they after me?" I finally manage to ask after a long time of playing with the words in my head.

"We don't know that for sure. But whoever it is, I assure you that we will protect you. You can see how bloodthirsty the twins are." The queen now points to Dan, who have just arrive, and Ren, outside.

"Sorry, but you cannot blame me for what I feel right now." Says Dan as he clenches his blood-smeared hands. "And my queen. I am here to inform you that we were able to capture one of the rogues. Suppose to be two, but the other one committed suicide before Prince Frederick could stop him."

"And where is he now?"

"In the lower cell. King Luke is with Prince Fred while casts a spell on him so he cannot commit suicide."

"And did you find anything?"

"Yes. It seems that they were aware that if they were captured and forced to talk, the only person they could talk to was their target."

"No! Absolutely not," Ren growls and punches the invisible wall. "No way we would let them lay their filthy eyes on her after threatening her."

I don't have to be a genius to figure out that they were referring to me. "So we have nothing. No other information other than the fact that they want to kill me and talk to me?" I ask.

Dan sighs, shifting from his standing position and running a hands through his hair, messing up his hairdo from the party.

"Unfortunately, yes. He only wants to talk to you—no other person in the room. But don't worry, Rose. We will find another—"

"Then I'll do it." I volunteer. I have no idea where these words come from, but it seems like something is compelling me to go. Maybe I will get some answers why the name Ferius has a strong impact on me.

"Absolutely not! Rose, you have done a lot of stupid things and this will not be one of them." Nate begins to protest, followed by nods of agreement from the others, including my aunt.

"For once, I agree with Prince Nathaniel." PRINCE Ace mumbles.

"Ace, don't start with me," I warn him before turning to my aunt to plead. "Please just let me do it. Just bind him with chains so he can't hurt me. And I'll talk to him at a far distance." There is something about this encounter that is telling me to dig deeper. It feels like something darker than I imagine is behind all of this. I can't explain how I know it, but I just get this tingling in my blood.

"My dear, I cannot risk that. I thought I lost my blood relatives forever until you came—"

"Oh, don't you start with that because you kidnapped me. I did not come here willingly." I remind her.

"But it cannot be a coincidence that it was you that I had to kidnap. It was your fate to let me kidnap you."

A moment of silence falls into the room while we all stare at my aunt. I guess I am not the only one who thought that it is strange for my aunt to admit that she kidnapped me so proudly. Even Ace's eyes were wide with shock before he quickly hides his expression by looking the other way.

"Seriously. That sounds so disturbing." Is all I manage to say without offending her too much. "But I have to do something. There's something about the name—"

"Rosalie, I told you that you are forbidden, and that's that!" When the queen raises her voice, Custard stirs awake and jumps off of my lap, growling lowly at my aunt for yelling at me. I get to my feet so I can look at my ant squarely in the face.

"I am sorry. You may be the Queen and my great whatever aunt, but my life is being targeted, not yours. I am involved in this mess, so I have the right to get some answers." I start to walk past her. "Let's go, Custard."

I am getting tired of waiting. This growing anxiety inside my chest is telling me to go. I'm not sure if it's just me or maybe there's some other force out there beckoning me to leave, but what I do know is that it might have something to do with my ancestors.

"Ace, if you would be so kind. Please." As the queen gives out the order, Ace suddenly grabs me by the shoulder to stop me.

"Let go of me!" I yell. Custard seems to be agitated and starts barking at PRINCE Ace. When Ace did not glance at him, Custard lunges and bites his leg. Ace grits his teeth in pain.

"Somebody do something about this dog, or I will." He warns. Nate takes action and grabs Custard off of Ace.

"That will leave a mark," Nate says, eyeing Ace's bloody leg.

"Hold her still." The queen commands while she runs and stands before me.

"Why are you stopping me?!" I demanded. I try to headbutt Ace from behind, unfortunately, he is too skilled for me to hit. He is too strong and my only ally is being held by Nate. "Let me do this for myself."

The queen only looked at me with remorse.

"My dear, you have the spitfire of my brother-in-law." She says it sadly. "And that is what got him killed. I will be damned if I let any one of my family die again. Now, go to sleep, dear. We'll keep you safe."

The last thing I remember is her opening her palm and blowing blue powder on my face.

Escape Plan

I was in my room by the time I awoke, along with Custard. I couldn't leave the castle and go for a walk. Nope. I was incarcerated.

In some ways, yes, but I do get visitors now and then.

The room is cleaned after the servants bring me food and clothes. The princes would come to see me as well, but I refuse to speak with them. I wouldn't even give them a second glance. They'd just sit in my room and talk about how they're assisting the queen in figuring this out without jeopardizing my safety. But I know they had no luck cracking the captured rogue every time they come. I understand they're just worried about me, but how can they be when they have no idea what the enemy has planned for me or why they want to kill me?

All I did for three days was read and play with Custard. It turns out that he likes ear scratches, which I recently discovered.

Not to mention the fact that I noticed that we have a psychic connection. I discovered it when I was too lazy to call out to him, I simply said his name in my head and heard him grumble in annoyance in response.

My familiar has an attitude problem—that or he's just as moody as me from being locked away.

After the princes' visit on the fifth day, I realize I need to speak with that rogue. That means I'll have to flee my room. Unfortunately, my room is under a spell that prevents me from leaving. I've been studying for a few days and have discovered that such spells have loopholes— ~~yes, I study~~.

If the spell requires me to remain in the room, I may be able to cloak myself. It's only a theory, but I gave it a shot.

Since Custard is also locked up with me, I tested my theory on him. The cloak that I wore last time is still in my closet. I brought it out and wrapped it around him. By the time dinner came, I had asked

Custard to try going out of the room carefully when the servants had brought me my meal. It worked.

Now all I have to do is make a strategy. One thing I've noticed is that everyone has a schedule here. I have schedules for my meals, baths, and visits. I was able to lay it all out easily. My only problem is how to get the key to my room from them. I bet that the princes would have it since they would be my last visitors for the afternoon before it would be handed to the servants. My plan is for Custard to steal it from the outside.

The eighth day has arrive, and it is time for the prince's arrival. All I have to do now is figure out how to make a hole in the pocket where they keep the key so that Custard can get it on their way out. My plan has a 40-60% chance of succeeding, but it is the best option I have, given my power limitations.

The door to my room opens, and I want to curse my unlucky stars when I realize whose pockets I have to destroy to get the key.

PRINCE *Ace, on behalf of all the good things in the world...I HATE YOU!*

Prince Ace removes his coat and places it on the coat rack beside my bedside table before he goes dragging a chair to sit at my side.

"The others are busy, so I am stuck with you as you are stuck with me." He starts to explain himself even though I did not ask.

I look away and clutch the small knife I stashed beneath the bedsheets.

I have no idea how I'm going to do this! This guy has hawk-like eyes! Before I even have a chance to rip his coat pocket, he'd figure out what I am up to. This means I'll have to reschedule my plans for another day.

Damn it! I barely slept last night preparing for this day.

"Ugh!" In my frustration, I accidentally knock the book on my table, and it hit the ground with a loud thud. Ace immediately runs and picks the book up.

"What the hell are you doing!?" He yells at me. "Books are precious artifacts for learning, and you just throw them away because I am keeping you company!?" He flares up in anger, and he inspects how much damage I had caused to the book.

At that moment, I realized that I was not so unlucky after all.

PRINCE Ace is a bookworm.

What's better way to piss off a bookworm than to drop books? Emphasis on the word *books*.

My drama queen mode is on!

"For goodness sake! It has been eight days! EIGHT DAYS." I got up from my bed and start heading toward my bookshelf. It breaks my heart to think about what I am about to do, but I have to keep my priorities straight. "You guys found nothing, and now I am stuck here with you. This is hell in real life!" I let out a frustrated grunt, and—with all my might—I push the bookshelf until it falls on the floor.

PRINCE Ace let out a curse as he runs towards the fallen shelf to rescue the books. Making sure that I bought myself enough time, I kick a few books as far away from my target as possible.

I'm so sorry!

"You guys can't do anything right!" I try to sound angry as I hastily and quietly make my way to his coat and tore off the stitches of the pocket. I made sure that I left a few stitches that would hold it for a while so it wouldn't be too obvious.

'Alright, Custard. Once this mean elf goes out, make sure to follow him out. Wait for him to lock the door and pocket his key again. If the key doesn't fall, I left a hanging strand that you can pull to unravel the stitch at the bottom of the pocket. Once you have the key, you slide it to me from the bottom, Okay?'

Custard grumble worrily in response.

'Hey, hey. None of that attitude! We need to work as a team, remember?'

"You don't have to bring all your frustrations out on the books, you brainless monkey!" Ace insults me just as I finish unraveling the stitches of his coat.

I was too focused on fixing the coat to make it look untouched that the only insult I could backfire was, "Your mom is a brainless monkey." I realize my mistake, so I quickly move away from the coat just in time as Ace glances in my direction.

"Seriously?" He questions me with an eyebrow raised. "You come up with nothing and start insulting my mother?"

I want to hit myself for being this stupid. But what can I do? There is no turning back now.

"Oh, so what? You're going to cry?" I start mocking him. "You gonna come cry to your mommy, PWINCE Ace?" I smirk because I know I struck a nerve when I reminded him of how he got turned into a kid.

Ace let out a disgusted sigh. "You are annoying."

"You are annoying."

"Now you're acting like a kid."

"Now you're acting like a kid."

"Honestly, being locked up turned you from a brainless monkey to a broken parrot."

"Your schedule is a broken parrot."

Ace shakes his head. "I cannot even insult you without being disgusted by your comebacks. I am out of here."

"Oh, yeah. That's right. Go to your mom and tell her that PWINCE Ace needs his nappy nap because Rose hurt his feelings." I need to stop. Even I am cringing with my insults. At this point, my reputation is going to get ruined.

He picks up his coat and makes his way to the door. Using my physic link with my familiar, I order Custard to follow Ace.

"The only thing that you are hurting are my ears. It would be best to put you on a leash tomorrow and have you walk around the castle to socialize."

"I don't want to hear the word *socialize* from someone who doesn't even socialize himself!" I manage to yell at him before he closes the door. "I got the last word!" I sang to myself.

I think he is right, though. I need to talk to someone other than Custard, or else I'm going to go *crazy*.

Custard is trying to communicate with me through our link. And you know what he says?

'Master, I got you the key. The door. Under.' At least, that is how I translate Custard.

"Oh, what a good boy, Custard," I pick up the key and unlock the door. Custard enters back to hand me the cloak so we csan exit together. Once I got past the spell binding me to my room, I can't help but lay down on the floor and curl up like a baby. "Ugh, yes! I miss the outside world!"

'Master! Please stop...' Custard starts poking my cheek with his paw.

"You are such a killjoy." I sigh sadly. But he is right though. I need to keep moving if I don't want to get caught.

I get up and start moving along with Custard. When we reach the lower cell, I found that it is heavily guarded.

Oh, don't you love it when you think you've got everything planned out and something *out* of the plan just pops right out?

'Okay, Custard. You go left, and I go right. There's only two of them.'

'Master, do you think you can take one of them out? You can barely kick off your shoes. No offense, master.'

'So, can you take them both?'

'You haven't even figured out how to return me to my fighting form...'

'So both then?'

'Master, you command me, not the other way around.'

'Hey! You're hurting my feelings.'

'Why don't I just become their distraction while you sneak in, Master?'

'B-but. It's too dark. I don't want to go alone.'

'You can do it, master!' Custard looks at me with sparkling and encouraging eyes as he wags his tail. *'You're brave.'*

And this is the part where I know that he is bullshitting me. He knows that I am a coward at heart. He just wants to leave me that badly.

'Okay, fine! But promise me that you will catch up.'

'I promise.'

Custard nuzzles my leg for good luck before running towards the cell guards. He starts barking at them a few times to catch their attention.

"Hey. What are you doing here?" One of the guards snaps and focuses in attention on Custard. In response, Custard runs and bites the guard's leg. The guard grunts and attempts to strike Custard with his spear. Custard, my good little boy, decides that he wanted the spear. He grabs it with his mouth and pulls it towards him when the guard swings in his direction.

With Custard now wielding the spear, he starts to entice the guard to pursue him. To ensure that the two of them would follow him, he dashes over to the other guard and trips him with the spear he had obtained from the previous guard. When the second guard is knocked back, Custard jumps on his chest and scratches his face before fleeing as quickly as he can. The guards, understandably, become enraged and chase him.

I draw the magic cloak around me as I try not to laugh at what I have just witnessed.

Geez, if Custard can taunt them that easily, just imagine what an actual human can. Security here sure is lacking.

I dash off and search every cell for the rogue. Blood and rotten flesh fills the air, making me want to vomit. I couldn't see where I'm going because the only light source in this area were lit torches.

Seriously, they have all the wizards and witches in the palace, and they cannot even provide a proper spell to brighten the place?

"If I were a killing rogue, where would I be?" I whisper to no one.

"Probably in an underground cell, wondering if the person outside is the princess or not."

History

I stifle a scream and immediately turn to where I heard the voice. It's coming from one of the cells.

I grab a nearby torchlight and hesitantly approach the bar walls separating me from my assassin.

Once I get a good look at his face, I have to look away or else I'll puke. Even though I only got a brief look at him, I cannot forget how dirty and bloody he is. He's wearing nothing but some old ragged shorts that were wet from urine and blood. Some of his nails are missing from scratching the stone walls. His face is bruised badly with a lot of dried blood that you could hardly tell if those are his hair or blood.

"To what do I owe the pleasure of having you visit a lowly rogue like me?" I can just hear him smile in amusement at my presence.

"You know why I'm here." I have to cover my nose and mouth to not smell the odor of this place. "I heard that you are under a spell to only talk to me if you were ever captured and couldn't kill yourself. Now tell me. Why is it so important that only in my presence must you reveal your true objective?"

"Once upon a time—" He starts.

"Oh, for goodness sake, I do not need a damn story!"

"Sorry, your highness. But all of these do not make sense unless you learn of your ancestors' sins."

"What sins?" Now I look at him with curiosity.

He smirks. "I suggest that the princess sit since it might be a long tale."

"No thanks. I prefer standing." I say nothing about the smell of pee, blood, and rot around the place. Who would even want to sit in this place?

The man scoffs. "Suit yourself." He says. "Once upon a time. King Varon had a loyal and trustworthy adviser. His name is Ferius, whom you might now know as the king of Tereu."

"He's the rogue King?" I accidentally interrupted him. "If he is serving King Varon, does that mean that he is a tamer?"

"Very good, your highness." The man claps like he is trying to compliment a child.

"Yes, he is. But as of now, his status is a bit complicated. As you may know, the Tamers were the most powerful race a long time ago. Their familiars come in different forms and shapes. Some have cobras, others have leopards, and others have griffins."

"Griffin? As in a mythical creature?"

"Not a myth. You cannot see them anymore because they are extinct." He says. "Ferius is a greedy man. He knew that if they wanted to, they could conquer the whole kingdom. All he had to do was convince the king to see the gift the gods gave them."

"Let me guess. King Varon refused?"

"Always on the good side, right? But yeah. Your great-great-great-great-grandfather refused and threatened to strip Ferius of his title as chief. Ferius was furious and called the king a coward. You can only imagine that Ferius still didn't give up on conquering the lands. He gathered men from every race who would be willing to accompany him on his conquest. He found witches that could help him give more power to his familiar: Qioura. His lion." He sighs. "He asked them to merge Qioura with the other spirit animals he had stolen from other tamers. By stealing, I mean severing the bond of a familiar and its Tamer by killing the tamer."

I flinch. I feel sorry for the other familiars back then. I only just got used to Custard, and it would pain me to imagine if someone abused Custard like that.

"The witches were successful, of course. Now Ferius has the perfect weapon to kill Naga, king Varon's familiar. They created a chimera that only Ferius could control."

"I have heard of this before," I say, knowing how the story would end. "He destroyed Gija. They massacred an entire kingdom and killed my ancestors—or so you thought." I whisper the last part with a smirk. "This is a waste of my time. You're just telling me what I already know." I start to leave.

"But don't you wonder what happened to the king Varon and Naga? How did they die? And of the chimera?" The rogue taunted, stopping me from leaving.

I pause, contemplating on whether I should listen more to the story or not. Then, after some careful internal debate, I decided to head and listen to the rest.

"Go on." I urge him.

"Like you said; Ferius succeeded in destroying Gija, but not without a price. King Varon wanted to make sure that the abomination was stopped. So, with the help of a few witches of his own, he cast a spell on Ferius. With the help of Naga, King Varon was able to seal the Chimera inside Ferius. A curse that would slowly eat him as time passes. King Varon used his royal blood as a protective seal that cannot be undone. Of course, king Varon knew that Ferius couldn't undo the spell since the only blood relatives he had were either or had escaped to another realm—a realm where no one can enter because Queen Elizabeth protects it."

"But," I pause. "I'm king Varon's relative." I whisper, realizing what kind of danger I'm in.

No.

Not just me, but also my family back home.

"Is….is King Ferius planning on using my blood to release the Chimera from him!?" The man in front of me laughs maniacally. "Answer me!"

"Dead or alive, as long as he can get enough of your blood to release his Chimera." He smirks, looking at another part of the cell where I am just noticing approaching footsteps. "Well, about time you got here. I was bored trying to distract her. I'm bad at telling stories."

A hand suddenly grabs me from behind and covers my mouth when I start to scream.

"The way you delivered your story was horrible." The man behind me says. I couldn't see him, but I know that he is wearing a palace guard's uniform.

The palace has been infiltrated!

"At least it's true. Hey, are you bringing her back dead or alive?"

"Alive, I guess. The king would be pleased to kill her himself."

No. They can't bring me back to Tereu. I refuse to be a means for thekingdom's destruction!

I thought back to my parents and sister in my realm. I haven't even told them how much I loved them back when I had the chance. I took my time with them for granted. I thought I had all the time in the world. I had not even fully bonded with my family. Back on Earth, I was selfish. I wanted to be alone and could not wait to live independently and away from them. When I was taken away from my world, I got to live that life. But it was so lonely without them.

I need to go back. I have to go back. I have to survive until I can return to them—by any means necessary.

I dig my fingernails into the face of my assailant. As I draw blood, the man behind me screams. I take advantage of the opportunity and draw his blade from its sheath and slash his right leg. "You can't take me. None of you can. If I can help it." I say before feeling another presence lurking in the shadows, but this one isn't a foe. It's just lurking in the shadows, ready to strike at my command.

Even on his bleeding knee, he is laughing. "How cute. You think a small girl like you can stop a big angry vampire like me?"

'Master.'

Since that one time in the woods, I hadn't felt this strong of a connection with Custard. It's terrifying, but I'm confident and trust my spirit beast.

"Yes, I can't fight you." I admit, tossing the sword to the side. "But he might." I point in the shadows behind the man. The man arches a brow before he quickly grabs fallen torchlight and comes face to face with a grown and ferocious white wolf.

The man lets out a terrified scream.

"Your friend here told me that Tamers were the most powerful race a long time ago. And I want to know why and how?" My eyes narrows. Truth be told, I am hoping that he would answer my question because even I have no idea how tamers are considered to be the most powerful race in this realm. That fact has be curious and it filled my mind with a lot of questions.

"I'm sorry, your highness. I-I'll leave. I will never harm you again!" The man trembles in fear as he looks at Custard.

"You serve the rogue king—the very person who killed my blood relatives. They took the familiars from their tamers to create a lethal beast that could destroy kingdoms. The king wants my blood, and you ask me to spare you?" I scoff. "You killed people!"

"Mercy!" He pleads.

It was weird. Custard looks like a wolf. Larger than a werewolf. This guy is a vampire—an undead. How is it that he is so afraid of him?

"Why are you so afraid of him?" If we're being honest, Custard is larger than the twins when he is grown. When the man did not respond, I turn the man in the cellar. "Why are Tamers so powerful?" The man in the cell is shaking in fear and would not even look at me.

"It's not the tamers, but the royals of Gija! You, the royals of that kingdom, are an abomination!" He yells frantically.

Then, I hear the other man scrambling to his feet. As I turn my attention back to him, he throws the torch in my direction. Custard flicked the torch away from me with his massive tail, snarling at him for trying to hurt me. The man is breathing hysterically and quickly turns away to run, but Custard lunges at the man.

"Custard, don't!" None of this was in my plans. I simply needed some information. I don't want to injure anyone, but as I watch Custard go for the man's throat, I'm starting to doubt that our easy escape from this situation was anything more than wishful thinking on my part.

Bloodline

"WHAT ARE YOU DOING HERE?!?" Nate appears beside me out of nowhere. I didn't say anything as I am frozen on the spot while looking at the scen before me.

White mist is coming out of the man. At first, I thought that it was smoke from the torch, but it clearly isn't since Custard seems to be eating it.

"Rose, make him stop!"

"I-I don't know how!" Even though I am not the one getting attacked, I still panic. My wanders to the man in the cage. He is trembling in fear, making me turn to Nate in desperation. "Nate, I don't know how to Custard stop!"

Nate sees the panic and fear in my eyes. His eyes soften, and he places a reassuring hand on my shoulder. "Try to stay calm and command him. He should listen to you."

I turn to Custard. "S-stop." Custard's ears only flinches, but he did not stop.

"Try again. This time, make it sound like a command and not a request."

"Custard, STOP!" Abruptly he stops. A tight sensation runs through my head, making me dizzy. Suddenly, I can hear screaming.

The same scream comes from the man that Custard attacked, but it seems far away like an echo.

"What happened here?" My thoughts broke when I hear Ren and Dan coming, but the loud ringing in my head is too hard to ignore.

"What is Rose doing here!? And why does she look constipated!?" Dan demands.

Ren growls when he sees the man that Custard previously attacked on the ground. "Brother, there's a rogue!"

"Oh, my gods. What happened to this guy? He doesn't seem injured, but he looks dead."

I decide to investigate after hearing that remark. Custard takes a step back to allow the twins to carry the rogue. The man has no injuries, according to Ren's description. However, his face is pale, and his eyes shake as if he is in pain. He's drooling and trembling with fear. I don't want to look at him anymore because he looks so bad. Instead, I look at Custard, who has shrunk back to his normal size, and walks back to me, looking ashamed.

What did he do to him? Is this the reason why he called the royals of Gija an abomination?

I hear Nate making a sound beside me. "You guys take that guy to Fred. I need to get Rose out of here. Come on, Rose." Nate guides me out with Custard trailing us from behind. Nate lead us out into the garden, where we sit on one of the benches.

For a while, we sit in silence. Nate figured I needed some time to collect my thoughts, which I appreciated. Even Custard wasn't even making a sound.

"I know you want to be alone," Nate says. "But you have to understand that I can't leave you right now. Not after what happened." He gives me a small smile of comfort. Even though it is a small gesture, I still appreciate it.

"I have no idea what just happened," My breath shakes as I say the words. "I know what I was doing before, but when that guy showed up, I knew I must not let him get me, so I panicked."

"So getting attacked by that guy wasn't part of your plan?" He says teasingly. Then he pauses like he just realizes something. "Wait. How did you get out, and where the fuck were the guards!?"

Oops.

"Um..." I start thinking of a quick excuse. I don't want to put the guards in trouble for my actions. "Actually..." I trail off when I see the frown on Nate's face. He's mad, alright. Even I can see that.

I avert my gaze and hope that he wouldn't suspect me.

"Rose, please don't tell me that you did something to the guards."

"Okay, *I won't*." I agree immediately, still not looking at him.

"Rose, do you realize that you could have endangered yourself by doing that? Well, scratch that. You *did*." I am well aware of how serious he is about this, so I did not attempt to lighten the mood.

He sighs, "We tried to keep you out of danger, yet you come running towards it. How can we even protect you?"

"Yeah, protect me by locking me up. Make me a prisoner in my own room." I roll my eyes. "At least I'm doing something. I have the initiative to find answers to why I am in danger instead of asking others to do the job for me. I may be a princess, Nate, but I don't have to sit pretty all the time. And it is a good thing that I did not." I whisper as dread starts seeping into me when I recall my conversation with the rogue. "What I found out is worse than I thought. Worse than any of us could have imagined."

"Then, I suggest that we head back to the office and have a meeting on this matter." PRINCE Ace, who was in the pavilion the whole time, says.

Nate and I scream in surprise. Both of us would have bolted if we did not recognize his voice.

We didn't notice Ace because he was standing where the wall's shadow fell. My gaze then shifts to the book he was holding. I can't read the title, but I do realize the character of the writing on the book that he's reading.

Those are fucking Japanese novels! Can he even understand them?

"Are you the ghost that keeps appearing when there's bad gossip in the castle?" I ask sarcastically, earning a scowl from the book-loving elf.

Ace narrows his gaze at me before shutting the book close. "What are you sitting around for? Didn't you want to say that you don't want to sit still and do nothing? If you have useful information, it is best to relay it to the queen immediately."

While Nate and I exchange glances, Ace begins walking back to the palace. PRINCE Ace led us to the queen's office, where she summoned us for a meeting. Only a few trusted guards, princes, the king, the queen, and myself were present. Guards were stationed at the doors and windows in case an unintentional attack occurred during our meeting. Only the queen and I were seated face to face. The princes stands behind me while the king is behind his queen. Custard slept on my lap as I informed the queen of my newfound knowledge - that a dangerous spirit lives inside of the rogue king.

Only the princes were surprised when I revealed that the rogue king is actually a tamer. Of course, since they lived during that time, the king and queen were not. The fall of Gija was apparently not well documented in history books. Furthermore, they kept it as brief and uncomplicated as possible because it only stated that the rogue king was a vicious man. Anyone unfamiliar with the story assumed Ferius was either a vampire or a beast man. Those who knew who he was were sworn to secrecy not to bring up the dark past, which had been declared taboo.

"Your highness, I do not mean to accuse you of anything, but you knew what Ferius was all this time, but you did not tell us?" Dan ask. And for the very first time, I hear him ask a sensible question.

"I did not know that it would matter." The queen shamefully lowers her head, not knowing how to respond to all of it. "But if what Rose says is true, then she must be heavily protected from now on. I never knew that the chimera was still alive, and only their bloodline is the key to unleashing that beast. If only I had enough power to bring Rose back to her world, then I would."

The room fell silent at the mention of bringing me back to my world. Somehow, I am not ready to depart yet. This is my family's history.

A dark and dangerous history that could destroy this world as we know it. But can the danger in this world affect our own?

As if reading my mind, Nate asks. "Even if we can send her back right now, won't the King look for another way to enter her realm and kidnap her? Especially now that he knows that he can undo the spell on him."

"There is that possibility. I never thought about it." The queen seems concerned. It was so out of character for her to look troubled like this. "Perhaps it is safer for her to remain with us for a while. Rosalie, what do you say?"

"I want to stay until all this is over. I have a younger sibling back home, and I can't let the rogues target her instead of me. And I can't let him know that I have a family back home." I whisper enough for their adept ears to pick up my words. I delicately stroke Custard's fur. Right now, I know that my family is safe as long as I am here. King Ferius would not think of going through the trouble of locating my family from another realm. At least, not when he knows I'm here. "I don't want to involve my family, so I'll stay."

The queen nods at my resolve. "That's very brave of you." She smiles kindly. "I apologize that if it were not for me, you wouldn't be in this predicament. But all I can say is that I am still happy that I have met you." The queen gets up from her seat and heads over to me and gives me an embrace.

Someone sniffles behind me, and I turn to see Dan and Ren whipping tears from their eyes.

When they see me looking, Ren blushed while does the opposite Dan glowers at me. "What? Haven't seen a grown man *cry* before?"

Wow.

The queen and I both laughe at how silly the twins look. They always have a knack for lighting the mood, no matter how serious it is. The queen decides that it is about time for her to discuss the next course of action based on their newfound knowledge, so she dismisses us, saying that I need not stress about this matter anymore. I didn't even argue about it this time. I have enough fear about the tamer's history and enough about King Ferius and his Chimera to make my ears bleed.

The princes and I quietly left the queen in her study. Well, by princes, I meant all except PRINCE Ace, who wanted to discuss something with the queen. Custard woke when we left the room and was running around ahead of us, constantly looking back to make sure that he could still see me.

Ren starts to clear his throat. I look up to see him giving me a scowl for some reason. "I hope this will be the last time that you put yourself in danger like this again."

At that statement, Nate laughs. "We all know that this won't be the last. It doesn't matter what we say. Rose is just not a proper lady who would sit and look pretty all day."

I scoff. "If you guys already knew that, why would you still insist on having me locked up in my room."

"It's for your—"

"—my own good. I get it." I cut Ren off and sigh in frustration. "But if it wasn't for my rebellious action, we might never have found out about the King's true purpose. And besides, keeping me in one place is more dangerous since the enemy would know which area to target. Have you guys ever thought about that?"

Ren shares a look with Nate as if I had slapped them with a cotton glove. Dan's laugh is what finally breaks the silence.

"My sister is amazing, isn't she?" He comes up beside me and pulls me close. Ren stares at his brother's hand on my shoulder, making Dan's smile grow. "Tell you what, sis. I have an idea that would benefit us both."

I am standing too close to Dan that I have to push him off. "Stop calling me sis. I don't want a stupid brother." I tell him and earn a snort of laughter from Ren. "And what kind of plan is this?" I immediately regret my question when I see Dan's smile growing. As if sensing my fear, Custard barks somewhere ahead, and by the sound of his nails on the ground, he is running towards us.

Dan grabs my hand and pulls me down the hall before I can react. Ren and Nate are also intrigued, but they remain silent. He leads us to a strange part of the palace, close to the palace door, where the corridor is lined with steel armor holding unknown war weapons.

"I think I just figured out your brother's intentions, and I don't like it," Nate says to Ren grimly. I look back, and I see that Ren is fuming in anger directed at his brother.

I was so busy looking at them that I bumped into Dan's back when he stopped.

"Here we are! The weapons room." He announces and throws his hands in the air for dramatic effect.

Weapon Room

A massive wooden gate stands in front of us, reinforced with metal to keep it all together. The doorknob is made of black steel and resembles a snake biting its own tail to form a circle.

I didn't get it at first, but it suddenly dawns on me when Dan turns to give me a wicked smile like he is confirming my guess.

I squeal excitedly, clapping my hands in delight.

"Am I going to get a weapon?!"

I hear Ren clicking his tongue behind us in disapproval. "I thought she would be against this."

Nate gawks at Ren in disbelief. His lips starts moving so fast like he can't decide what to say to him at that moment. Finally, when he did, he yells, "DO YOU EVEN KNOW HER!?"

In response to my earlier question, Dan just gives me a wink. "But of course. Just in case we aren't around and you are forced to fight, at least you have the means to defend yourself."

Dan pushes the door made of oak wood open. It makes a loud creaking sound as it bursts open. The inside of the castle is illuminated by the same glowing orbs that illuminated the outside. They light up hundreds of thousands of pieces of silver and metal as soon as they glow, making me take a step back. Armors, battle axes, and shields adorn the walls. There are racks upon racks of swords of various shapes and sizes. Thick wooden tables line the center, which are adorned with bows of various materials. I assume they were forged by different blacksmiths based on their design. There are a few more weapons I didn't recognize, but I'm sure they're just as deadly.

There was one weapon that made my heart skip a beat.

I release a very long and exaggerated gasp. "Oh my gosh!" I scream and run before Dan can stop me. I head to the center rack and pick up a sword that has 3/4 of its blade curved. "It's a khopesh!" I say.

I'm more hyped about it since I read about it in a book. After taking ahold of the weapon, I start running back towards the princes.

"*Brother-you-better-stop-Rose-right-now.*" Ren is talking too fast for me to decipher his words. Nonetheless, I hold the sword in front of me while showing it to them. "Look!" I hold it out towards them with the pointed edge pointed at the princes.

Dan quickly draws a large shield from the table, and the three of them hide behind it. Dan pokes his head out and laughs nervously.

"Yes, Rose. You are correct. That *is* a khopesh. A very **deadly** weapon that can *skewer* our heads. Now, **please** put it back." I must be tripping, but why does it sound like he is begging?

"Can I keep it? It is a little heavy, though. But maybe a few practice swings can help me get used to its weight. Don't you think?" I swing the weapon left and right like a golf club. It isn't the move I want to make, but I couldn't do anything else because it is too heavy for me.

Ren and Nate kicks Dan away from the safety of their shield, so Dan quickly grabs a dagger and points it at the khopesh.

"Rose, you are going to cut your legs if you keep doing that!" When he warns me.

A gruesome image of my legs being chopped flashes through my mind, and I quickly release the khopesh. The three princes scramble to their feet in a panic as the khopesh flies through the air. They forgot about the shield and ran around with their hands shielding their heads. However, the khopesh is heading straight for me, not them.

"Eek!! I yelp when I am suddenly tackled to the side by Nate as the khopesh drops harmlessly on the floor. My back is against the table, and I am trapped between the wall and Nate, who is currently looking at me angrily.

He glares at me, and all I do is give him a sheepish smile. Suddenly, a dagger flies in between our faces, but it is closer to Nate's face than mine. It struck the armor, stopping its trajectory. Nate quickly pushes me behind him while he turns to face our attacker, but it is only Dan who is giving him a sinister smile.

"Oops. My hand slipped when I saw you touching a *Rutledge*."

"I'm not a Rutledge." I remind him.

"Are you crazy? That could have hit us!" Nate bellows.

"Really? I was only aiming for you."

"I thought you said it was an accident?"

"Oops." Dan innocently places a hand over his lips.

When another knife flies in our direction, almost missing Nate by an inch or two. Nate shoots Ren a venomous glare. Ren's smile is reminiscent of his brother Dan's, but it is twice as menacing.

"For some reason, my hands slipped." Ren grins, clearly trying to provoke Nate like they always do. Soon, they are exchanging profanities, which I couldn't hear because my focus is already elsewhere.

Ren threw a dagger, and I began seeking for it since it was smaller and rounder. Not sure if the blades were particularly sharp or if Ren's throw was particularly forceful, but I find it wedged against a stone wall. For whatever reason, I push the idea out of my mind and instead focus on the disk-shaped object buried in the wall. It comes out with a good tug, and I suppress a gasp as I realize what it is.

"Both of you, get off of me now! I am serious." Nate shouts at the twins angrily.

"Oh, but we are serious. YOU DARE RUIN MY FUTURE PLANS FOR MY BROTHER!?"

"Shut up, brother. I cannot think of ways to torture him with your yelling."

"You idiots! Let go of me." Nate persist.

"Why should we?"

"Nobody is **watching** Rose!" At Nate's words, the three princes looks at me just as I wave the new weapon I hold in my hands.

"Guys, look! I found a *shuriken*." I scream with excitement. "Does that mean ninjas are real!? Can I learn a *shadow clone jutsu*!? Imagine hundreds of me running around. Oh! That is just marvelous. Maybe I will learn how to run on water."

"Ah-ha..." Ren gulps. Sweat forms on the young werewolf's forehead. "I don't know what kind of weapon is a *jutsu*, but don't throw that thing if you don't know how to use it."

I felt a little offended by his words. "Hey, I have watched all seasons of a ninja show to know that they throw their shurikens like this." When I raise the weapon, preparing to throw it, the princes sucks in their breaths.

"No!!" They all yelled in unison before rushing towards me to grab the raised weapon.

Unfortunately, it's too late.

I throw the star-shaped blade, but instead of it going straight like I want it to, it suddenly makes a curve and hit the tip of the battle axe held by an empty amour. When nothing happens, we all sigh in relief, before the princes glowers at me.

"I think you have had enough of a tour of the weapons room." Ren shakes his head, massaging the bridge of his nose like he is driving away a headache.

When I am about to raise my voice in protest, we suddenly hear a huge bang and turn to see that battle-axe smashes into rows upon rows of armor, spears, swords, and shields. Finally, as everything is winding down, the final axe strikes a great sword that is coming straight for us. As each prince pulls me, all heading in different directions, we became immobilized. Because of that I am forced to close my eyes until I hear the clang of metal against metal. When I open them, I see that the princes have their swords raised to parry the falling great sword.

"Who the hell made that large sword!?" Nate demands as soon as they move the great sword to the side. "Nobody even uses it."

I shyly tug Ren's sleeve. Ren looks at me, his face relaxing with relief "Are you okay?"

I nodd in response. "I do think I have had enough of touring here. Can we leave?" They all seem grateful for my request and they all looks like they are about to fall to the ground from fatigue.

"For the record," I add as we are heading for the door. "I do think that ninjas exist in this world since none of you denied it."

"What are you—" Nate starts to speak but is cut off by an even larger and angrier voice.

"WHAT IN THE WORLD HAPPENED HERE!?" At the sound of the angry PRINCE'S voice, we all stop and look fearfully at the exit. There stands a very angry-looking Ace with Custard cowering at his feet. When Custard sees me, he immediately hides behind my skirt.

"Custard, you're the one who's supposed to protect me!" I hiss at him.

"I want answers!" PRINCE Ace demands again, making us stiff up.

Only Nate has the courage to answer him. "Well, Dan had this idea of giving Rose a weapon of her own so she could protect herself if we couldn't." Ace raises a questioning eyebrow at him, urging him to tell him more. "Well, Rose got too excited, and... well, let's just say that she wasn't ready yet. It was a bad idea."

Ace is pondering his words when he notices a servant passing by. With a quick raise of his hand, Ace beckons the servant over. "Gather the soldiers and have them clean this mess up. It is their punishment for leaving this room unguarded. I do not tolerate slackers." He says.

"It's okay. We can clean this up. It's our fault that we made a mess in there." I volunteer, and the others solemnly agree with me. However, despite our sincerity, Ace doesn't seem pleased. To be honest, I wasn't surprised, considering what a heartless man he is.

"Oh, don't worry, you will have your own punishment. I do agree that you should learn how to defend yourself. You cannot rely on your familiar alone. So I suppose that in order to learn, you need proper teachers who can teach you the basics—ones who are capable and have experience. You three!" Ace addresses the three princes with me, who are secretly sneaking away—the traitors!

"Y-yes?" Dan bats his eyelashes at him innocently.

"You all have your wish. The three of you will have the task of teaching this barbaric girl how to fight as your punishment."

"Barbaric!? I'll show you who's barbaric!" I grab a nearby fallen mace and raise it over my head, but the three princes gather and grab the raised mace, preventing me from killing the demon elf PRINCE.

Ace seems unfaze by my actions and gives me a disgusted look. Oh, how I wish I could headbutt him so hard that his eyes would roll back into his head.

"I will go and inform this to the queen." He expresses his displeasure with the damage we had done to the weapons room. "Tomorrow at dawn, since you all seemed excited about it. If I don't see you all by then, expect a far worse punishment." With that said, PRINCE Ace left us dumbfounded.

"I do hope he is kidding." Ren murmurs.

"I don't think he is, brother." Dan replies, looking defeated.

"Great. Training at dawn. We'll show him the fruits of our labor. How hard can it be?" I pump my fists enthusiastically.

It's probably like gym class anyway, or martial arts class, right? If it is, it should be fun.

Three pairs of eyes locks on mine, and the longer they stare, the more lifeless they have become.

"What have we gotten ourselves into?" Nate buries his face into his palm, looking like he is about to cry.

New Morning Routine

"Rose, wakey wakey! Time for trainey." Ren and Dan were cheerfully singing as they knock on my door.

Currently, I am a bit grumpy because their knocking did not stop. I sit up and glare at the door. Custard is stirring beside me, not happy to be woken up either. When the twins burst into the room, I rubbed the sleep from my eyes and bloody murder when they decided to open the curtains.

Now I understand why Nate finds them annoying.

I hiss like a cat and crawl under the covers of my blanket. Custard has obviously detected my distress and is now on high alert. When he realizes there is no danger, he returns to sleep—like master like a beast, I suppose.

If there really is something that my familiar and I have in common, it's patience.

"Rose, the sun is barely rising. You are not a vampire, you are a tamer so act like it." Ren says. I couldn't see him through the covers, but I could sense that he was smiling.

"Oh yeah? Then how should a tamer act?" I retort. It's then followed by a very long silence since Ren couldn't think of a response.

Dan snorts. "She got you there, brother."

"Shut up, Dan. You are not helping." Ren growls at his brother. "Rose, I will count up to 5, and if you won't get up willingly, then I will have to take you with me. By force."

"Wow, that's something I would like to see." I hear Dan sigh dreamily, so I uncover my head to give Dan a disgusted look.

"One." Ren starts to count and earns a glare from me.

"Two." I roll my eyes. He's a pussy. He would never resort to kidnapping.

"Three." He continues. I stuck my tongue out at him and went back into the covers of my bed.

"Four."

I hope they'll give up soon. I just want to go to bed.

"Five. Okay, that's it." Ren moves to my side and starts rolls me until I am wrap in my own blanket like a cocoon. Afterward, he throws me over his shoulders and carries me out of my room. Custard grunts uncomfortably in my cocoon as he is kidnapped alongside me.

"Must you be dramatic every morning?" Ren complains when I continue to struggle.

"Must you all have to be such *early birds—or dogs!?*" I retort before letting out a scream near his ear.

When the full force of my scream reaches Ren's delicate ears, he yells in agony. Someone suddenly removes the sheet covering my face and puts an apple in my mouth.

"There. Now the pig is ready for roasting." PRINCE Ace gives me an annoyed expression. His hair is unkempt, as if he'd just gotten out of bed. He looks at us all as if we were peasants.

Truth be told, it is the first time that I have seen him this tired. "At the very least, if you're going to kidnap someone, do it right." He mumble something grouchily and turns to return to the library.

In turn, I spit out the apple. "Hey, you stupid bookworm, you can't just shove an apple into someone's mouth!"

"I just did. Now I don't see why youmake such a big deal out of this. Honestly, first order of business and I get to see your face. What a bad start." He breathes out, turning away to avoid looking at my face. "What a pest."

"Let me at him, Ren! Let me at him!" I start squirming, making me look like a worm in my blanket cocoon.

"Rose, hold still." Ren sounds like he is having trouble keeping me on his shoulder as I continue to wiggle like a worm.

"Don't even try to bother me." PRINCE Ace says, without turning back. "You should focus on your training, because as you are now, you can't even touch me. Not with those heavy legs of yours." He smirks arrogantly before he enters his beloved library's doors.

"Well, that was anticlimactic." Dan slouches in disappointment. I don't know if he was expecting a fight or something, but if he was, he better blame Ren for the lack of it.

"One of these days." I grit my teeth. "One of these days I will make him bend the knee to respect me."

"I totally agree with you, Rose. But I hope you do not mean a proposal with 'bend the knee'." Ren and I both turn to look at Dan, who has a concerned look on his face. Ren slaps him on the back of the head because I am still in my cocoon.

"Stop talking nonsense." Ren chides his younger twin.

"Ren, please let me down. I can walk on my own." I say, earning a doubting look from him.

"Yeah, right. You're just going to run away again."

"Nope." I shake my head even though I doubt that he can see me. "I am eager to make that PRINCE pay for all the bullying he did."

"Um...I guess that is great." I can't tell if he is convince or afraid of me, but nonetheless, he finally sets me back down on the ground.

I stand up straight. The blanket falls from my body and onto Custard. "Come on. It's time to train." I cheer and start marching to the training grounds, but pause when I notice that the twins are not following me.

When I look at the two, their eyes are avoiding me. Well, Dan is looking at his brother amusingly, while Ren is covering his red face with one hand.

"What's wrong with you guys?"

Dan simply chuckles when Ren doesn't respond.

"You two should save that outfit for your honeymoon." He comments. His eyes still focuse on his red faced brother.

It is then that I became aware of what I am wearing—a nightgown with an extremely low neckline that expose far too much skin as considered in this realm. And the hem—well, in my era, it was pretty standard, but in this era? Well, let's just say that it is a no go.

I quickly snatched up the blanket and wrapped it around my body. My cheeks flush with embarrassment as I realize I've been caught in this outfit. Custard has finally awoken and is staring at us with interest.

"Meet us downstairs by the stables when you are ready. 10 minutes or I'll come and pick you up." Ren hastily says before leaving and dragging his twin sibling along with him.

When they left, all I could think about was Dan being a weirdo and Ren being the normal one—well, at least the most normal one between them.

It took me about 8 minutes to get to my room, brush my teeth, wash my face, and change into clean clothes. Since this day is supposed to be for training, I chose a shorter length dress and wished I had a few pairs of pants or leggings. I can only imagine the torture I'll be subjected to once the training begins.

Custard stifles a yawn, and I believe he'd rather nap than join me on my training. Unfortunately for him, because I am a tamer, so he will have to go through the training with me.

By the time I arrived, the princes had already begun stretching. When I saw them in their hunting outfits, I was envious. The twins were dressed identically in forest green tees, slacks, and hunting boots. Nate was dressed in a maroon v-neck tee that hugged his body and highlighted his muscles beneath. He wore his shirt tucked into his brown cargo pants, unlike the twins.

They wave me over as soon as they see me walking over to them.

Nate grins. "I thought you'd never come."

"The bed was tempting me, but I figured that you guys wouldn't even let me sleep in peace even if I ditched you guys." I yawn, thinking about my bed in my room.

"You're right. After all, this is sort of our punishment. Ren was supposed to deliver your uniform, but he forgot about it." Nate shrugs, like he already expected it to happen.

"Uniform?" I ask, and it is only then that I notice the neatly folded clothing that Nate has in his hands.

"I also brought you your shoes. Sorry if you have to go back and change. I'll come with you and carry your stuff." Nate offers.

"It's okay. I can change in the stables assuming that no one's inside?"

"Just the horses and the smell of horse dung."

"I'll take my chances." I say. "Come along, Custard. You keep watching just in case these guys get any ideas." With my fresh pair of clothes in hand, I head for the stables to change. They weren't kidding when they said that this place was full of horse dung. Even Custard was sneezing just from being here. I quickly undressed and changed into the long-sleeved white shirt and brown slacks that Nate brought for me. I remove my sandals and put on my riding boots while holding my breath because the environment is giving me a headache.

"Come on, Custard. Before we faint." Grabbing my discarded dress and sandals, he quickly got out of the stables. "Never again will I change in that place. Ever." I declare to no one in particular.

As I cough and wheeze to get some fresh air into my lungs, the princes laugh at me like they find my distress amusing. From the looks of it, it seems like they have just finish their warm-ups.

"Leave your clothes on that crate over there so we can start." Dan gives the order, so I obey and quietly follow him. Since I didn't know how to stretch my muscles, Ren instructed me to follow him as he stood next to me.

"All right, Rose. We need to build your endurance before we can teach you proper self-defense. We're only going to run and do a little muscle work for a week." Nate explain to me with a smile. It seems like he is the leader for today's training session. "Today is our first day so we will go easy on you. But if you are late tomorrow, or even consider not showing up, you will be penalized."

"What? I thought this was just training. Why is there a punishment!?"

"You need discipline as much as you need training. My brother, on the other hand, can make sure you're not late by coming to your room and picking you up." At his suggestion, Ren's face turns bright red before elbowing Dan's ribs.

"Stop talking nonsense!"

"Enough!" Nate yells at the twins. I thought for sure that the twins would retaliate and talk back at Nate for yelling at them, but it seems like they just behaved, which is a huge surprise for me. Nate returns his attention to me. "For this day we shall take it east and run a full ten laps around the castles' perimeter."

"Are you friggin' kidding me? Ten laps?" The castles' property and its lawn alone are equivalent to five of the world's largest arenas, and they want us to do 10 laps?! "You guys are joking!"

"Why? Is it too much?" Ren tilts his head to the side, looking concern as my face turned pale white.

I gape at Ren for his question. *These guys are monsters!*

"Of course it is! Do you really need to ask me that?"

Ren rubs his chin for a moment before looking at the other two princes. "Should we do 3 lapses first? I don't think Rose can survive even five. "

"We can make adjustments." Nate rubs this chin like he is considering Ren's suggestion. "But sure. For now, we can three. Now, since we all finished stretching our muscles, I think that it is time for us to run."

Liliana

The prince's method of training wasn't easy. I keep getting left behind. This run was nothing like my normal run at the school gym. This was more like hiking and a marathon combined into one. We had to go through the forest, which is part of the castle's perimeter, through rocky paths, and even through little rivers in the garden just to finish one lap. It doesn't help the fact that the princes were too fast for me to catch up, so from time to time they would slow down to wait for me.

To say that I was embarrassed was an understatement. Custard didn't seem bothered by running. In fact, I felt his excitement through our bond and I am somewhat happy that at least one of us was having fun.

On the second lap, I was already panting and struggling for breath. One lap was equivalent to running 15 complete laps around the school's track or maybe more. I couldn't say because I never completed a 15-lap round of the track. My knees finally gave out when I was halfway through the second lap. Custard pauses and starts sniffing my face in concern—or maybe he is checking if I am dead or not.

"Boy, just leave me here to die." I roll on my side, not even caring what's on the ground anymore because all I want to do is rest.

You thought having all those adventures out in the woods helped me build my endurance, but I guess it's different when you actually do the running instead of horseback riding.

I don't know how long I stayed there, but I could feel Custard tugging at my hair, urging me to keep going.

"Go away, Custard. Leave me alone." I moan and let out a yelp when someone nudges my arm with the tip of their boots. I know that it wasn't Custard since it was too forceful for him. And there is only one being who is sick enough to do that.

"Watch it!" I glare at PRINCE Ace.

"I thought you were dead." He says, looking a little disappointed.

"Nice to see that you care."

"I was actually planning to bury you if you were dead. But I can still bury you alive if you want." He offers *kindly*.

I use my elbows to push myself up so I wouldn't have to keep looking up at him. "Well I—" I make an attempt to stand, but my knees werestill so tired that they easily gave out.

Instead of helping me, PRINCE Ace casually steps sideways to avoid me and I fall face-first on the ground. I'm actually grateful that he did because I don't his help.

"Don't do that cliché move on me." That's what he said after I spat a few dirt off of my mouth.

"Trust me. If I were to choose between falling down a cliff or into your arms, I would rather choose the cliff." I wanted to punch him, but my legs won't listen. Even thinking about standing is already making my head spin.

I'm too tired to do anything!

"You have been out in the sun for too long, and you seem dehydrated. Try crawling to that tree shade over there." He points to a certain spot with a lot of shade.

"Wow, cool idea." I say in a daze. "But as you can see, I can't even move! I'll do that later."

"You really are a pain." I hear him mumble before I feel him grab me by the back of my shirt.

"Hey!" I let out a protest when he starts dragging me over to a shaded area.

"Dude, at least carry me and be gentle!" I complain when he throws me at the end.

He ignores my comment and throws something at me. It hits me in the face before it falls on my lap. It is a bota bag.

"Drink up before you die." He says before walking away before I can see the expression on his face.

Dang it. What sort of face was he making? I need to know maybe he poisoned the water or something.

I mean, why else would he have a bota bag with him?

But what if he did not poison it? Does it mean that he ~~cares~~?

"Don't get the wrong idea." He calls out, pausing and addressing me like he might have read my mind. "You are still to choose the future king and I'll be damned if you die before you crown one of us!" After saying that, Ace turns back and hastily walks to the castle.

Yeah, what was I thinking? An arse PRINCE like him doesn't care about anyone except for himself and his own gain.

Well, at least now I know that it doesn't have poison.

I start to drink the water. Immediately, my body starts to cool down. Having the cold liquid touch my lips felt so good that the pain in my head started to recede. Custard, who followed me, nuzzles beside me as I start to feel well enough to fall into a peaceful sleep.

✳✳✳

"She's dead! My sister-in-law is dead." I can feel someone crying over my head, making my brow twitch in annoyance.

Great. The twins found me.

"Brother, what are you talking about? Sister-in-law?"

"You! You good for nothing sibling. How can you be so....so blind! Now she's dead and you don't even feel anything?"

"No....?"

"She's not dead. I can hear her heart—"

"Oh, shut up, vampire." Dan cut him off. "Don't you see her as more than a friend?!" I can only assume that Dan was talking to his twin.

"Of course, I see her as more than a friend. She's been my best friend and I care about her a lot, so stop bothering her while she sleeps!"

There was a pretty long silence after that, and after a while, I started crying. I open my eyes and see the princes staring at me.

I can't help it. I feel so moved!

I look at Ren through tear-filled eyes. "You really mean it? I'm your best friend?"

I feel so happy!

Dan looks at me with sympathy. He kneels down beside me and carefully rubs my back to comfort me.

"Rose, I'm so sorry for my brother. I really am. I tried to clue him in, but my brother is too dense. I have known for a while about you two and—"

I slap Dan's hand away while I jump to my feet to face Ren. "You're my best friend too! I am so happy that you and I feel the same way." I beam at Ren, a gesture which he returns happily.

"Awe. Come here you!" He opens his arms and invites me for a hug.

Feeling better after the short nap, I leap straight into his chest for an embrace.

"Best friends!" We both yell happily. Soon, Ren carries me and starts to spin us around.

"OH MY GOODNESS!!" Dan yells, making me wonder why he sounds so frustrated. Isn't he happy that Ren and I are friends? "I FORGOT HOW PERFECTLY DENSE YOU TWO ARE. YOU GUYS ARE REALLY SOULMATES INDEED!" Dan starts kicking rocks everywhere like a child having a tantrum. His little outburst makes Ren and I stop our mini celebration of friendship.

"Geez, what's his problem?" I ask after Ren sets me down so we can stare at his brother.

"No idea." Ren replies.

Since none of us knew what was happening, we turn to Nate.

"As much as I hate seeing you two hugging each other, it's better if you guys figure it out. Besides, it would feel so much better if you guys were serious about being best friends." Nate smiles politely at Ren and I.

"Of course!" Ren and I say the same thing, which irritates Dan more as he kicks the bota bag while Nate's smile only seems to grow.

"Ow! Hey, watch it." Someone yelps when the bota bag hits the stranger's face. "I came here to see how you two were doing, and this is the welcome I got? Geez. You guys never change." A maiden in a lavender dress strolled towards us. Her short, dark curls swayed as she did.

I was perplexed, and only Ren and Dan's expressions suggested that they knew who this person was when I turned to look at the princes. The pretty lady stopped right in front of us. Her yellow eyes sparkle as she curtsies. "You must be Princess Rose."

"I-um....I'm sorry, but I am not familiar with you." I say apologetically, hoping that she wouldn't be offended that I do not know her.

"She's our childhood friend." Dan answers me. He also seems troubled, which is odd. Beside me, I can see that Ren stiffens at the sight of her. It only doubles my confusion. I mean, they were supposed to be happy, right? She is their childhood friend.

Despite the tension in the air, she still smiled politely. "My name is Liliana Nightshade. As you can guess, I am from Sanver as well."

"Nice to meet you." I nod at her in greeting. I suddenly become aware of my appearance. I don't think I smell that bad, but beast men always have sensitive noses. I just hope that I don't stink that badly for her to criticize me. "You came here to visit the twins?"

"Yes, but more so, I came here to visit Renevier Rutledge. My fiancé."

Vision

"Um...you're his....fiancé?" The word taste rough in my mouth. It's weird saying it out loud especially when I am referring it to Ren's fiancé.

"Yes." Liliana smiles politely. The girl is like a bright sunshin, making it harder for me to believe that she's going to be a Rutledge bride. "Where is Ren, by the way?"

I wince, looking at the twins with pity. It's really a shame. One of them already has a fiancé, and she can't even tell who's who.

Dan shys away from the background while Ren glowers. When he sees me looking at him, his cold expression washes away.

"Whatever you are thinking, it's not what you think." His voice sounds a little shaky and I could not understand why it seems like he is explaining himself to me.

Liliana takes notice of the twin beside me. She beams, clasping her hands together while looking pleased.

"Ren, there you are!" She sounds joyous as she moves between us to grab Ren's arm. Custard whimpers and snaps at her legs when she accidentally steps on his tail, but before his teeth could sink, I immediately pick him up.

"Liliana, now is not the time. Let go of me." Ren looks desperate while trying to move away from her, but it seems like Liliana has a tight grip on his arm.

It makes me feel horrible watching them. Although Liliana is undeniably beautiful, it is unacceptable that she can't distinguish her fiance. I think it's only fair that the twins become engaged to someone who can tell them apart. Someone who is not put off by their appearance or their naiveté.

Dan comes up alongside me and put a hand on my shoulder. "My brother may be dim, but he only has room for one love. Well, when he realizes it." He shrugs.

I give him a pitiful look and extend my arm to touch his shoulder in return when I realize what he meant.

"Must be hard that he loves Liliana more than you."

"Excuse me?" Dan gapes at me for a while before shaking his head in resignation. He sighs and instead looks at Liliana and his brother. "Lily, I take it you just got here? Have you met the Queen yet?" Dan asks.

Dan catches Liliana's eye, and she gives him a short glance before pouting her lips into a narrow line.

"U-um. Yes, I just arrived." Call me crazy, but I think she is avoiding Dan's eyes. Even though it was a brief greeting between them, it makes me wonder what Dan did in the past that makes a girl such as Liliana seems uncomfortable.

Ren seizes the occasion to speak to my subconscious at that precise moment.

'You won't believe this, but Lily likes my brother and not me. She's basically just using me to get close to him.' He says, and I give him a weird look.

"Dude. That is messed up. Is he dense or something?" I lean close to him so I can whisper. The story seems so absurd that it makes me second guess if I am in a fantasy novel or in a romantic comedy sort of novel.

"Long story. I'll tell you later." He replies.

"Ren! Come and introduce me to the queen." Before Ren and I could talk more, he was dragged away by Liliana.

"Alright." Ren seems annoyed at this, and when they pass by Dan, Ren grins wickedly and grabs his brother.

"Brother, why don't you come with us? Liliana would love it if you could come." Because of his teasing comment, Liliana stomps on his foot.

"Have fun! I'll keep the princess company." Nate smiles and waves while the twins head back to the castle. Nate looks amused and satisfied when he sees the twins reacting violently when they realize that I am going to be alone with Nate, but he cannot do a thing since Liliana is dragging them away.

"Oh, man. That was so satisfying." Nate laughs, wiping a tear from his face. "You know, it's never too late to choose me, you know. I could make you happy."

I don't know what he is referring to so I am just guessing that he means that I should pick him as king of Thalia.

"I could make you cry if you don't stop." I eye him manacingly.

"I feel like I'm being threatened by a potato." He chuckles. "You are so adorable that you can't even tell when a person likes you."

"Who likes me?"

"Me."

"Lies."

"I wouldn't give you Cloud if I didn't." He mumbles under his breath, making it hard for me to catch what he says.

"What did you say?"

"Nothing." He pouts, puffing his cheeks when he addresses me. "You know what I think? I think you have selective hearing."

"No, I don't." I deny.

"I would confess my undying love for you, but Prince Fred is watching." He says.

I gasp, moving my head from side to side and trying to search for a handsome warlock prince. "Did you say Prince Fred? Is he here? Where!?" At that moment, I realize that it was a trap set up by Nate to prove his point. "Oh."

Sad to say, but I could not hide my disappointment.

Nate's eyebrow twitches in annoyance, but he immediately wipes off with a forced smile. "What if Ren likes you and he's your soulmate?"

"It can't be. He said it himself that we are best friends."

"Maybe he just doesn't realize it." At that, snorts and covers his mouth like he is trying to hide his smile.

"Dude, what kind of idiot do you take him for?"

My question made Nate burst out laughing. "Oh, man." He shakes his head. "You have no idea what an idiot that mutt is." He sniffs and wipes a tear off of his face. "Everyone must have realized it by now, but you guys. Well, I guess it's for the best. It gives us all a fair chance."

"Nate, sometimes you say a lot of monologues. You know that, right?"

Nate points a finger at me as if to prove a point. "See. Selective hearing. What if I say that PRINCE Ace likes you romantically?"

"I will punch you, and I am not kidding." I deadpan.

"What if Prince Fred likes you?"

I start to retract my fist and become a little bashful just thinking about my dream prince liking me back.

"You really think so? I mean, come on~!" In my embarrassment, I slap Nate's arm, making him stare at me coldly. Then, I see him pouting and making a puppet with his hands to mock me.

"Blah, blah, blah. Fred, Fred, Fred. No Nate. Even though Nate is always there for you." He says it in a weird, feminine kind of tone.

"Stop acting like a kid, Nate."

"Oh, stop acting like a kid?" Suddenly his face becomes serious when inches his face close to mine. "If you want me to stop being a kid, then I might show you my....adult side." His eyes and voice change dangerously low like...like a ~~pervert~~.

I look at him warily and eye him cautiously.

Nate's expression turns back to normal when he chuckles. "See, Princess. I can stop acting like a kid, but I'm pretty sure that you won't like it. I mean, I could lock you up so no one would dare lay a finger on you, and only I could visit you." He says it in a joking, manner, but something about his eyes makes me think that he might actually do it.

"Dude, you sound crazy. Go away."

Nate gasp, placing a dramatic hand over his heart. "Rosalie Amber Stan, you're hurting my feelings!"

"Nathaniel Denver, you're scaring the crap out of me!"

"Touché." He laugh before he begins to wrinkle his nose while smelling the air. "Hey, I want to go take a shower. I assume you do too. Want me to carry you to your room?"

"Nah. No thanks. I can manage to walk on my own."

"Then I'll walk with you." He hums happily as he starts to accompany me. Custard is merrily strolling alongside us when, all of a sudden, he shivers and collapses to the ground.

"Custard!" His tiny paws are trembling ferociously, and he is whimpering in agony. As soon as I touch him, a sharp pain shoots through my head. I collapse to the ground, unable to breathe because of the pain.

"Rose!" Before I hit the ground, Nate caught me. He kneels down with me still in his arms. "What's wrong!?"

I couldn't respond to his question because images started to cloud my head that it is starting to hurt. Nate takes that as a cue for an emergency when he starts to carry me and Custard in his arms.

"I don't know what's going on, but it's going to be okay. I'll go and ask for help." He is trying to use a gentle voice on me, but it is clear that he is terrified from the slight shiver of his voice.

I don't know how far he went or how far we got before he started screaming for the servants to leave or call the queen, but he sounded panicked the whole time. All I remember is that the pain was so intense that it seemed to be tearing my brain apart.

"You're heating up. Damn it!" He starts screaming again. "Move! Open the door. Move it! I SAID MOVE!" I hear the loud bang of a door bursting open when Nate kicks it.

"Ready a cold towel!" He orders before he gently sets me on the bed. "Rose, wait for me. I'll call the queen."

However, I did not want him to leave. I was scared of what's happening to me. I grab onto his hand and squeeze it tight. Nate gives my hand a gentle squeeze in return, as though he understood.

"You! Get the queen and hurry. I don't like yelling orders or repeating myself. Go NOW!" At his words, I hear the scurrying of feet out of the room.

I scream once more. Unfamiliar images keep flashing through my head. Even though my body is warming up and I am perspiring, I still feel cold. Nate hold my hand.

"Rose, if you're just squeeze my hand as hard as you can, I won't mind." I was afraid to open my eyes, but when I did, I saw a vampire shivering and looking worried.

I manage a weak smile. "Are you...crying?"

He tries to smile and hide his tears, but he failed miserably when his lips start to quiver. "Are you turned on with me now? Are sad boys your type?" He jokes, but I can tell that it is a weak attempt to lighten the mood.

Custard squirms beside me. At that same moment, I smell blood. Nate's eyes widen. I place a finger under my nose and when I bring it into view, I see blood on my fingertips.

"No." Looking back at Nate, he appears to be more afraid of my situation rather than me. "You can't leave me too. You can't!" He squeezes my hand gently and rests his head.

My head starts to ring once more as a fresh wave of images hit me. I cry out even louder. It feels like someone is showing something into my head. The pain is unexplainable that tears start to stream down my face.

"Where is she?"

"What happened to her?" Ren kneels beside me on the bed, bringing his face to the same level as mine.

"I'm not sure. She just started to collapse." Nate tells them briefly what happened earlier, but I can't hear what he told them exactly because the pain has me distracted.

"Call all the doctors in the kingdom immediately. This is an emergency." The Queen orders as soon as she arrives and gets a good look at me.

Breathing became more difficult.

I have no idea what any of these images are or what they mean. I repeatedly see two lights crashing into one another. I can hear yelling and an unnatural scream.

Where is this coming from?!

"She won't need a doctor." Ace casually enters the room. "Just dump her in a bathtub."

"What do you mean she won't need a doctor?" I can hear the wolf in Ren's voice when he screams at Ace. "She's in pain. I know you don't like her but to let her suffer this much and throw her in a bathtub? Are you a monster?!"

"Brother, calm down." Dan chides him. "I know you're worried, and so are we."

Ren tries to calm himself and let out a low growl. In spite of my frailty, I extended my hand and pull at his sleeve.

"C-Calm down or I might deck you. All your screaming is making my head hurt."

Ren seems to realize his mistake and begins to gradually calm himself.

"Are you done? You did not even let me finish." Ace snaps after a long moment of silnce. "Her condition is the same as mine. Remember, her powers have been locked up for a long time, and it was only recently that she obtained whatever her powers were when the little mutt came." He points at Custard.

"So what are you saying then? We should separate Rose and Custard?"

"We can do just that." Ace says like he is considering it. "But for a tamer, it might kill her too since we don't have much knowledge about them aside from the ones recorded in the books. I propose that we cool her off in the bathtub. As for her growing powers, I suggest letting the earth absorb some of it."

"How do we do that?" The Queen asks.

"I might be able to help. I can manipulate the nearest tree in this room to reach out to her and absorb the abnormality in her power."

"But there aren't any trees here."

"Then we do it in the garden. There's a pond there."

"I got her." Ren says, carrying Custard and I with him. Everyone left quickly and headed to the garden. I shuddered more when Ren carefully placed me in the pond. Due to his small size, I raise Custard a little bit to prevent him from drowning.

"Whatever you're going to do, do it fast." Ren pleads.

PRINCE Ace moves quickly to my side and places both of his hands on the ground next to me. "Since we're outside, I can manipulate the underground roots. This is much preferable."

I could feel the underwater roots and vines entangling Custard and me. Ace seems to be closely observing me when he cuts my finger with a dagger.

"ACE!" Everyone shouts.

"It's PRINCE!" He yells, seemingly annoyed. He glares at everyone—yes, even the queen—before pointing the dagger at them. "I told you all countless times that it's PRINCE Ace! Just to let you all know, her body is not like the elves who have connections to the earth. Her powers can only be absorbed through her blood. Do you all understand? Or do I have to let you all experience it with a bigger wound?" He threatens them.

"You guys can handle this. I'll leave my niece to you guys." The queen murmurs, seemingly scared of the PRINCE holding a dagger.

"I cannot believe he just threatened the queen."

"He should be in prison right now."

"Look at him with the dagger. I think he likes it."

"Does he always carry a weapon with him? What a psycho."

At that last comment, I hear them all scream in terror.

"You crazy PRINCE! Why'd you throw the dagger at us!?"

I close my eyes. I feel a little dizzy. Nearly all of my pain has subsided, and I can already feel myself getting better.

As soon as I fall asleep, I have dreams about the images that have suddenly started to become more distinct, as if they had been some long-forgotten memories in the back of my mind.

Linked Dream

I dreamt of blood.

A drop of blood falls onto a cup. The images wavers and soon, a new scenario appears.

A dark and a light figure dances around one another. I was perplexed, but the more I concentrated, the clearer the images became.

The darker figure has the front body of a lion and the back body of a goat. It has two heads. No three. At the very front, it has two heads. One is a lion, with its fangs smeared with dried blood, and the other is a goat, its longhorn sharp and erect. The other head is at the back—or more likely to say the tail. The snakehead is hissing and snapping at the air, trying to intimidate its opponent. My heart pounds inside my chest as realization dawns on me.

It's a chimera.

I focuse on the other figure. It appears to be a a large version of Custard when he transformed back into the woods. Only this other wolf is bigger. What's weirder about it is that this particular wolf has blue tattoos all over its body like runes.

Something tugs at the back of my head. I know this wolf. Something tells me from my connection with Custard that this wolf is…

"Nagga?" I form the name with my lips in a whisper. As soon as I mention its name, the white wolf turns its head towards me. Its ears perks in recognition, and its tail wags slowly.

Nagga is a majestic wolf. He is so beautiful and mesmerizing to look at that I can't seem to separate my gaze from him.

Suddenly it snort as if saying.

'Took you long enough.' I hear it saying at the back of my mind. Looking at where Nagga is looking, I realize that he wasn't talking to me. He referring to Custard, who suddenly appears at my side.

Suddenly, Nagga raised its head in the air and howls. The wind rushes towards me and I am pushed back.

***

I jolt up from my bed with a heavy gasp. A chill falls down my spine when I recall the dream I just had.

I look around me. I am back in my room and fully changed into my pajamas. My head still has the remainder of the pain from my headache. But it's much more bearable now and I can finally see that I wasn't alone in my room.

Nate is sitting on a chair with hand supporting his head. Dan is sprawled out on the couch while Ren squats on the ground next to my bed. And PRINCE Ace…

"Took you long enough." As mentioned, Ace is there. He sits on a sofa beside a balcony with a book in hand. "I thought you would never wake up."

"Must you always look like a villain?"

He raises an eyebrow. "Must you always be a damsel in distress?"

"I hate you."

"Right back at you." He starts to straighten his posture when he addresses me. "You've been asleep the whole day yesterday. You must be really hungry. You didn't have anything to eat."

It's true. I have not eaten since yesterday and…

"Wait what!?" My brows furrow at what he said. "I was asleep the whole day!?"

At my outburst, the princes woke up. They all jump up in alertness, all looking ready to unalive a perpetrator.

Geez. These guys are always ready for battle. I'm kind of jealous of their reflexes.

As soon as the princes saw me, they all jump near the bed, which woke up Custard. The poor baby wolf immediately runs into my arms as the princes begins to crowd around me.

"Are you okay?"

"Does your head still hurt?"

"Ren was beside you the whole time. Fun fact." Dan earns a hard slap on the face from Ren.

"That's because you wouldn't share the couch, you greedy bastard!"

Even Ren and Dan's bickering couldn't cheer me up this time, but still, I give them a small smile for consolation. "I'm feeling better now. Thank you." I turn to Nate, who has his brows drawn into worry. "Thanks for helping me yesterday."

Nate places a fist on his lips and looks away for a second.

Is he trying to hide his smile? I don't know.

Ah, nope. He is just coughing to clear his throat.

"Does that mean I get a kiss?" He offers instead.

"Sure. My fist is ready for your lips. Pucker up, Nate!" I smile with a raised fist.

"If you want to kiss Rose, you have to kiss me first," Dan arrogantly challenges Nate. I believe that he was sure that the vampire would back out of his threat, which is a pretty bad move considering that it's Nate that he is talking to.

"Brother, you are sick in the mind." Ren looked at his brother with disgust.

"It's for your own good. Don't you judge me!" Dan places a hand on his sibling's shoulder.

Nate contemplates Dan's words and taps on his chin. He looks at me, winks, and then he turn back to Dan. "I think it's worth it. Come here, Ren."

"It was Dan." I corrected Nate.

"Okay. Dan, come here and pucker up." Nate reaches out to grab Dan's cheek. Dan sees him coming and jumps back with a completely disgusted and horrified expression.

"What are you doing!?" He screams.

"If I have to kiss you to kiss Rose, then I wouldn't mind." Nate has a crazy look in his eyes when he says this.

"You are sick!" Dan screams in both panic and disgust.

"I do hope that you guys are not going to involve me in whatever game you guys are playing. Nobody is kissing me." I calmly tell Nate and Dan, who are running around the room chasing each other.

Dan pauses for a brief moment after hearing my words. "That's true. Except for my brother."

"Don't drag me into your stupid schemes, brother. Rose and I are best friends."

"YOU TWO ARE POTENTIAL M—" Before we could find out what Dan was about to say, PRINCE Ace gets up. He probably snaps because he could not finish the book that he was reading a while ago with all the noise in the room.

"ENOUGH!" He yells.

Ace glares at each and every one of the princes before he locks eyes with mine. He walks in my direction, looking as pissed off as ever.

"You. What is it?" He starts to interrogate me for some reason, which leaves me utterly confused.

"What is what?"

"Tell us now what you're hiding." By the looks on his face, he probably knows that I am worried about something.

How does this guy get a sense when people are hiding something? Is that also part of his magic or he's just very perceptive?

"I don't know what you are talking about." I avert my gaze, not ready to talk about the dream I just had.

"I have been watching over you since you woke up. You seem troubled. Tell me, did you dream of something?"

"I'm not in the mood to talk about it right now."

"So you had a troublesome dream. And judging by your expression, it's not just an ordinary dream. I know a linked dream when I see it."

"A linked what?" This time, I look up.

"Someone or somebody was calling out to you, trying to send you a special message or a warning. It's rare, but I have seen some gifted elven folks having it."

I despaire even more after hearing those words. It only solidified the bad news that I am holding.

"Can we talk about this a little later? I want to eat. Frankly, I need more time to remember the dreams." I say, looking away from the rest of the princes. I wasn't lying about what I said. The dreams still seem a little vivid in my memory. I am afraid that if I try to immediately force myself to remember them, it will slip out from my grasp.

Custard snuggles closer to me and comforts me. I may not be wise at solving dream codes, but for some reason, Custard and I have the same idea.

"Just focus and tell us what you do remember." Despite my request, Ace still bark a demand. "It would be better for us to hear them now before you forge them by any chance."

"That's kind of hard as they still seem a little fogged up." I says, getting up from my bed so I can leave my room. For some reason, I kind of feel a little suffocated with them around. I need to go somewhere quiet. Unfortunately for me, finding a secluded place is harder, especially when Ace is blocking my path.

"If it's important, then we need to know. Now." He inches his face closer to mine, I don't know if he is trying to intimidate me into answering, but it only angers me more.

Why can't he understand that not everyone can focus like he can?!

"Back off!" Ren gets to my side and snarls at Ace. "She said she wanted to eat. Unless you want her to starve to death. I appreciate you helping her when she was sick, and I am sorry for calling you a monster before. But can't you just be a little more sensitive to her situation? She's not accustomed to this world, so magic has a different effect on her, both physically and mentally."

Ren's use of the word "mental" makes me hope he's not referring to my vast array of stupid actions. Still, I appreciate him taking my side.

Ace looks at Ren coldly. While I am standing behind him, his gaze falls at Ren's hand that is pressing against my arm. Ace grounds his teeth together and moves away from the door.

"Do what you want. If she becomes sick again, you take care of her." He left after that, but not before slamming the door behind him.

"I see." Behind us, Dan hisses under his breath, looking displease. "Another love rival. Damn it!" We hear Nate face-palming himself after looking at Dan.

For a moment, I can finally breathe easy. The hands at my sides shake, and I squeeze them together nervously. My mind kept going back to the chimera and Nagga, which is probably the only clear memory that I have at the moment.

My head jerks back to my bed, remembering my little wolf spirit. Custard is sitting on my bed looking at me as if waiting for a command. Looking at him, I can tell that we have had the same dream.

"Custard, come here." I beckon and notice how shaken that little wolf is when he walks towards me. I pick him up as soon as he's in front of me.

I still can't get over the fact that the Chimera is alive, but something about that information is lacking. It feels like there's one part of the dream that I am forgetting.

Try as I might right now, I really can't recall.

I look at Ren and the others, who are still giving me worried looks. I try to smile to hide the worry on my face.

"Well? Are we going to sit and gawk all day or are we going to eat?"

Chimera and Nagga

Except for the king and queen, we all ate together at lunch. And of course, PRINCE Ace. Everyone was quite quiet except for Liliana, who is coaxing Ren to break the silence because it was starting to get really uncomfortable.

It was challenging not to ignore them since they were both seated across from me. Sitting opposite Liliana, Nate appears to be having a good time. He takes it upon himself to hand over plates of food to her saying, "Ask him to try these. These are his favorites. Feed this to your fiance, will you?"

I noticed Dan isn't eating, so I look at him. I see him stare at Liliana, making my brows furrow curiously.

Something is odd about our little wolf boy.

I looked at Liliana, wondering why Danny boy might be interested in looking at her.

Strange. I wonder what Dan is up to this time. I must be missing something.

I look at Dan again. His hand is clenching his fork.

I wonder who he wants to stab at, this time.

I catch a glimpse of Liliana feeding Ren before turning to face Dan, who is now slicing into his steak and taking a sizable bite.

Why would he look at his twin with such a gaze—

Finally, I gasp, after realizing the only possible reason for such a behaviour.

I believe that it's because of my suspicious grin that Dan takes notice of me. When Dan sees me laughing at him silently, he starts to choke on his food. Very quickly, he snatches the bottle of water before him and chugs it down.

"Geez. What are you, a serial killer!?"

A teasing grin is still on my face when I start to point at him. "You cunning little boy." I giggle secretively so that only Dan can see and hear. "You actually like—"

Before I could finish, Dan shoves a huge slice of stake in my mouth and drags me out of the room while yelling,

"Oh, no. She is choking. I will save her. Do not follow us or she may die seeing your ugly faces." He says dramatically as he drags me outside.

Whether the others cared or not, I couldn't tell because I was busy trying not to die from choking.

He releases me as soon as I am able to take a deep breath again. After recovering from nearly choking on the steak, I take it from my mouth and begin nibbling at it, which is a huge NO on table manners. It is probably the reason why Dan is giving me a look.

"You can seriously eat anywhere, can't you? We need to work on your manners." Dan chides me.

"Hey, you were the one who dragged me all the way here." I remind him and finish off the rest of the steak. He hands me a napkin to wipe the grease off of my hands, which I gratefully take.

"If I hadn't, then you might have said something that would make me want to deck you." He grumbles. Seeing Dan looking this troubled is kind of worrying. Usually, he would be that one to cause an ice-breaker at this very moment.

"So," I say teasingly, moving closer to him on the bench that we're sitting on. "You like her? Liliana I mean."

"W-what? Don't be ridiculous! I have no such feelings for her." I don't know what to think upon seeing a very bashful Dan. This is the first time that I'm seeing this side of him that I want to cringe. I really want to, but for his sake, I control myself.

"Are you being serious right now? You just—" I didn't get to finish what I was about to say when a hand covers my mouth.

"Hey! What are you guys doing there?" Ren suddenly pops up behind me. "Oh, hey, brother. Mind if I take Rose for a bit? I need to speak with her." Ren did not even wait for his twins' reply while he dragged me away to who knows where.

What is happening with the world and why am I continuously being kidnapped!?

"Alright. I think it's safe to talk here." He whispers after we get a good distance away from his twin brother.

Getting the hint, I bite on his hand, which still covers my mouth. He lets out a yelp and finally releases his hold on me.

"Would you mind telling me why you dragged me here?"

Ren stares at his hand that I bit before looking at me with a scowl. "I can't let you ruin my entertainment."

"What entertainment?"

Upon my question, Ren grins and sits with an arrogant stance. "Well, child. Once upon a—"

"Oh, just go straight to the point!"

"Hey, hey! Patience, my dear. You wouldn't know if I didn't start from the beginning."

"Oh-heavens-kill-me!" I groan.

"It all started 10 years ago—the first time we met Liliana." Ren goes into narrator mode, which makes me roll my eyes. I badly wish that I can fast forward whatever story he is about to tell me.

"Let me guess. Love at first sight?"

"Jealousy is appreciated, but only at the right time." He glares at me for interrupting him before composing himself to continue the story. I have to fight the urge to grab a rock and hit his head with it because he looks so arrogant and my patience isn't that great in the first place.

"As I was saying, the first time we met Liliana was during a conference for the higher-ups. Her parents brought her along with them to formally introduce us. She was a very stubborn girl and wouldn't bother to talk to us at first. That afternoon, Dan and I realized that she was missing."

"A boogeyman took her?" I says and earn another glare from wolf prince. "Fine, fine. Please continue."

"Dan and I went our separate ways, but naturally, as the paranoid big brother, I was also concerned for my younger sibling, so instead of going in the other direction, I decided to follow him. It wasn't long until he managed to find Liliana. She slipped and got stuck in a tiny crack. Of course, my brother managed to save her." Ren starts tearing up at this part like he's being a proud older brother. "Do you remember that I told you that Liliana actually likes Dan and not me?" I nod. "The reason for that is because Dan gave my name instead of his when Liliana asked which twin he was on that particular day." Ren let out a heartfelt laugh. "The little idiot! It was obvious that they had made a bond at that time."

"Hang on. They made a bond?"

"It's what us Beast Men do. It's kind of like our inner spirit telling us that we have found our soulmates. At that time, their inner beast was telling them that they were potential soulmates."

This time, I was getting more and more confused. "Ren, I don't get it. If at that age, their beast was telling them they were potential partners, then why is Liliana your fiancé and Dan being a weirdo in denial?"

"I can't say Dan is in denial—more like he is dense. Fortunately, Liliana does get it. She knows exactly who saved her that day. That whole fiancé charade was just to make Dan jealous and snap him out of his idiotic state."

"So you mean," I trailed off. "Dan is in love, but he doesn't realize it?"

Ren nods. It wasn't that long until the both of us doubled over laughing. "Oh man, I know you guys are idiots, but how can people not tell when they are in love?" I laugh.

"I know, right?" Ren laughs. "I mean, Dan has his wolf to tell him about his soulmate, but he is too dense to figure it out."

"I bet his wolf must be frustrated."

"For sure. All those years—"

"Rose!" Our conversation is cut short when we see Nate running towards us. "Rose, it is urgent. You must come to the Queen's office." Looking at Nate's grim face, it appears that it must really be an emergency.

Ren and I look at each other one last time before we follow Nate.

Everyone is already at the Queen's office by the time we arrived.

"Rose." The Queen turns to me the moment I enter the roon. "We have information about the rogues." She makes a sign with her hand toward a chair in front of her. I take a seat and patiently waited for what she would say. Whatever it was, I deduced from the furrows in her brows that it wasn't good. "The rogues intend to use your blood in a ritual." She halts. She turns her attention to me and tries to read my expression.

"Um." I start awkwardly. "Don't we know about this already?"

"Stop being rude in front of the Queen." PRINCE Ace hisses.

The Queen clears her throat, the universal language to attract everyone's attention. "As I was saying, yes, King Ferius needs your blood, but there is a very special item that they need to acquire a chalice of some sort. We have no clue what it looks like—"

I am suddenly thrown back into my dream at the mention of a chalice. There's just something about the word that makes a click in my memories.

"—there are a lot of magical chalices." The Queen continues, but my mind is already elsewhere. In my dream, I saw a cup. But what I believe was a cup isn't a cup after all.

It was a chalice that was being filled with blood.

"We don't know that color or what material was used for it—"

"The chalice is made out of wood. Oakwood. The very first one." I interrupt her. The words just came out of my mouth; I'm not sure how I know the specifics. As the images from my dream begin to manifest clearly at this precise moment, my heart races rapidly.

In my dream, Nagga appeared. He wasn't just a symbolic image. No. It's letting me know that the Chimera isn't the only thing trapped in the rogue king's arm.

I look up at the queen with shaking hands as I ready myself to tell her the news.

"Queen, I think Nagga is alive.."

How to confess

"This is not it. This chalice is made out of stone, not wood." Nate sighs and returns the book with the image of a glass chalice to the shelf from which it was taken.

"Prince Nathaniel." PRINCE Ace glares at him the moment he catches Nate shoving a book on a random shelf. "If you do not know where you got that book, you should just leave it on a desk and let the bookkeepers handle returning it."

"I'll..." Nate trails off and takes the book from its shelf. "I'll go hand it over to the librarian then." He takes off rather quickly and quietly.

I decided to look at the other shelves. My mind is staring blankly at all the titles before me. It's like I can read, but the words don't make sense.

It was after my talk with the queen that we decided to do some research about the wooden chalice. No one had heard of it, but they didn't doubt me either. But aside from that, the news of Nagga being alive was more of a shock.

***

"Nagga's alive and so is the chimera?" The queen says with a grim expression. "I can't say if it is a good thing or a bad thing."

"Your majesty, what of the chalice?" Dan asks. "Shouldn't we focus more on that?"

"I agree. We should get a hold of it before King Ferius does. Assuming he doesn't have it already." says Ren.

"I mean no offense, but maybe the wooden chalice is just symbolic? Since it is made out of wood, maybe it means the very first magical chalice?" Nate inserts.

"Unlike witches and warlocks, tamers tend to have clearer prophetic dreams since their spirit bond tends to translate it for them because they share the same dream." PRINCE Ace says. "I may have remembered something about it, but I am

not sure if I read it in this library or in the library back home. In any case, I would send a letter to my brothers about it."

"That would be a big help, but please refrain from saying anything unnecessary. I would like to keep this matter between us. I don't want anyone to know about it or it may cause an uproar." says the queen.

"As you wish, your highness."

"I—" I stutter. It was the first time I spoked since talking about my dream. "I would like to excuse myself and do some reading in the library." I proposed. My voice came out in more of a whisper than I intended to. "Since this is basically about me and whatever chance of survival I have, I would feel more comfortable knowing more about it."

"I'll go with you." Ren says.

Actually, I am kinda busy—" Dan starts to say, but is cut off by Nate.

"I would like to come too."

"On second thought, I am not busy at all." Dan grits his teeth and says it.

"I'll head over to my room to write a letter. I'll see you all in the library, I suppose."

***

My train of thought is interrupted the moment Ren waves his hands in front of me. "Hey, Rose?"

"What?" I focus my attention on Ren.

He grins and points at the book that I am holding. "It's nice that you want to learn how to cook, but you are reading it upside down."

I look down and blush. I close the book and place it on the shelf casually. "If you tease me, my fist may slip and hit you in the face." I smile sweetly.

"Wow, someone is moody. Relax a little. You know all of us are here for you, right? Even demon lord Ace."

I let out a sigh and give him a small smile. "Thanks, Ren. Who knew you could be sensitive at times."

Ren gives me a lopsided grin. "Can I take that as a compliment?"

We hear a small sort of giggle coming from one of the shelves across from us just as I'm about to respond. I catch Ren reaching out to knock a few books off the shelf while gritting his teeth in irritation. Two books fell on the ground, and I stared at them with a horrified look.

I sure hope Ace won't show up now.

"Hey, *chuckles*." Ren glares at his brother through the hole he made in the shelf. "What's so funny?"

I can see Dan batting his eyelashes at Ren when I look through the gap. "Nothing, brother. I am just happy. Am I not allowed to be happy?"

"With a face like that, then no."

"True, true." He nods. "I cannot be happy with a face like this. All the ladies keep chasing me. It's like I have no *privacy*."

"Why you little—" Ren apparently decided that it was a good idea to jump into the small space between the shelves to grab Dan. By doing so, he is knocking all the books off the shelves. He grabs Dan's shirt and pulls him in, his hands reaching for his neck. Dan starts screaming like an idiot, making the situation much worse.

By now I know what is about to happen, so I slowly back away from the scene in the hope that if *HE* somehow catches us, I will not be involved.

My back hit someone, and based on the furious breathing I'm experiencing, I already know that getting away is now nothing more than a pipe dream.

Curse those twins!

I still tried to clear my name when I turn to face him. "Just so you know, I have nothing to do with them."

"Oh really?" Ace raises a brow.

I nod. "Really. In fact, I have never seen them in my entire life." Sometimes, when we are in a very bad situation, it is good to pretend not to know the perpetrators.

"Why is there a cookbook here? It's *on the wrong shelf*."

"Hey! It's not wrong. Cooking is not far off from dess—" I immediately bite my tongue as I was caught in the PRINCE'S trap.

I immediately change my expression. Maybe I can still turn this around.

"Pfft! I know, right? What kind of *idiot* would make the mistake of putting a cookbook in the dessert aisle."

"*You*." He says as he raises an eyebrow at the twins, who are now looking terrified at Ace. "And to the both of you. Get out. Now. Or would you like me to escort you three?"

"But the queen is my aunt. You can't—" Ace cuts me off with his piercing glare.

"Why, *princess*? I was kindly asking you to leave. I was not kicking you out."

"You call that *kind*?"

"In my current state of mind? *Yes*. I did offer to escort you out."

This guy is a lunatic. "What about Nate?" I point out.

Now that the three of us are doomed, I plan on dragging as many people as I can.

Nate is just standing behind us and appears perplexed as to why I am pointing at him. It seems like he has just arrived at the scene. Poor guy.

"Nate will be staying here."

Nate flinches when he starts to realize that he might be stuck alone in the library with a fire breathing demon.

"Actually I—" Nate starts to come up with an excuse to leave, but Ace cut him off with a look.

"You are more useful than the three of them combined, so you will stay here."

So long as Nate gets into trouble for a different reason, I don't really have any objections.

Ren, Dan, and I walk out of the library quietly so we will no longer provoke Ace.

"Great job guys. Maybe we can help look for the chalice by digging up holes in the garden." I say, smiling and pressing my hands together as if I am saying it out sincerely.

The twins catch my sarcasm and exchange looks of regret before I quicken my pace and turn away from them.

The library was starting to get stuffy anyway, so I guess that it is a good thing that we get to head outside. I ignore the twins, even though they continue to follow behind me. Up until I heard a recognizable howl, I did not pay attention to where I was going.

Custard is running in my direction with his tongue hanging out. Because he left bite marks on the book's cover page, Ace effectively expelled him from the library earlier.

"Hey, Custard." I bend down and pick him up. The moment I pick him up, he nuzzles my neck in a comforting manner.

It was only then that I started to take note of my surroundings. I was headed to the garden pavilion without even noticing it. I decided to take a seat on one of the chairs that had recently been placed there for tea time. Ren and Dan are still following me while continuing their talk, which I have just started to become aware of.

"I am telling you, brother, you should trust me more. I will be your wingman." Ren says proudly.

Dan rolls his eyes and scoffs. "And what makes you think you are qualified to be a wingman?" Dan gives his brother a very doubtful look while placing his cheek on top of his hand. "You don't even know your *feelings*. Heck, I bet that even if your wolf bites you in the ass, you will still consider your mate as a friend."

"Wow, Dan. Are you speaking from experience?" I stare at him.

"Well, at least one of you is less dense." He mutters. He sighs and looks at his brother. "Unlike you, brother, I clearly know my feelings. But do tell me what you know."

"I know that you like Lilliana, and you are currently confused about your infatuation with Rose and your bond with Lilliana."

It might be my imagination, but I think I saw Dan's eyebrow twitch. "Oh my, oh my. How could you say that *I* am infatuated with Rose?" He grits his teeth and asks, his eyes dangerously wild and wide like he is just moments away from going crazy.

"You seem so happy when you see her and react violently when another guy approaches her," Ren says, looking extremely confident.

"And do not get me started when you were *stalking* her earlier in the library."

I want to say it was stupid, but the atmosphere here seemed a little dangerous considering Dan's veins on his forehead thatseem like they are about to pop.

I should just stay out of this conversation for now.

Dan's breathing seems a little heavy, but he ss still giving his twin a sweet and deadly smile that Ren seems oblivious of. "Anything else?"

"Just some advice."

"And what kind of advice?"

"Lilliana is your true mate and not Rose. I know you like Lilliana. Stop denying your feelings and just listen to your wolf."

At this point, Dan stood up so quickly that his chair fell.

"Listen to your wolf—the audacity!" He screams and immediately stops himself. Then, in a slightly calmer tone, he says, "You should be taking your own advice why—" His face is turning red with anger that I am afraid he might burst. "Please excuse me for a moment."

Dan has turned his back on us. He takes a deep breath and lets out a scream that causes Ren, Custard, and I to jolt in our seats.

"WHAT HAVE I EVER DONE IN MY PAST LIFE TO BE PUNISHED LIKE THIS!?!?"

After a few more outbursts, he finally stops screaming. After a while, he gives us a slightly more energized look as he turns back to us. Ren and I look at him as if we are looking at a serial killer.

At this point, I am extremely convinced that Dan is bipolar.

"So," Dan says cheerfully. "I would just like to clear out some things."

Ren and I are so afraid of him at the moment that we can only nod to signal him to carry on. "I am not interested in Rose aside from her being my sister."

"So you being jealous of a guy approaching her is because you are acting like an overprotective brother?"

I cough. "Siscon." I say under my breath.

Dan glares at me. "Yes. Rose will be an adorable sister of mine."

"I knew it. Your mother and father plan to adopt me. Aha!" I point at them like I have just solved a mystery. Well, it's not like it's a mystery since they are making it too obvious for me.

"Why do you seem so proud as if it is true!?" I can hear the frustration in Dan's voice as he facepalms.

"Brother, is this true?"

"Where did you guys—" Dan slaps a hand to his face in defeat, again. "Forget it. You guys really are perfect for each other. Anyway, I know Lilliana is the mate that my wolf chose because, unlike *someone* in the family, I am not dense."

"Pardon?"

"No need to worry about that. But I do need some help." Dan says. His face looks like he is plotting something. "You see, I need to see for myself how to confess. Oh, *dear* brother of mine. My one and only, *dear* brother, would you please demonstrate how a confession works?"

Something tells me that the mischievous twin is up to no good again.

"Um...sure?" Ren slowly gets up. "First of all you—"

"No, no, no. I am an idiot who cannot follow easily with mere explanation—"

"Brother, you are a prince, you ought to get used to it by now."

"No! I want a demonstration. As in, act it out." As Dan says, our eyes met. I flinch, and I swear my whole body is telling me to run.

"I–I have to feed Custard." Just as I manage to get on my geet, Dan catches my wrist to stop me from leaving.

Ah, crap!

"Oh, I know. How about you act like you are confessing to Rose? That would be a really good example." By this time, I swear that Dan is starting to lose his mind, judging from the deranged smile on his lips. "I'll take Custard for you. Now, go and show me how to properly confess." Custard let out a small whimper as soon as Dan takes him.

Now Ren and I are awkwardly facing each other while Dan watches from the sidelines.

"Anytime now," Dan waves at us to continue.

To my surprise, Ren suddenly grabs my hand, making me gasp in surprise since I was just thinking of ways to leave this place.

"Lilliana—"

"No, no. She's Rose, not Lilliana." Dan corrects.

"Rose, I... I like—" Ren pauses and searches my face. "I like how your hair pales under the sun. How your silver-blue eyes come alive when you laugh."

Is this how he thinks confessions are? Because I also don't know, but it makes me want to run, even though I hate running. It's terribly cringe worthy!

"I-I…..I-I l-l.." Ren can't seem to get his words out, and Dan looks like he has the hiccups just from watching his brother struggle.

This is undoubtedly going to take forever. I should just act this instead and get this over it.

This is how it's done! I'll show them.

Rather than letting him hold me, I reach out and take both of his hands. "Prince Renevier Rutledge! I am in love with you with all my heart and soul. Will you accept my love?" I declare dramatically.

The scene goes silent, and then we hear a very startled gasp off to the side. This time it wasn't Dan, but a housekeeper bringing tea and treats on a tray.

Happily Ever After

"Y-your highness, I sincerely apologize! I didn't mean to interrupt. I saw your highness here and thought that I should bring some snacks so..." She hurriedly places the tray on the table, bows, and rund. "Congratulations, your highness!" She yells before I can stop her and clear up the misunderstanding.

Dan is laughing so hard that he is clapping his hands and looking like a complete idiot. Ren, on the other hand, is flushed with embarrassment as I stand there trying to process what just happened.

"Oh my, what a show." Dan gasp, leaving me disappointed that he did not choke on his spit.

"I agree. I guess this is the new norm? The girls confess to the guys since the guys are all wimps." Lilliana, who is suddenly sitting beside Dan and eating a macaroon while watching us, says.

Dan chokes on his tea when he sees Lilliana next to him.

Serves him right for drinking tea without putting his pinky out.

Lilliana just stares at Dan's reaction and casually handed him a napkin from the table to wipe his mouth. Dan's face is bright red while it is now Ren's turn to laugh at his brother.

I suddenly have an idea. A brilliant one at that.

This would be the perfect opportunity for Dan to express his feelings to Liliana!

As if reading my mind, Dan gives me a disapproving look as I start to drag Ren away, but not before grabbing a few macaroons that I wrap in a napkin.

"Ren and I would like to feed the fish in the pond. And no, you may not follow us. Bye!" I give Dan a thumbs up before leaving.

Ren seems to understand what I am doing and follows me without protest. I thought he would have said something to his brother to tease him, but he never said anything.

"Wait." Ren abruptly comes to a stop and pulls me down another path, where we continue to circle until we reach the pavilion's back. Even though we are partially hidden by the bushes and quite a distance from the pavilion, we were still able to see Dan and Lilliana.

"I can't hear anything."

"I can hear. A little." Ren says.

"But if you can hear them, doesn't that mean they can hear us too?"

"Lilliana is a lynx. She can't hear us, but my brother might. Fortunately, he is too flustered for him to notice us."

"Not fair! I wanna eavesdrop too."

Ren smirks smugly at me. "Well, too bad you're not a wolf."

Is he being racist right now or just being boastful?

Wait, a wolf.

That reminds me. I have Custard! I started to reach into our connection and poke Custard to wake up.

'Master?' I can feel him yawn at being woken, but he did not complain.

'Hey. Sorry to wake you. You are still in the pavilion, right?'

'Yes, Master. I am with the other wolf prince and a female cat. I'll come to you soon.'

'No, no. Stay there. Is there a way for me to listen to what you are hearing right now?'

'Yes, Master. If you wish, I can share it with you.'

'Great! I'll be counting on you.'

'Okay, Master.'

I turn to Ren. This time, I am the one wearing a smug face. "It seems that I can hear what Custard can hear. I may not be a wolf, but I *have* a wolf." I boast, even though what I just said seems like it does not make any sense at all to him.

I want to boast more, but the connection that I have with Custard starts to take into effect and I began to hear Dan and Liliana's conversation.

"*-thought you liked Ren since you thought I was him.*"

"*You honestly think I am stupid enough to mistake you for Ren?*" Lilliana says. "*It is true that you gave me a false name when you saved me, but my lynx bonded with you and not with him. I know the soul to which I am bonded to.*"

"*Then why—*"

"*Because you are too stubborn for your own good. You keep avoiding me and refusing to acknowledge it, so I turned to your brother for assistance. I pretended that he was the one who saved me back then and pretended to be in love with him. All the while, he would pretend to be ignorant and play along.*"

"*Well, that play you and my brother were in went too far to get engaged.*" Dan sounds a little irritated and looks away.

"*There was a little bit of a misunderstanding with your parents. We cleared it up and they luckily agreed to keep it a secret from you.*" Lilliana laughs nervously. "*I also cleared it all up with my parents, so Ren and I are only engage in word and not in paper. By the way, did you know that your parents agreed immediately to break off Ren and I's engagement? It would seem that Rose is Ren's—*"

Custard suddenly sneezes and temporarily cuts off our link.

DANG IT!

"What? What?" I look at Ren. His mouth is hanging open in shock. I nudged him to get his attention. "What did she say?"

Custard had to sneeze at the best part!

"I-I don't know. Your wolf suddenly sneezed, and I couldn't hear it clearly." Ren is acting strange and he is somehow turning red.

Suddenly, the link was back.

"*-too dense. Both of them. You do not know the pain I have to go through everyday.*" Dan sighs.

Lilliana merely chuckles. "*At least they seem to get along in their own way.*" She let out a sigh. "*By the way, I am leaving tomorrow.*"

They are quiet for a moment until Dan clears his throat. "*Lilliana I...*" He didn't finish.

"*It's fine, Dan. If you are not ready to say it. But I will say it first. I—*"

"*I love you, Lilliana.*" Dan cut her confession off with his own.

Ren and I both gasped and covered each other's mouths. I have the urge to gather all the flowers around us and sprinkle them on the couple at the pavilion. I stop myself, of course, because it would ruin their moment.

I can see their silhouettes a little and make out Dan holding Lilliana's hand to his chest. "*I hope you can feel the sincerity of my words. I love you, and I am sorry for being stubborn and hurting you. I am sorry for not telling you this sooner. The truth is, I already formed a bond with you a few days before the incident. That is how I found you.*"

"*Well, since we are being honest with each other, I guess it is only fair to say that I liked you before our bond was even formed.*"

"So all this time I was a third wheel? Wow, what a childhood. Ow!" Ren winces when I pinch his cheek because he is distracting me from the beautiful scene unfolding before us.

"Shut it!" I tell him.

"*All I am saying is I love you too, Daniel.*" Then Lilliana and Daniel's head draw together until they were kissing.

"OH MY—" Before I can shout my glee and expose us to the two lovebirds, Ren slaps his hand on my mouth.

"Weren't you the one who just told me to shut up!?" Ren hisses.

What!? Can't I be happy and excited for his brother now!?

Still, he does have a pretty good point.

The two finally separated, but their foreheads were still touching. "*Lilliana, I decided to come with you tomorrow. I would personally want to escort you home and tell both of our parents. I don't want you to bear the burden alone anymore.*"

"*What about the selection for the future king?*"

"*Do you really think I can be king if you are not my queen?*" Dan laughS softly. "*I do worry about my brother. How will he react? And there is also the problem about his—*"

"You can go, brother!"

Ren suddenly burst out of our hiding spot before I could stop him. He suddenly marches out to where the lovebirds are, that I have no other choice but to follow him.

Our cover has been blown. I guess it is futile if I still hide. I might as well go over and congratulate the two. I just hope that they won't be too bad if they learn that we have been eavesdropping on them.

"I have a hunch that you two were close by." Dan leers at us.

"I am the older brother. I should be the one worrying about you and not the other way around. You go and do what you like. I will support you."

"Brother, it is natural that I worry because—"

"Go home. If you guys decide to get married right away, then better send an invitation." Ren smiles sincerely, his gaze falling on Dan and Liliana's intertwined hands. Still, despite Ren's thoughtful words, Dan still seems worried about something.

"Brother, worry about yourself! You don't even—"

Ren places a hand on top of his brother's head. "I get it. I get it. The wolf really did bite me in the ass and I ignored it. I understand now. Thanks." Ren winks at his brother like he is passing on a secret to him.

Dan's mouth is hanging open in shock.

"E-Excuse me for a moment." Dan turns his back on us and screams yet again to no one in particular. But I can tell that it is a happy scream.

"**FINALLY**!" He screams, making me think that he might be losing his mind at this moment.

After he finishes yelling like a hooligan, he turns to face us with a crazy grin. It seems like everyone is extremely happy at this moment, which fills my heart with contentment. It seems like we rarely get to have moments like these, so I figured that it was best to enjoy them while we can.

Lilliana suddenly comes close to me and gently hold my hand. "Rose, I cannot wait for us to become sisters in the future!"

"I knew it!" I pump my fist in the air. "Ren and Dan's parents really are planning to adopt me!"

All smiles fade and are replaced with grim expressions.

Dan is massaging his temples, Lilliana has a blank look of shock on her face, while Ren is stifling a laugh and shaking his head.

"Now I get how you feel all the time, brother."

"Well, it is your problem now, so you better hurry up and fix it before it is too late. That vampire has been acting cheeky, so you better watch out."

"Am I missing some inside joke or something?" I ask while listening to the two brothers exchanging words. Ren and Dan did not answer and instead looked away. Lilliana smiled and placed both hands on my shoulder.

"I do not blame you since you do not have a beast inside of you to bite you in the ass. In due time, I guess." Lilliana shrugs.

"Well then, I have to go and meet up with the queen and file my resignation. Shall we get going?" Dan offers his hand to Lilliana as they both start to head back.

Watching them both walk away made me sad at the realization. Dan will be leaving, just like Fred. But at least he is doing it for love, so I guess I should be happy. But I can't help but feel sad.

It saddens me to think that tomorrow will bring about another void.

Ren suddenly pinched my cheek. "What's with that face? Cheer up. They haven't left yet."

"Yeah, but I will really miss them."

"I will too. But if you ever miss Dan, then just look at me." He grins.

I shake my head. "No. You can't be Dan. And Dan can't be you. Just because you're twins doesn't mean that you are the same person."

Ren looks at me softly as a smile slowly finds its way to his lips. He grabs my hand and kisses it. "How could I have been such an idiot when you are this adorable. And this is exactly why—" He trails off as his face starts to inch closer to mine.

"Ren? P-personal space?" I stutter and move back. Upon seeing my reaction, he grins mischievously.

"—it's so fun to tease you!" He suddenly rubs and messes up my hair before running away.

"You dork!" I yell, trying to fix the tangles that he caused on my hair. "If someone sees—"

"If someone sees that, then it would be another issue. Yeah, yeah. I'll handle the rumors, so don't you worry. I'll beat up anything that gives you worry."

I stand there and watches him move before he winks and heads back toward the palace.

'Master?' I feel Custard beside me.

"Custard, I don't know what is happening, so never leave my side."

Somehow, there seems to be a plague that makes everyone act weird today. I just hope that I won't get that disease or whatever.

Party Prep

"Nate, any more running, and this training will do me more harm than good." I pant. It is freaking **6 a.m**! I want to sleep more instead of running for who knows how many laps already.

Nate slows down a bit and runs back to join me. He wasn't even breaking a sweat and simply gives me a teasing grin. "Rose, you do know that you only did 5 laps, right?"

"Only…five you say?" I can barely let out the words. "You're saying that as if running five laps is normal."

"It is."

For you guys that is, I want to yell at him.

"Admit it, Nate. You're just here to torture me."

"You should be thankful that I volunteered for you. Aside from Ren, who is currently busy planning his twins' farewell party, there is PRINCEAce, you know. Or would you like me to call him instead?"

"Oh, my! The weather is too great to sleep in. Nate, let us jog some more!" I suddenly felt motivated to run after picturing what kind of torturous training I would get if this bloodsucker decided to call the demon lord. Custard, who is running beside me, whimpers in protest.

In the end, we did three more rounds before Nate realized how tired I was. He accompanied me under one of the trees, where a picnic blanket and basket were prepared.

"Here, drink." He hands me a cup filled with water. I took it and drank it greedily. I cough when the water went down the wrong pipe.

"And that is why you should drink in sips." He gives me an amuse look when he hands me a napkin. I didn't respond when I take the napkin and wipe my mouth with it. I watch as Nate takes a bowl from the basket and fills it with water for Custard. Custard wastes no time as he greedily drinks.

"Just like your master." Nate chuckles, and I feel astonished to see Nate petting Custard affectionately. Custard stops drinking his water and stares at Nate's hand before he licks it.

Alright. Something fishy is going on here. Custard would not normally let the other princes pet him, nor does he like any of them.

"What kind of drug did you feed him? Fess up, Nate."

"How rude. I love animals. You see, my horse is always in good condition. Even Cloud."

My gaze wanders to the castle before I sigh. "It doesn't seem real."

"What do you mean?"

"Dan is leaving." I shift from my sitting position since my legs are starting to fall asleep. "I mean, isn't it going too fast?"

"Well, from what I have heard, it's long overdue. Plus, they are mates. It's their tradition."

"It's kind of sad not having him around."

"Peace and quiet for me." Nate mumble, making me reach over and hit him. Nate just laughs. "I'm kidding! We still have the other twin, who's equally annoying."

I shake my head, grinning a little. "Be honest, Nate. You still can't tell them apart."

"How can I even do that when they do their best to confuse everyone? Are we even sure that Dan is leaving and not Ren? Or is Daniel actually Ren? Or Ren is Dan, who is pretending to be Dan? Or—"

Before he could continue, I shoved a sandwich into his mouth. "Just stop talking before you also confuse me." I get up and dust my pants. "I think I should go since we're done with the morning training. I want to help with the party. It's the least I could do for Dan."

Nate nods. "I'll follow after cleaning up. See you there." He waves.

The maids hastened to help me clean up as soon as I entered my room. The bath felt really good as it washed away all of the fatigue and sweat from my body.

I chose a light blue dress that would be ideal for a laid-back party. It was a sleeveless dress with a delicate ruffled strap. Even though the dress doesn't have a corset, it accentuates my curves. I wore some short heels since the queen couldn't see them and they would be hidden by the dress.

The maids helped by tying my hair up in a side ponytail with some side braids. Little flower ornaments are decorated all around the braids.

Once I was done, I headed to the ballroom, where the farewell party for Dan will be held. It was a small party just for us since we couldn't do a proper one because of the limited amount of time. The ballroom itself was beautifully decorated. There was a space in between, and rows of long tables with pastel pink and white tablecloths were lined. Pastel blue and purple cloths were hung from column to column, adorned with flowers.

When Custard notices the setup, he yips joyfully and runs around to inspect the space.

So much for a simple party.

I see Ren standing by one of the tables set up. I headed over to him to see what he is looking at.

"Hey." I greet him.

Ren stiffens up. He turns around, accidentally bumping the table and cursing.

"Sorry, I didn't notice you were already here." He smiles at me in greeting.

"I thought I should come early and help you with the preparation, but I think you had it all figured out. Great job, by the way." I nod in approval at the tables full of colorful desserts, which all seem to look like flowers in pastel colors. "If you don't mind me asking, is Dan or Liliana into pastel colors and…flowers?" I ask as I take note of the theme in the room.

Ren sighs and rubs the back of his head. "About that. While I was preparing for a more simple layout, a certain PRINCE told me that it was too plain and he would help out."

I stare at Ren. Something about the way he said PRINCE gave me a hint of who it is, but that character of him helping out seems too unreal. "Is it Prince Fred?"

Ren's face darken for a second before he bites his lips. "No."

"Prince Nate?"

"He was out training with you."

"It can't bePrincee Dan. And PRINCE Ace is too prideful to help out."

"What are you doing here?"

I let out a loud and unattractive gasp when I hear his voice behind me. I turn around to see Ace glaring. "Why do you always do that!?"

"I have no time for a stupid plebian like you. Move." He moves past me and heads for the maids, who were busy decorating.

"More flowers! Bring in every kind. Light colors are better. If I see anyone putting flowers with colors that don't match the theme, then I will feed it to you!" The maids trembled in fear as they continued to work. Ace kept on barking orders at them.

I lean into Ren and whisper. "Is it me or is he taking this a little serious?"

"It makes me wonder who Dan's actual brother is. I mean, he puts more effort into this than I do."

"Maybe he saw your hosting skills as lacking."

"Hey!"

"You two!" Ren and I flinches when Ace turns his attention to us. "If you guys are not going to help, then get lost. This place needs to be perfect!"

"We'll help!" Ren and I said it at the same time. Even though Ace scares the hell out of me, I still want to take part in this for Dan. I don't want to send him off without doing anything after all.

A small movement near the north entrance draws my attention. It is Nate heading in our way, but he comes to a halt when he realizes Ace is in command of the venue. Very carefully, he turns around and quietly makes his move to leave.

The coward! No way am I letting him escape.

"Hey, Nate. You're finally here to help!" I yell and Ace immediately turns and spotted him. Nate flinches and glares at me for revealing his escape plan.

"You. Hurry up and get in here. You and the mutt will be in charge of the cutlery. As for the stupid female over there, help the maids with flower arrangements."

I want to argue and make a comment about him calling me stupid, but seeing as though he is in a foul mood right now, I think it won't be a good idea. Besides, this party is for Dan.

Or at least, that's what I thought until our *visitors* arrived.

Daniel

I was wrong. This party wasn't for Dan. And the reason why PRINCE Ace was helping out was for a very different reason that does not involve Dan.

It was clear to me the moment our surprise guests entered the room—Ace's siblings.

"Hello, brother. Good to see—"

"Nora!"

Ah, there they are, the Feradin siblings. The older brother and crown prince of Tordis, Eltur, had his stunning silver hair down. His left ear was adorned with a golden, jagged jewel. For a crown prince, he was dressed in a plain white shirt with a leather vest and some black trousers. Darem, the second prince, wore the same clothing, but his golden-brown hair was tied into a ponytail - showing off his pointed ears. Alongside them was Nora, the youngest sibling, who was dressed in a plain white dress. As always, she looks like a mini version of Ace, but as a girl. Her hair is tied into pigtails and is decorated with lavender flowers.

PRINCE Ace quickly moves past his older brother and comes to pick up Nora, who is waiting for him with her hands up in the air. Nora laughed happily as he easily lifted her up.

"Bwother!"

"I knew he was too eager for this party. Now I know why." Ren mumbles.

"I can't believe that you're still surprised." I say.

"I can't take this scene. He's too..." Nate backs away with a terrified expression. "...happy! Are you guys even seeing this?!"

"Nate, this is not the first time we've seen him like that. But yeah, it makes my head hurt. He's so out of character." I look at Ace again.

Ace starts twirling Nora around, and...

...laughing.

Ugh!

"Oh my God! My eyes." I suddenly scream. The image burned itself into my mind and the sound of his laugh becomes an endless echo. "Make it stop!"

I'm kind of being overdramatic, but when you see a guy who has the energy of a demon prancing around like a happy clown, it is kind of hard to swallow.

"You guys are overreacting. It's not that weird." Ren says. His eyes avoiding the scenery in front of us.

Wow. The audacity of this guy to say those words when he's not even looking is unbelievable!

Nate and I share a look. It seems like we both have the same idea when we nod at each other at the same time. Nate creeps up behind Ren, grabs his arms, and forces him to face the Feradin siblings. My hands moved to his face as I forced his eyes open.

Ren screams. "Let me go!" He tries to shake Nate off, but the vampire is surprisingly strong.

"Burn it, mutt. Burn it into your brain!"

Ren screams and continues to struggle. Meanwhile, Nate and I hold our ground to make sure the image of a happy PRINCE Ace would seal itself into Ren's brain.

If he has one, that is.

"Leach, what are you doing to my brother?" There's a pause as the main character of the day arrives. Dan walks towards us, holding Liliana's hand. Liliana is busy looking at the room decorations that it takes her a few seconds to notice us.

"You guys arranged a farewell party for us?" Dan asks.

Ace takes a pause and gives him a look.

"What do you—" Ace begins speaking, then he stops abruptly, as if he's just remembered something. "Oh yeah, I guess it's your party too."

"Too?" Dan has an unreadable look on his face for a second. Then he sees the older Feradin brothers and frowns. "Oh, what brings the two of you here?"

For some reason, Dan and the Feradin brothers seem to always be at each other's throats, which always makes me wonder if wolves hate elves or maybe it's just Dan being anti-social.

Eltur and Darem Feradin gives him a smug look. "Oh look. It is the soon to be obsolete prince."

"If I'm obsolete, then what should I call the two of you, who didn't even make the cut to be a candidate?" Dan smirks in satisfaction when the two brothers give him a glare.

"Well, you are out of the game, but our baby brother isn't," Darem argues.

"That argument doesn't even make any sense. And my twin is still in the game."

"Is he though?"

"See how close they are right now."

Eltur and Darem's gazes suddenly landed on the three of us. Eltur gasps and gives Nora a look.

Nora smiles and wiggles her foot to signal Ace to put her down. She gives Ace a sweet smile and grabs his hand while suspiciously making her way over to us.

"Wose!" She beams and practically runs while dragging Ace behind her.

"Hey, Nora." I let go of Ren to face Nora. She releases Ace's hand and brings both her hands up towards me. "Do you need something?"

"Up! up!" She says. When I didn't respond, her facial expression fell.

A shiver suddenly goes down my spine, and I look up to see Ace glaring daggers at me. Nora had her back to him, so she couldn't see what her brother was doing. Ace points at his sister and makes a gesture of an embrace, then he brings his thumb to his neck and makes a slicing gesture. It was a sign that if I didn't carry his sister and continued to upset her, then he would kill me.

I gulped and bent down to carry Nora. She squeals in delight and turns to face her brother, who now has a soft smile on his face.

What a scammer.

"I can see bwother better now." She smiles.

"Indeed." Ace reaches out and pats her head affectionately.

Can he stop making that expression!? It's really disturbing and so out of character of him.

"Bwother Wen!" Nora smiles when she sees Ren.

Ren approaches my other side and grabs one of Nora's hands as she reaches for him. His other hand pats her head. "Good to see you again, Nora."

All of a sudden, Ace grabs both of Ren's hands, pulling them away from Nora. "It's PRINCESS Nora to you." Ace says darkly to Ren when he sees that his baby sister is blushing at Ren's touch.

I forgot. Nora likes Ren, which makes him all the more protective of her when Ren's near.

"R-Right..." Ren says, slowly and starts backing away.

I overheard Darem and Eltur laughing. I look in their direction to distract myself from Ace's weird expression. I follow their gaze only to find Dan enraged. He grumbles something under his breath and gives Liliana a look. Liliana nods and gives him a thumbs up.

"Go for it." She smiles encouragingly at him.

I give Dan a skeptical look when he comes over to me. A moment later, he has his hands up and beams sweetly at me.

"Up! up!" He says, imitating Nora.

I scrunch up my face and grimace at him before taking a step back. Shortly after, there's an awkward pause.

Ace breaks the silence a short while later. He grabs Dan by his collar and in a very menacing voice, he whispers, "Are you mocking my sister?"

"Of course not! I was just trying to use my charms as a younger brother." Dan turns to his twin and gives him a pleading look. "Brother, help."

Ren has his face cover and is looking away from him. "I have never met you. Please don't speak to me."

Ace releases his hold on Dan and gives him one final glare before returning to my side. Dan pouts and goes to Liliana for comfort.

Well, now it got boring. Maybe I should go and cause a little havoc while no one is volunteering for entertainment.

A bad idea suddenly forms in my head, and I grin mischievously. I look at Nora. "Hey, Nora. Who is your favorite brother?" I say cheerfully, which catches the attention of the three Feradin brothers.

"Bwother Aish! He is cool and has pwetty powers." Nora says it bluntly. It made me feel sorry for the two older Feradin brothers, who were now sulking in the corner. Dan did not miss this opportunity to laugh at the two fallen Feradin brothers.

"Now, who do you like more? Your brother Ace or Ren?" I grin mischievously while looking at the two princes for their expression. Ace glares piercingly at Ren after hearing him being compared to him. On the other hand, Ren simply covers his face as he gestures for me to stop.

I grin wider when Nora seems to take her time thinking. Actually, I was pretty scared at the moment because she really looked like she was considering Ren. If she does, then this party will also become a funeral for Ren.

"Bwother Aish. He is mowe good wooking and mowe stwong."

Ace seems to glow with pride and smirks at Ren. *'I win'*. His look says.

Ren laughs before turning to me with a pout. "Thanks, Rose. It really made me swell up with confidence there." He says it sarcastically, but I could see a hint of relief in his eyes. He probably knew that he had survived getting murdered by Ace in his sleep.

I grin sheepishly at him. I did—kind of—expected Nora to pick Ace, but I did not expect her to actually compare them based on their looks or even their strengths.

I mean, *ouch*.

This time, it was the Feradin brother's turn to laugh at Dan's solemn face.

I decided to break off the awkwardness that soon followed.

"Okay! We should start the party with words of gratitude towards—"

"A fallen comrade?" Nate suggests.

"A good for nothing sibling?" Ren inserts.

"A dead mutt," says Ace follows.

"Hey!" Dan protests at their descriptions of him.

"A fallen—I mean—" I glare at Nate, who started all of it. "A departing friend." I finish.

"Dan, you're one of the craziest princes I have ever met. I can't tell you how thankful I am for all that you have done. You taught me so much—"

"It wasn't easy. But Ren did most of the work." I bit my lip at Dan's sudden interruption.

Hold on, Rose. Don't kill him before he departs.

"—I wouldn't be where I am without your help. You even risk your life to save me. And for that, all I could wish for is your happiness. Do visit us again." I smile upon finishing my speech.

Dan stands there looking at me with his hands in his pocket. He gives me a genuine smile, and I could faintly see the sadness in them.

"I will. Don't you worry. I just can't leave you alone, especially when your etiquette is still lacking." He teases.

I ignore his last remark while I laugh along with him. I turn to Nate and give him a nod to go next.

Nate rubs the back of his neck before stepping forward. "I know you are not fond of me, but I consider you a comrade. Even though you and your brother are annoying, I still respect you both as princes."

Oh my God.

"Nate?" I whisper.

Nate shushes me while the others began to laugh at him. "I am glad that you're finally taking another step in life. I hope you'll grow more as a person worthy of respect."

"Oh my God, Nate!" I whisper a little louder.

"What?!" He sounds pretty annoyed that I kept on interrupting him. He's going to regret that since I am just trying to help him.

"That's Ren you're talking to." I say, not even bothering to be discreet anymore.

Dan, Eltur, and Darem doubles over laughing. Liliana covers her mouth as she laughs while Ace is busy watching Nora clapping and laughing.

"Aha ha." Nate sheepishly looks at Dan. "Same message. I hope you heard that."

"Got it. I respect you too. Just don't get in my brother's way." Dan flashes a gleeful grin and throws up two middle fingers in his direction.

"I'm afraid I can't do that." Nate smiles and flashes him the same gesture.

I look at Ace hesitantly, gesturing for him to go next. Nora sees me and gives her brother a soft nudge. Ace sighs and faces Dan.

"Bye." That is all he says.

"Bye..." Dan replied awkwardly.

"What?" Ace turns and gives me a raised brow when he sees me looking. "Did you expect me to say something more?"

"Good point. I shouldn't have." I mutter.

Well, at least he said something.

I turn to Ren instead and gives him a thumbs up, a signal for him to go next. Ren rubs the back of his head bashfully.

"Daniel, I hope you'll do well on your own. We always knew that a day would come when we would have to go our separate lives. It's just too hard to imagine. I mean, we're always together. Look, we even became a king's candidate together." There is an exchange of mournful smiles between the two brothers when their gazes meet. "I just didn't think that we would have to separate so soon. Not like this..." Ren trails off. "But I really am happy for you!" He turns to Liliana. "Take care of my brother, will you? He's kind of stupid."

Liliana laughs but gives him a short nod. "Of course."

"Stupid? You didn't figure it out until you were eavesdropping—" Before Dan could finish, Lilian covered his mouth with her hand.

"That's enough spoilers from you, dear."

Ren and Nate went around and hands each of us a glass of juice as soon as everyone said their farewell message to Dan.

"To Daniel Rutledge. May he be blessed with happiness on his new journey." Ren clinks his glass in a toast to the group.

"See that? They're a loving sibling." Eltur comes to Ace's side along with Darem.

"Go away. My only sibling is Nora." Ace states unequivocally that he does not wish to speak with them.

"What? No fair." Darem pouts.

"Why can't you love us like you love Nora? WHY WON'T YOU LOVE ME!?"

"I'm hurt!" Eltur dramatically makes a gesture that bumps Darem's glass of juice. The contents spills on Darem's white shirt.

"A f*ck!" He curses.

"Fwak!"

My family and friends stare at Nora, who is still in my arms, and gasp.

"Fwak!" She repeats.

I must be hearing things. No way would Nora—

"Fwak."

Oh sh*t, she did!

When I look up, I see Ace holding his wine glass so tightly that it has shattered. When he looks at his older brothers his eyes narrow and take on an angry expression.

"Nora, t–that is b–bad!" Eltur stutters upon seeing how angry Ace is.

"Why?" Nora asks curiously. "I sometimes hear bwother Eltwur say fwukin bwits." Eltur screams in horror at Nora's revelation. He grips his silver hair and uses it to hide his face. His white skin turns even paler as he glances at Ace.

I must admit that it looks funny, but I feel sorry for Eltur at the same time.

"Just what kind of language do you use in front of my sister?" There's venom in his voice—a menacing aura emanates from Ace that I step back just so I'd have Nate and Ren beside me in case things go out of control, I can always offer them as sacrifices.

"Eltur, Darem, outside." Ace commands as he carefully approaches his older brothers.

"N-no thanks. It's comfy in here." Eltur shakily lifts his wine to his lips and pretends to look at the decorations in the room.

"N-Nora! Come here to your big b-brother please?" Darem desperately calls for Nora, who's currently the only one who can save them now.

"But you said to stay with Wose."

"Change of plans! C-come here, our adorable angel."

"You dare command Nora!?" Ace demands. "From now on, you will not touch her, look at her, or even speak to her. You simply nod!"

Dan seems to enjoy this as he is laughing and clapping at the same time. "Serves you right, you cheaters." He cheers, thrusting his hands in the air. "You see that, Lily? We win!"

What is Dan even talking about? Are they having a competition or something?

"Ace is scary." Nate comments.

"No sh—" Before Ren can finish what he is about to say, Nate and I cover his mouth with our hands.

The three of us nervously look at Nora, wondering if she heard Ren. Her eyes gleam in curiosity at the unspoken word.

I see Ace pause from harassing his siblings and turn in our direction. He looks ready to kill and slowly makes his way to us.

Crap!

"What. Did. You. Say?" I know that Ace is scary, but when it comes to his sister, I can almost feel like Death is lurking behind him.

"N-no sheep!" My voice squeeks when I think of an excuse. "W-we need sheep meat!"

Nora smiles at her brother, who now seems to be calming down. I let out a sigh of relief.

"Scary siscon." I mutter under my breath. I temporarily forgot that I was carrying Nora in my other hand for her to hear me.

"Sishcon!" Nora repeats my word. My hand quickly flies to her mouth before Ace can hear her.

Can this child give me a break!?

"Nora, I want to live!" With trembling lips, I murmur her. When I finally do look up, I see that Ace has a grim look on his face.

"Just what are you teaching my sister?" He says in a sinister voice.

I see my familiar, Custard, hiding under the table. I willed him to come and help me, but he just brushed me off.

'Sorry, Master.' He apologizes and runs away. That coward!

After closing my eyes, I hoist Nora in front of him. After a while, I noticed that Ace had removed Nora from my arms and was carrying her himself. As if daring me to object to the kidnapping of his sister, Ace shots me a glare.

Nora taps a hand on Ace's cheek. "Bwother, why awe you scawing Wose?" She pouts. Just like magic, Ace's facial expression changes.

"I wasn't." He answers. "Are you hungry?"

"Yep."

Ace then turns his back on us and walks away to prepare a meal for himself and Nora. Nora looks over her shoulder and waves cheerfully.

"What an angel." I cry as I realize that Nora did it on purpose to save us.

Dan suddenly pops up between Ren and I.

"So are you eating or what?" I laugh at his carefree attitude and follow the twins to where the food is being served. The rest of the day is spent playing, talking, and arguing between Dan and the Feradin brothers.

"If we win, you will not be invited to the wedding!" Eltur says.

"If I win, you can't even enter Sanver at all." Counters Dan.

"Your brother hasn't even made any progress!"

"Your brother wants to murder <u>she who must not be named right now</u>!"

And the bickering continues. Somehow, I am getting tired of listening to them arguing. When are they going to have a fist fight? I want some action!

Lily suddenly comes to my side. "I haven't talked to you that much, but I do believe that we will get along in the future. Sorry if I called Ren my fiancé. I swear it was all an act." She tells me.

"No worries." I still feel a little awkward talking to Liliana. She does seems like a nice person so I am hoping to be friends with her. I never had any close fe,ale friends in this realm yet.

"I didn't hurt you by doing that, right? If you'll hate me for it, then I can understand." She says sadly. Dan and Ren seems interested in our conversation all of a sudden.

"No way. Why would I be upset about that?" I answer her.

"You're not offended?" Lilian seems surprised and studies my face closely to see if I am telling her the truth.

"Why should I be hurt in the first place? You didn't hit me." I wonder.

At the corner of my eye, I see Dan taking a deep breath, and forcing his twin into a hug.

"There there, brother. It's alright. I am here for you."

Soon, it was getting dark and Dan and Lily would have to leave soon. But before they left, Dan kept giving me a glance. "The weather sure seems dense around here!" He kept saying it every time our eyes met.

It was getting irritating for a while because it seemed like he was teasing me with the tone that he was using.

"Yeah, yeah. Please go while the weather seems nice." I clench my teeth together and say, to Dan's amusement.

"Rose." He says softly. "My brother might feel lonely from time to time. Please do watch over him in my absence." I briefly believes he is going to tease me, but when I looked into his eyes, I understood that he was serious. He is genuinely concerned for his twin.

"I'll help, of course." Nate suddenly appears and places an arm over my shoulder.

"Hands off!" Ren pinches Nate's hand off of me. "I won't be lonely for a while since we have our link. Do keep me updated." He tells his brother.

"Goodbye already." Ace interrupts us, looking bored as Hell while standing to the side and holding his sister.

"Aw, Ace don't be like that." Dan feigns hurt. "I thought we were comrades now."

"It's PRINCE Ace." He corrects him.

Dan chuckles lightly. "Well, I guess we're off now. We want to reach Sanver before it gets really dark. Be sure to keep me posted with letters!" We all exchange hugs, even Ace, who couldn't do anything with Nora watching.

Soon, their carriage was nowhere to be seen.

"Brother, we came here to deliver this to you." I look back and see Eltur handing Ace a couple of books. "I guess we should get going too."

"No." Ace stops them. "It's getting late."

Darem let out a gasp. "Brother, you do care!"

"I care about Nora's safety. It is not safe to travel at night. I only care about you two as her escort. Your job is to make sure that Nora gets home safe." He snaps.

I snort. Ace really cares about his sister. I see Nate looking at them with jealousy. "Must be nice to have that kind of relationship with your sibling."

"Aren't you close with your brother?"

"Yeah, sort of, but not like theirs. Or like Ren and Dan's."

Speaking of Ren, Nate and I turn back to see that Ren is being quiet. His gaze is still fixed on where his brother's carriage disappeared.

"I bet he misses him already." Nate whispers to me.

I walk towards Ren and place a gentle hand on his shoulder. "Ren?" I moved to look at his face and was surprised to see that he's crying. I see Nate moving towards us, and I gesture for him to stop. I figured that Ren wouldn't want anyone to see him in that state right now.

Nate and I had grown so close that he understood what I was asking of him with a single nod. He approached the Feradin siblings and led them inside, leaving Ren and I alone outside.

"I...I'm sorry. It just won't stop." He says in between tears.

"It's alright," I gently pull him in a hug.

"I couldn't...even tell him half the t-things I wanted to say. I couldn't give back to everything...that he has done for me." He snifles. "I wasn't even the one who...prepared the party!"

"No one is perfect, Ren. No one is perfect." I tell him and continue to pat his back.

By The Shore

"I said higher!" Ace barks at me during our morning training. He's currently teaching me the basics of sword fighting. At first, I was glad because it meant that my stamina would improve if they were willing to teach me something different. But now, I am dreading it.

I wasn't sure if I was just a bad student or if Ace was just venting out his frustration at me. You see, earlier this morning, his siblings had to go back, which meant he had to part ways with Nora. This siscon wasn't happy to see his beloved sister go, because he had a duty to train me.

"Give her a break, man." Nate suggests when he comes up behind Ace while giving me a look of pity. Nate has no reason to stay here, but he actually stayed when he saw my worried look when I found out that Ace was teaching me sword fighting. "Remember, she's just a beginner."

"She only swung 50 times!" Ace snaps. "When I was a kid, I did 3,000 swings!"

Amazing. What does he want? A medal?

I don't know if he was boasting or not, but one thing is for sure. He's a monster who swings 3,000 times. I wonder how much he can swing now that he's an adult?

Meanwhile, I am already panting. My white shirt is already soaked in sweat. I ran 10 laps today and took a few minutes of a break before my sword training began.

My arms are killing me! No wonder Nate insisted that we do some arm stretches and push-ups as warm-ups before. Maybe I should listen more to Nate from now on.

I slump onto the ground and drop the wooden sword. It was heavy, even though it was just made out of wood. If I can't carry this, then I wonder what would happen if I carried a real sword.

Ace regards my slumping form and sighs. "It would seem that wielding a sword is not the right weapon for her. Let's drop it and change weapons." He says with a shrug.

I give him a look as if I wanted to strangle him. If only my hands could move, then I would.

"Then what weapon do you suggest would suit her?" Nate asks with his brow raise.

Ace looks at me and ponders for a while. "Most probably a weapon that can block weapons and attack at the same time. With her weak arms—"

"Hey!"

"—I suggest blades that are light. Something that she can swing easily. Twin swords would be nice, but with crescent guards." Ace observeS.

"How about hook swords? It has a guard, a blade, and with her terrible luck, she can simply use it to trip enemies."

"You guys make it sound like I get into a lot of trouble." I complain.

Both Ace and Nate gave me a look with their eyebrows raised. I pout and shut my mouth since my opinion doesn't matter to them anyway!

"I think the hook swords would work, but we have to be careful about the end blade. She could stab herself accidentally and **die**." Ace thought out loud. His eyes suddenly widen at the idea and he seems pleased. "Let's give her the hook swords." He suddenly sounds inspired.

I narrowed my gaze at him, knowing fully well why he suddenly agreed. "You're actually hoping that I will accidentally stab myself and die, aren't you?"

Ace looks away. "It's perfect." He said firmly.

Nate giggles uneasily. "I do think that it's perfect. I mean, she can defend herself from the enemy even if they sneak behind her with the end blades. I'll just have to find a wooden version of it for training."

I honestly have no idea what kind of weapon they were talking about. But as the village idiot among them, I trust that they know what's best for me. At least I trust Nate's judgment and not Ace's.

"So!" I clap my hands together. "If we're done here, can I go back and sleep?"

"Actually." Nate crouches in front of me to hand me a bota bag full of water. I take it from him gratefully as I start to drink. "I came here because I wanted to tell you something regarding your powers—the ones that royal blooded tamers as you possess."

"What about it?" I ask after a few gulps of water. Sadly, I am still thirsty, so I kept drinking.

"Royal tamers can take away a supernatural's power and turn them into a human."

I spit out the water that I was drinking at the shocking revelation. In front of me is Nate, dripping wet from the water that I had just sprayed him with. I gave him a sheepish smile as I apologize.

"That..." I pause as I recalled the image of the large Custard eating smoke when he attacked the rogue. "Are you telling me that our spirit animals, royal spirit animals, can take the essence of what makes you...unnatural?"

Nate, after whipping the water from his face, nodded grimly. "Rose, the human civilization that you know of was actually created by the royal tamers."

I stare at him. "Nate I—" I look down abruptly, unsure of how to respond. I take a deep breath as I try again. "You mean to tell me that the humans were originally from this world, but after having their powers taken, they were sent to that world?" I shake my head. "Then why don't humans have any supernatural powers?"

"When a tamer takes their essence, then it is permanent. Their children cannot inherit anything that they no longer possess." Ace speaks and gives me a look that I am unable to read. "I guess that explains why you humans have stories about wolves, vampires, and other supernatural beings."

"Oh gosh." I clutch my head as I let this sink in. "This information is too much. In other words, the human world is just like a place for banishment in this realm!"

Ace and Nate look at each other in surprise. "If you put it that way, then I guess so." Nate scratches the back of his head, looking equally as disturbed as Ace.

"And that is why it is important for you to train your powers. You can actually take our essence if you are not careful." Ace says. "While the wooden hook swords are being made, we can practice how to control your powers."

I raise an eyebrow at him. "Do you even know how to train me despite having limited knowledge of my powers?"

"I'll teach you the basics of controlling magic. I am pretty sure the basics are the same."

"You'll teach me!?" I gasp and glance at Nate for help.

Nate raises his hands in defeat. "As much as I want to help you, I can't. Vampires have physical strength and agility. We don't have magic, except for our fast regenerating ability."

"You know who else has magic? Fred!" I gleam with hope.

"I'm right here." Nate leers at me along with a bitter smirk on his lips. "And too bad for you. He's busy and he doesn't have the time to visit you." He starts to pout and cross his arms over his chest.

Ace sighs. "Listen, I do not wish to teach your untrainable butt either. But we do not have a choice. If we can no longer protect you, then you have to protect yourself. For now, you can't do that without your familiar. And all those times that you use your powers are when you're in danger. You have to learn how to control it. You know what happens when King Ferius gets a hold of you? It will become a disaster. You can potentially stop him, but if you're as weak as you are now, then it is the end for us."

I look at the ground. Sadly, Ace was right. In order for all of us to survive and to ensure the safety of the whole kingdom, I must not get captured. We can't let King Ferius release his chimera and repeat what happened in the past.

"Alright." I agree.

Ace nods, pleased with my answer before turning to one side.

"Hey, mutt. Get over here and bring that wolf." He barks his orders at Ren, who was peacefully sitting under the shade of a tree. Custard is sleeping on his lap as he strokes his fur gently. Poor Ren.

It's the first time that he and Dan have been separated. He has been feeling a little depressed since this morning, so I have asked Custard to stay at his side and keep him company.

Ren stared vacantly for a moment, then got to his feet and walked toward us while carrying Custard. He puts Custard down next to me. The brown wolf cub yawned, yet continued to be awake. I could tell he was expecting something because of the way he looked at me.

Ace crouches down in front of me. His hair slightly covers his eyes as he looks down to meet my gaze.

"Close your eyes." He orders me. "If you fall asleep, then I will hit you."

"Well, that's reassuring." I close my eyes.

"Can you feel your bond with your familiar?"

"After locking me up after the ball? Of course, I can." I say smugly. "There was literally nothing else to do at that time other than to talk to Custard."

I couldn't tell what Ace's face looked like at that time since my eyes were closed, but from his grunt, I could tell that he wanted to deck me. "One of the most basic skills that every tamer 'had' is to feel their connection. Just by thinking about your familiar, you can tell where they are."

"Um, he's right beside me." I say.

"You're not even trying!" Ace snaps. "Focus!"

I badly want to roll my eyes, but thought against it since I do not want to test Ace's patience with me while I can't see him. While I was concentrating, I feel a slight pull to my left.

"I can feel him, but he somehow feels far away? Am I even doing this right?" I ask and patted the ground where I last saw Custard. It is empty. Where is he?

"Don't you dare open your eyes. You're doing fine, so just concentrate." Ace sighs. "Another one of your skills is to see through your familiar's eyes and hear through its ears. It resembles my power, but yours is only limited to your familiar."

Tapping into Custard's hearing ability was easy since I had already used it when I was eavesdropping on Dan and Liliana before.

But seeing through Custard's eyes? It took me a while, but I was finally able to do it.

It feels weird to see myself through Custard's eyes. He is being carried by Nate as they stand under a shade of a tree.

When did they get there?

"Now." Ace continued with his lesson once I told him that I was successful. "Try summoning him. Make him appear beside you."

"Appear? How is that possible? And how do you know this information?"

"It's in the book that I asked my sibling to bring." He huffs. "Now focus!"

Geez, what a temper.

I try to focus and urge Custard to appear in my arms. Nothing.

"Can you give me a hint? It seems that it is not working."

"Try again. Imagine him in your arms."

I tried. Nothing. *Again.*

I open my eyes this time. "I don't think it's something that is possible? I mean no offense, but maybe the information in your book is a lie? Like some of the kings in the elven history, maybe the tamers altered some truths too." I suggest.

Ace wasn't happy, but he looks like he is considering that possibility as well. "You know, the queen should be the one to train you since she knows more about tamers bu—" Ace pauses. His eyes suddenly widens in panic and fear as he turns in the direction of the forest. I follow his gaze and see the forest dancing even in the absence of air.

Ace has the magic to sense and see his surroundings through his gift. I can only guess that he saw something unpleasant because of how his face morphed at that time.

"No." He mutters and starts running. "Nora!"

Nora? Was he using his powers to spy on his sibling?

"Hey!" Despite my aching muscles, I get up and run after him. He's running towards the stables, where our horses are running around in a large and enclosed fence. Ace let out a whistle, and I see Midnight's head perk up in attention before running towards his master. Midnight jumps over the fence to meet with Ace. The elf prince jumps and swiftly rides his stallion into the forest.

I glance at Cloud and try to imitate Ace's whistle. I thought that Cloud would do the same trick as Midnight, but her ears just twitch a bit before she continues to eat.

Of course. What did I even expect?

"You haven't trained Cloud yet." Nate laughs and leads me to his horse. He hopes on Ryde and places Custard on my lap after helping me get on the saddle.

I noticed Ren getting on Garius and staring at us. Nate returns his look after catching his gaze.

"Let's go."

We start to follow Ace into the woods.

I was thankful that I was wearing trousers and high boots so it was comfortable for me to ride. Ace is already far ahead of us, which made Ren and Nate speed up their horses.

"We're gonna lose him." I say. I don't think I would have been able to keep up with them if I was riding alone. I am still a beginner when it comes to horse back.

"That stallion is too fast. Excuse me, but hang on tight." Ryde's speed suddenly increases, and I have to close my eyes due to the rush of wind on my face.

It wasn't long after we exited the forest that I noticed we were slowing down. When I open my eyes, I realize we are on a sandy beach just past the town at the palace's main entrance. Ace jumps off Midnight and runs towards his brother, who are now unconscious right before us.

"This is bad." Ren gets down from Garius as his eyes start to wander everywhere. "I don't smell Nora anywhere."

Nate comes down and assists me in getting off Ryde. We got to where the Feradin brothers were quickly, where Ace was trying to wake up his brothers.

"Eltur! Darem! Wake up." For the very first time, I saw the concern on Ace's face towards his brother.

"Brother?" Darem wakes up and coughs water out of his mouth. "Nora." He says weakly.

"Are you well enough to talk?" Ace starts to raise his brother a bit to help him get into a comfortable position.

"Don't mind me. Help…Nora…" Ace places a hand on his brother's forehead, then he starts to feel his pulse. His brow starts to crease. "You've been poisoned, haven't you?"

"It's just a paralysis poison. They…hit me with a small dose. Eltur, on the other hand, took a lot when he tried to take on the Atla Generals."

Ace's eyes narrows. "Did they take Nora?"

Darem nods.

"Why?" Ace demands. His gaze looked dangerous by the second.

Darem looks at the ground in shame. "It's our fault. Nora wanted to walk on the beach. She said that she feels a lot of dark energy coming from the ocean—distressed auras that it made her uncomfortable enough to go and look." His wet golden brown hair covers his eyes in shame. "Before we knew it, five generals from the Alta kingdom came and took Nora. Eltur and I tried to stop them, but we were powerless when fighting in the sea. I tried pulling them using my psychic ability, but they poisoned me. Brother Eltur's fire elemental spirit was no use, so he decided to take them on in combat. As you can see…" He gestures towards a bloodied and badly beaten Eltur on the sandy ground. "We couldn't do anything. I'm sorry." He whispers. "I know that you'll do it without me asking you but, Ace, please. Save Nora."

Ace looks at his distressed brother and places a hand on his shoulder. "It's not like you did nothing. You were able to inform me of the situation. That alone in something." Ace grits his teeth. "Those bastards who took my sister will pay. They will regret the day that they set foot on land and took our sister."

Nate, Ren, and I watch as Ace guides and helps his brothers to ride on Midnight. Seeing their struggle, Ren comes and help him carry Darem. They place Eltur on midnight and help an injured Darem next to him. "Ride Midnight and find your carriage. Knock some sense into the guards for not following you. After that, go back to Thalia and have the royal doctors treat your wounds. I will come back with Nora." Ace says. It seems like Darem wants Toto argue, but figures that in his current state, he could no longer be of use. Curtly nodding, Darem drives Midnight in the general direction of where I believe their carriage is.

"So, what's the plan?" Nate asks after we got closer to Ace.

In response, Ace gives him a look. "The plan is for you guys to go home."

"Ace—"

"It's PRINCE!!"

I roll my eyes. "PRINCE Ace, this is Nora that we're talking about—your sister. Do you honestly expect us to leave you alone knowing that your little sister is in trouble?" Ace gives me a look. "And please, you should know by now that whenever one of us is in trouble—"

"Mostly you." The three princes cut me off. *Well, it is at least nice to know that they would all agree to something.*

I purse my lips at the sudden alliance of the three. "Yes, I admit that I am an accident-prone person, but the point is, we are here to help each other—to help you. So again, we ask you, what's the plan?"

Ace studies all of us. It was as if he was thinking whether or not we were joking.

"First of all," He says, shifting his gaze towards the massive boulder on the shore. "Why don't you come out of your hiding spot, you little brat?"

The Second Prince of the Sea

Nate is there in an instant, dragging a small child who was hiding behind the rocks. The child is dressed in white seaman pants with a belt made of sea shells and braided seaweeds. His hair is what catches my attention first because it is an ocean blue color. His green eyes glows with fear when he looks at Nate.

If we were in the human realm, Nate is going to face some serious child abuse issues—not like he is tryingt o abuse the child anyway.

"What is a sea folk like you doing here?" Nate wonders as soon as he gets a good look at the child.

"A sea folk?" I look at Ren for answers.

"People of the sea." Ren answers curtly. "Sorry. I don't know much about them as well. They never show up in social gatherings, and they aren't in any trade agreements with the other kingdoms. Not much is known about them. Even seeing one is rare enough."

"Mermaids exists!?"

"Rose, you guys literally fought a mermaid a while back!"

Oh, right. That one mermaid who was so obsessed with killing men. How could I have forgotten about her?

Ace charges towards the boy, who is now cowering in terror. "Do you know something about the whereabouts of my sister? Answer me or else!"

"PRINCE Ace." Nate stops Ace from grabbing the child, who appears to be about 6 years old. "He's just a boy. Don't be too hard on him." Ace grits his teeth but backs away.

I headed over to Nate's side while he was trying to calm Ace. Meanwhile, I place a gentle hand on the boy's hair both out of curiosity and pity.

"Hello!" I greet him once he takes notice of me. "Me. Name. Rose." I gesture to myself. "They," I point to the princes. "Nate. Monster. Ren. Custard. We. Come. In. Peace. Your. Name?" After my introduction, I can hear multiple face slaps in the background.

The child gives me a curious look. The fear in his green eyes is gone and now replaced with puzzlement.

"My...My name is Zeraph Bastian." He answers me.

My jaw drops as soon as I hear him speak. I glared at Ren for an explanation.

"Why didn't you tell me he could speak normally!?" I turn to face Ren with a slightly flushed expression out of embarrassment.

Ren looks like he is trying to fight off a laugh whil raising his hands in the air. "Hey, I said it was *rare* for us to see them. I never said that they *could not* speak our language." He points it out.

Okay, that's a valid argument. Why didn't I think of that?

The kid keeps glancing at the ocean, and somehow he seems worried. "I know where your sister is, but it is not safe yo talk here." The child says nervously to Ace. The elf prince looked back at the ocean and frowns.

"Fine. There's a town nearby. We can talk there." Ace proposes before heading off into the direction of the village.

The rest of us follows them. Nate, Ren, and I are a few blocks away because Nate and Ren had to pick up their horses.

The town was distinct from the one on Thalia's outskirts. It was tedious. The females wore masks to cover their faces and were accompanied by one or two males. Normally, I would not mind such behavior, but seeing how they cower when they see us, it strikes me as odd. It seems like the town is not that friendly to strangers.

The princes must have noticed it too, because they decided that we should head to an inn and lay low until we figure out the problem regarding Nora. We headed to the nearest inn when a petite girl suddenly approached us.

She's a small child who was about 10. She taps my arm and gestures for me to come closer. Hesitantly, I complied.

"Miss, please wear a mask or something to cover your face." She says, pointing to the cloth on her face.

"Why?" I ask.

"It's for your safety." That was all she said before she ran away.

Nate suddenly taps my shoulder and hands me his handkerchief. "Come here. I don't know what their deal is, but there's a sign that says, *'women with no mask cannot enter.'* " I let Nate tie his handkerchief over my face before we enter the inn with the others. We let Ace rent a room for the four of us. It was small, but it easily accommodated us. Once we were safely inside, Ace turned to the kid.

"Talk. Who are you?" Ace did not beat around the bush and quickly interrogates the kid as soon as we are all in the room.

Zeraph nervously fiddles with his hands while under Ace's intense gaze.

"I'm...I'm the second prince of the Atla kingdom."

Ren almost falls out of his chair at Zeraph's revelation. Custard barks at Ren for dropping him and comes running towards me, jumping on my lap.

"Holy sh—" I throw a pillow at Nate before he could continue his curse. Damn vampire. Can't he see that there's a kid in the room?

Ace narrows his eyes at the child. "What is the second prince doing out here on land?"

"It's because of my father." Zeraph drops his gaze from Ace. "He keeps taking women into the kingdom of Atla to either be his concubine or be the crown prince's bride."

Upon hearing this, Ace's grip on the back of a wooden chair tightens.

"What...did you say?" Ace breathes dangerously, and the rest of us has to back away knowing that he is going to explode at any second now. "Why did my sister, who's only 4 years old, get captured!?"

"It was probably for me, so I can choose my future bride..." I move closer to Zeraph, fearing what Ace would do to him after that confession. I don't even know what I could do for him if Ace decides to grab him, to be honest. My body just moved on its own.

Ace punches a nearby wall which instantly cracks. When Ace attempts to lunge at the child, Nate and Ren jump to their feet and hold him in place. "You better tell me how I can get my sister back, or, so help me, I will make sure that you will never see the light of day again!"

"Women!" I was sitting beside Zeraph when he suddenly grabbed onto me to hide from Ace. "Beautiful women. If one of the generals sees a beautiful woman, they will take you to sea." The child says quickly under Ace's glare.

"That is absurd," Ren says. This time, it is his turn to give the kid a suspicious look. "You, as the son of the king, why are you here telling us all of this?"

Zeraph is silent for a moment and looks at the ground. "My father, King Corona Bayrus Bastian, is a mad man. He kidnaps women, abuses my brother and I, and he is making shady deals with another kingdom." Seeing the shaken look on Zeraph's face, I don't think that there's any reason for us to doubt him. The boy looks traumatized. "One day, my father suddenly had one of his...moods and locked me up in a cage for weeks. My brother, Prince Mereum, got me out and sent me here on land to escape. I'm currently a fugitive in our kingdom."

"Is that why the women here wear masks? To avoid King Corona Bayrus?" Nate ask. Zeraph nods solemnly in response to his question.

Ren shakes his head in disgust. "I can't believe such a king exists."

"Do you know this shady kingdom that Atla is dealing with?" Ace interrogates him but with a calmer tone this time.

"No..."

"Do you know another way to infiltrate Atla? Considering the shady deals that they are doing, I doubt they would welcome us even if we sent a formal request."

"I can take you to the entrance using my magic, but I cannot lead you to where the captured females are since they are heavily guarded."

So only girls can enter the palace?

"I have a plan!" I declare smugly. I have seen this in a lot of movies that I just have to incorporate it into this world. "All we have to do is let them capture me. Then I will lead the captured females to the exit, where you guys can meet us. Easy peasy!"

The princes stares at me with dull eyes. Their looks tell me that there is not a single ounce of trust that they have for me, Prince Ace especially. He gives me a dead look and grimaces.

"First of all," He points out. "They only take *beautiful women*. And second, you're a big clutz who attracts all the negative energy in the world. Third, your sense of direction is awful, so how the—" Ace cuts off his cursing when he notices Zerpah. "—can you lure the women to the exit. Fourth, don't get me started on how you're going to deal with the guards. You can't even defend yourself. Fifth, **BEAUTIFUL WOMEN** only. Have you seen yourself in the mirror lately?"

Well, that was an awful lot of roasting.

"You son of a—" Nate quickly covers my mouth with his hands before I can finish cursing him.

"Well, Rose does have a good plan. How about we simply polish that plan?" Nate then glances at Zeraph. "Don't cuss in front of a kid."

Sure. I'm the only one that he patronizes!

"We follow my plan: save Nora!" Ace yells stubbornly and stomps his foot. Suddenly, he runs out of the room like a crazy siscon.

The princes, Custard and I follow him along with Zeraph. Ace heads out of the inn and suddenly marches into a nearby store for clothes. He kicks it open with a loud bang.

"I NEED A DRESS!" He yell at the store attendants, who all jumps at his sudden outburst. I pause right beside him, looking at him and wondering why he would buy a dress at this time.

The storekeeper takes a good look at me in my white shirt, brown trousers, and boots—my outfit every time I train.

"Is it for this lady right here?" The shopkeeper inquires with a professional smile.

"Are you blind!?" Ace scolde her, which makes the storekeeper flinch in surprise. "It's for ME!"

Our jaws dropped. The shopkeeper and her attendants even drop their things out of shock at what he said. Ace didn't look like he was joking either. If it makes matters worse, he also adds, "I need a long black wig as well!"

LADY Grace

It didn't take long until Ace *'came out of the closet'* — if you know what I mean — looking like a different person. All of us let out a gasp as we took in the sight of this beautiful creature in front of us. Long back hair that ended at his waist, a soft blue dress with long sleeves, and an army green cloak to cover his manly arm muscles. His piercing midnight blue eyes glinted under the bangs of the wig.

The attendant gives him some heels to pair with his dress. Ace didn't even say thank you to the man as he slipped them on.

"Oh my." I cover my lips to stifle my gasp.

"Well, I'll be…" Nate breaths, his eyes focusing intently on Ace.

"I must be hallucinating." Ren starts looking away and rubbing his eyes.

"If I didn't know that he is a man, then I would have proposed," Nate mumbles, earning a slap at the back of his head from me in order to snap him out of whatever spell he's in.

Ace looks…beautiful!

He looks like the most beautiful girl that I ever laid my eyes upon and I am not even kidding. His elven features, which gave him a sharp jaw and sharp ears, highlighted his looks. Not to mention how clear and smooth his skin was. There was a light layer of makeup on his face that gave him a pinkish glow, both on his cheeks and lips.

Ace stars walking as soon as he finishes clasping on the locks on the heels. "Damn these cursed shoes!" He grunts and started to walk forward. Once he did, he trips and starts to fall forward. Immediately, Ren managed to move quickly and catch him just as he fell.

I feel like my eyes are playing tricks on me because what I'm seeing right now makes my heart flutter. I don't even know whether I should laugh or start taking pictures!

Ren grabs Ace's waist to keep him steady, while Ace rests his hands on Ren's muscular chest. Ren and Ace's eyes met for a split second as his black wig swayed with the motion. Ren flushes unexpectedly while Nate and I hold hands as we take in the scene before us.

It felt like I was watching a scene in the movie where the male and female leads first met.

"I do not know if I should feel jealous or amused." Nate blushes when he looks at them.

"I do not know if I should feel amazed or insulted that he looks better than me."

Ace suddenly glares at Ren.

"Are you done?!" He snaps at Ren, not even bothering to look grateful that he helped him. "Help me up or I'll break your neck."

Fortunately, Ren finally realizes that the woman he has in his arms in a man that he quickly helps his settle back on his feet. Once Ace is back on his feet, he flips his wig back in place flawlessly.

"Let's go." He then gracefully walks out of the shop.

As we walk back to the beach, Ace fills us in on the plan.

The plan was for Ace to pretend to be a lady, while the rest of us are her/his(?) servants—not that we have any problem with that at all. While Prince Zeraph and Custard will have to hide somewhere. Of course, Ace still doesn't fully trust Zeraph that he let Custard guard him.

Ace will have to get captured and find the kidnapped females. Meanwhile, the rest of us, using Prince Zeraph's magic, will wait by the port of Atla tomorrow at sunrise. Zeraph already told Ace what to look out for to get to the port. Ace is smart, so I bet he won't have any problem finding his way around an unfamiliar kingdom.

Ace suddenly gives me a hat and a coat to cover my gender.

"Since your chest is almost flat, it won't be a problem." He says. If this guy didn't look the way he does now, I would have strangled him. He better be lucky that I don't hit pretty girls.

Ren places a hand on top of my head when I was growling in frustration. "Don't let his beauty intimidate you." He says.

I give Ren a pointed look. "Says the guy who was blushing earlier at Ace—"

"It's **LADY Grace**!" Ace snaps at us.

And there he goes with his titles. At least he is taking his roles seriously.

Ren, Nate, and I exchange glances like we are waiting for someone to go and say something about the title that he just came up with. Since none of us seems to want to say something, we just bow our heads at Ace.

"As you wish, LADY Grace."

"Shut your mouths and let's get this over with already. Stupid female attires!" Ace starts trudging to the beach in his heels. Ace grumbles the entire time because his heels keep sinking into the sand, looking more like a monkey than a proper lady at this point.

Ha! Now he knows how hard it is to be a lady.

Nate and I exchange glances. A mischievous smile spread on our lips and we push Ren towards Ace.

"Wolf boy, go escort the LADY."

Ren stumbles forward, looking back at us with a pout.

"Why me?" He whines. In response, Nate and I simply shrugged and left no room for argument for Ren. With a grumble, Ren complies and offers his arm to LADY Grace. The LADY gives Ren a look, briefly flips him off before accepting his arm. Together, they walk to the shore of the beach. Nate and I follow a few steps back.

"I feel like we're on a double date." Nate whispers in my ears.

"Focus, Nate." I remind him. "We are supposed to admire LADY Grace."

Nate draws back and grumbles. "I finally got my *screen time* in this chapter and this is how you treat me?"

Ace finally has enough of the shoes that he finally kicks them off. Ren, being the gentleman he is, bent down and grabbed the shoes for him. I grip my heart, and it keeps pounding in my chest so hard.

Why do I enjoy seeing them like this? They look good together!

I know that they are both straight, but something about the scene is addicting to watch!

The ocean starts to bubble, drawing our attention to it. Large men covered in sea green scale armor suddenly emerged. There were at least five of them in total. Nate subconsciously stood in front of me as a guard, but the men weren't after me. They have their gaze fixed at Ace—I mean—LADY Grace.

"Look what we have here. Another beauty." The man eyes Ace from head to toe with a pleased expression.

Bloody hell. The plan worked.

Now, all we have to do now is pretend to defend LADY Grace. Ren, like the good boy that he was, extends a protective hand over him.

"Go back! You may not touch our LADY." He says.

"Go back to where you belong, fish men!" I added in my failed manly voice and heard Nate snort in response.

The men didn't heed our warning and started to come after LADY Grace. As planned, we pretended to attack the men and lose on purpose. Everything was according to plan until this dumb idiot—not me!—started to beat up the generals when they attempted to grab him. By the time Ace is done, he shakes and dusts his hands together and not even breaking a sweat!

"How dare you peasants touch me with your dirty hands! I am LADY Grace, the most beautiful lady on the land." He flips his wig back gracefully.

I have to say, Ace just beat up those men while wearing a dress. I should really ask him for pointers on that.

"What is with this girl!? She's too strong." One of the men says and cuddles his bruised cheek.

"Maybe we should just give up on her."

Damn it, Ace! Get with the program.

I waved my hand enough for Ace to notice me. When our eyes met, I mouthed, *"For Nora."*

Ace thankfully got my message because he closed his eyes and sighed. Suddenly, he grips his hand and raises it dramatically.

"Ow. My nails broke. Ouch." He says without ZERO emotion and fall on the beach like a falling log. "I am injured, and I can't seem to get up."

Nate, Ren, and I facepalmed at how horrible this guy's acting skills were. It's like he's not even serious!

"I thought she hurt her nails? Why can't she suddenly get up?"

Damn this LADY Grace!

I sneakily crawl until I am behind one of the generals and yell, in an imitation of their voice, "Who cares? She's pretty!"

One of the men thankfully agrees. "Yeah. King Corona will like her. She is even brave enough to go without a *mask*. How *stupid*." At this, I see Ace glaring daggers at him but did nothing. Two men are able to recover and escort LADY Grace up. I watch as they drag LADY Grace to the ocean and waited.

Mission accomplished, I thought as I crawled back to where Nate and Ren were.

But, as we all know, I attract a lot of negative energy in the world. When a large clam emerges from the ocean where they were supposed to put Ace, a huge wave slams into me. My hat is washed away by the strong wave, and my blonde hair unraves in front of my face.

I was drenched!

"Hey! We have another girl here." I look up to see a general looking down on me.

An idea suddenly occurs to me when I remembered that they only take pretty girls. I start to cross my eyes and pull my upper lips back to reveal my gums, hoping to discourage them.

The general suddenly gives me a weird look. "She doesn't fit our standard, but maybe she'll be prince Meruem's type. We should still bring her along."

I turn to look at Nate and Ren and I see them mouthing, "Run."

I nod and grab a handful of sand before throwing it at the man before me, hoping to blind him and perhaps give me enough time to run.

Unfortunately, I miscalculated the wind as it blows the sand back to my face, blinding me in the process.

"I'm down! Princess is down!" I yell as I roll on the ground in pain.

"She's a princess!? Then she would be a perfect bride for Prince Mereum!" The sound of one of the men seem joyful and proud.

I feel them hauling me up to my feet. I can feel the water seeping into my boots as they half drag and half carry me through the ocean. I am able to open my eyes a bit to see that we are headed to the large clam, where Ace is being held captive by another sea general.

I smile sheepishly at him.

He's gonna kill me. I know it for sure.

Ace, who is still trying to kill me with his gaze, is thrown into the giant clam with me. I turn to the two princes on shore for help. They smile and wave at me sadly, knowing fully well that they couldn't do anything about my situation with Ace.

Suddenly, water begins to rise around us, forming a protective bubble when we begin to descend gradually.

I sit on my butt and study the magical wall surrounding us. Curiously, I touch the bubble. My finger went through the magical barrier, and I was touching the water. I drew it back to find my hands wet with seawater.

Ace grumbles beside me. I look at him and see that he is massaging his temples. "Can't you do something right for once?" He snarls at me.

"Hey, if you only followed your own plan, then we wouldn't be in this mess. Who says you can beat them up?"

"It was self-defense, you moron. That is how you should react when someone tries to capture you. I hope you paid attention to that."

"Yeah. The fact that I should scream 'Ow. My nail broke.' and drop on the ground. Please, I can do better than that."

"Yeah. You screamed that you were a princess. How *smart*."

"Look, pal. If it weren't forme, then they wouldn't even bother to capture you after you beat them up." I rub my hands on my shoulders as the temperature kept getting colder. Luckily, LADY Grace didn't say anything anymore.

I kept my gaze at the magical barrier. It was clear enough that I could see the outside. We were traveling under the sea and I wished that there were lights, because as we keep going further and further down, it was getting darker, and I could barely see all the beautiful corals and fish that we passed by. As it kept getting darker, the temperature also dropped. My clothes were soaking wet, and it didn't help my current situation at all.

"Listen." Ace starts to say something, but I wasn't really paying attention to him. I feel like my nose is itching for some reason. "Since this wasn't part of the plan, you have to fend for yourself. My top priority is Nora. You are nothing to me." He keeps blabbering, but I have already cut him off.

I want to sneeze, but the sneeze itself won't come.

My eyes started to water when I tried to focus and force myself to sneeze.wants

"Are you listening to me?"

This time, I look at Ace with tear-filled eyes, since I wasn't able to sneeze. I cover my nose and mouth with my hands and glare at him.

Can't this guy leave me alone? I want to sneeze, but I can't concentrate enough with his constant yapping.

As soon as Ace sees me, his eyes widen in surprise and a look of guilt briefly flashes in his eyes. I quickly look away since he isn't even talking. I might as well concentrate to get this over with.

At the corner of my eyes, I see Ace trying to grab me, but I slap his hand away.

Can he not bother me!?

Great. That sneezing feeling is gone, leaving a very uncomfortable feeling in my nose.

I wipe my eyes clean and sniff. I look back at Ace with a glare. It's his fault that I wasn't able to sneeze.

I expected him to glare at me for not paying attention to what he was saying earlier, but instead he appears surprised and taken aback.

His mouth is moving like a fish out of water. It's like he wanted to say something, but couldn't.

The calm carriage stops moving abruptly, making Ace and I collide. Luckily, Ace is strong enough to steady the both of us. Our gazes meet when I raise my head. His long black hair and piercing blue eyes stare at me, and I have to push him back because I was feeling insecure about his ridiculous feminine beauty.

I readied myself for the argument that was about to come for acting rudely towards him, but it didn't come. It was weird. He was acting weird.

"We're here. Get up, ladies." The bubble was suddenly gone, and one of the men escorted us. I got up and dusted my pants. I hopped off of the giant clam and looked back at LADY Grace, who seemed guilty about something.

"LADY Grace?" I call for him. He seems to snap out of his predicament only to meet my gaze. I couldn't exactly read his expression, but it looks like he is troubled and guilty at the same time. The look quickly vanished the moment he gave me a curt nod and got up himself. He walks past me without even saying a word.

Princess Mississippi Bloom Shakalaka

The Atla kingdom might be my most favorite place in this world. If it weren't for the fact that there's a *virus* named King Corona.

The kingdom itself was underwater—obviously. Ace and I must have bickered longer than we thought, because where we're standing right now is the seafloor. I looked up and saw the same huge magical barrier that separated us from the water. Tall coral reefs lined the place and were constantly being rained down with water. Large domes made out of sand and rocks lined with moss seem to all have a large shell in front of them. We have more than enough light to see our surroundings thanks to the numerous glowing jellyfish that are constantly swimming in the vicinity and enclosed in a bubble.

My ears were ringing at the drop of pressure underwater. I look at Ace, but he doesn't seem bothered at all. The men lead us along a sandy path that has shells as stone pathways. Ace—as LADY Grace—made sure that he stepped on the shells so his heels wouldn't sink as he walked.

We observe a large, multicolored palace surrounded by brilliant rainbow-colored bubbles. The palace is magnificent, and I would have loved it even more if one of the guards hadn't pushed me inside. The interior was beautiful as well. They have white tiles and shiny walls despite being an underwater fortress. The columns were decorated with tons of shells and seaweed. Not just the columns, but the whole area where the wall meets the ceiling. I was walking and looked up when I chanced to run into Ace.

I brace myself in anticipation that he would scold me, but he didn't. He simply gives me a look and returns his gaze forward.

He is acting really strange since we got here.

We soon pause at what I assume is the throne room. At the very top of the staircase is a throne made out of coral. A man with sickly green hair and a bulging stomach sits on it. He is eating some sort of fish while looking at us. Bits and pieces of the meat are stuck on his beard. He is wearing nothing at the top, but his white trousers look like they are ready to give up. Beside him is a man, seemingly as old as Ren and Dan, with long, light blue hair and cerulean eyes. This man is also shirtless and wearing the same white ripped trousers, but unlike that bulky man on the throne, he looks better in them.

"King Corona, Prince Mereum, we brought two new female prisoners." One of the men says.

The king stops eating as he regards Ace and I with his eyes. I suddenly found myself hiding behind Ace because his stare is getting uncomfortable.

"Beautiful!" The king bellows. "What is your name, young elf lady?"

Ace steps forward and gives me slightly more cover from the king. "My name is LADY Grace. I am a noble elf from the kingdom of Tordis."

"Brave young lady!" The king grins hungrily at Ace and I wanna laugh as I imagine what the king's facial reaction would be when he learns that the LADY is actually a PRINCE.

As if sensing my presence, the king turns his gaze at me. "And who are you?" He asks.

"I—um.." I actually haven't thought of a name, and I was stuttering in response.

Ah, crap. There's no way that I can tell them my name. For all we know, they might know of Rosalie Amber Stan. I don't need another kingdom to add me to their wanted list because I'm already on Tereau's.

"We heard that she is a princess, your grace." One of the men says, and I had to fight the urge to karate chop his head.

Dude, the king asked me, not you! I want to scream at him.

"A princess!?" The king looks at me. "She doesn't look like a princess."

"And you look like a virus, but you do not see me complaining." Unconsciously, I utter, and then quickly bite my tongue. I swear there are times when I despise myself for having a violent side. I really need to quit hanging out with PRINCE Ace.

Prince Meruem hides his laugh in his fist while the king seems like he would like to murder me. Well, he is not the first royal to give me that look, to be honest.

"What did you say? A virus!?" The king demands. "If you're that brave then maybe—"

"Father, you can't." Prince Meruem cuts off his father before we can even hear what he was about to say. "I'll take her." He says with a tired sigh.

"You will?" The king raises an eyebrow at him and returns his gaze to me, then back at his son. He looks like he is judging the taste of his son in women. I purse my lips so I wouldn't say anything more that would get me into more trouble. "Well, this is the first time that you have shown interest in picking a bride. Even though she is rude, she is a princess." Then, as if it reminds him of that fact, he returns his gaze towards me. "What kingdom are you from?"

Of course. Here comes the million dollar question!

"Unicorns." I say this in a deadpan tone. "But I can't show you my horn because I am away from the magical tree that gives me my power to morph. My mother, Queen Dis-is-a-lie Shakalaka, from the kingdom of Yadayadaboom must be worried because their lovely daughter, Princess Mississipi Bloom Shakalaka, is missing." It's amazing how much bullshit my mouth can produce. I am impressed with myself.

"Princess Mississipi Bloom Shakalaka from the Kingdom of Yadayadaboom full of unicorns? I have never heard of such a kingdom." The king is obviously doubting me. Even Ace, who obviously knows that I am lying, grimaces at me. I can't tell if he is impressed with me or annoyed to the point that he wants to hit me. I am guessing the latter.

If I am going to lie, I might as well go all out.

I take a deep breath and force tears to form in my eyes. *Think of dead puppies, Rose!*

I clasp my hands together as if I am praying. "Our land is precious and we do not let the others know of our mythical place! Only those who are wise and worthy shall receive the blessing of our holy goddess *Dairycream*." For dramatic effect, I sniffed and pretended to wipe away nonexistent tears. "Alas, I, Princess Mississipi Bloom Shakalaka, ran away because I was curious about the outside world. Our world is locked in a magical tree with no news of the other kingdoms. I dressed up as a man and became her escort." I gesture at LADY Grace, who is now giving me a warning look when he realizes that I am going to give him a background as well. "LADY Grace, the most beautiful girl on the land, gave me a home when she realised that I had nowhere to go. Before I met her, I suffered from hunger, loneliness, and depression. I experience the hardships of this world, but also the beauty that it offers. I cannot recall where the kingdom of shakalaka is but someday I hope to come home and be reunited with my family! It is thanks to the good—" I choke in disgust at my description of him. "—and kind-hearted LADY Grace that I survived this long."

As soon as I was done, the king and a few men were crying.

I guess watching all those cartoons when I was a child broadened my imagination. I knew it had its perks!

"Isn't it the Kingdom of Yadayadaboom? Why did you say Shakalaka?" One of the men points out my error in the story.

I flinch and give him a pointed look before I pretend to cry in despair. "I have been away for *three years* that my memory of my family and kingdom is fading."

"Oh, your majesty! We must help Princess Mississipi." One of the guards cried.

"Indeed! Such a pitiful tale of truth and bravery. This young princess has been through a lot!" King Corona sniffs, making me look away to hide my laugh. "She would be a perfect bride for my son." He suddenly added

Excuse me. **What?**

I stared at them in alarm, and I knew that I must have screwed up again.

"Princess Mississipi Bloom Shakalaka, as soon as we are wed, I promise to help you find your family." Prince Meruem says. My lips start to tremble really badly because I really want to roll on the floor and laugh, but at the same time I want to yell my opposition to this marriage arrangement.

"T-Thank you." I forced out the words while silently cursing myself and my stupidity for getting myself into this mess.

"These two we shall keep. Hide them in the royal quarters, where they will temporarily stay along with the others. We still need time to process their tokens."

Tokens?

I look at Ace to see if he knows what it is. He meets my gaze and shakes his head. The men start to lead us in another room with two large shells used as a door. As soon as they open it, we saw Nora, who is crouching and shaking in a corner. I grab Ace's hand as soon as I notice him starting to run towards his sister, because the guards are still with us.

"There are enough beds in the room. Tomorrow, once we give you a token of ownership, you will be transferred to your designated chambers. Please knock on the shell three times if you ever need anything." And with that, the men close the shell doors and disappear behind it.

I finally released Ace's hand and let him run towards Nora. I follow him slowly.

"Nora!" He yells and runs to his sister. Nora, who is crouching on the floor and hugging her legs, turns to look at us. She scream when she sees Ace and run towards me instead.

"Wose!" She cries. The poor little elf girl seem scared out of her mind as she desperately raises her hands for me to carry her.

I'm not sure who I feel sorry for more: Ace, who was rejected by his beloved sister, or Nora, who is terrified of her crossdressing siscon of a brother.

Ace, still dressed as LADY Grace, approaches us. Nora sees him and quickly buries her face to my chest. Poor guy.

I lean in and whisper to her. "Nora, the lady right there is your brother."

Nora cautiously raises her head to gaze at her brother, who is clearly upset. After closely examining his face for some time, Nora was able to identify her brother and squeals with joy. Because of how much she is wriggling, I had to give her to Ace, who is more than glad to take his sister away from me. I watched as the two siblings hugged for a while before I cleared my throat.

"You should probably start briefing her with the plan, don't you think?" I tell him.

Ace grunts but complies. I watch as he tells Nora about our plan. Ace is just at the middle of his explanation when the door suddenly opened, and in came Prince Meruem. He carefully closes the door behind him before facing Ace and I.

"Pwince!" Ace and I both look at Nora, who has just called out the crown prince.

Prince Meruem smiles and places a finger to his lips as if to shush her. "You guys seem to be close to each other." As soon as he says that I yelp in surprise when Ace pulls me to his side. He gives the prince a warning look. The sea prince must have sensed Ace's hostility because he raised his hands in surrender. "Lady, I—"

"He's my bwother!" Nora declares, addressing the sea prince.

A few seconds of silence linger between the group while Meruem tries to process Nora's words.

"You're a…guy!?" The look in Prince Meruem's eyes makes me wish that I had a camera so I could take a picture of how hilarious it looks. How I wish that the other guys could see this.

Ace gives Nora one final glance before turning his attention back to Prince Meruem. He lifts the wig with his free hand to reveal his natural hair, and he then gently raises his cloak to reveal his muscles. When Prince Meruem appears to be close to pass out, I suppress my laughter into coughs.

"I—" He pauses. "Well at least, it makes it easier." He mumbles and came closer to our small group. "I want the three of you to escape, and I will help you."

Ace and I exchange glances. We are wondering about the same thing.

"Why?" I ask.

Upon hearing my voice, Prince Meruem gives me a sad look. "Princess Mississipi, I know that we promised to search for your family when we are married, but I believe that you guys cannot stay here. The kingdom is already ruined the moment my father succumbs to his greed."

If this guy genuinely wants to help us, then I would really start to feel guilty for tricking him with my unicorn story.

"What kind of shady activity? We heard about it from your brother, but he couldn't give us a clear explanation about it."

"My brother? You've met my brother?!" The prince gasp and grasp my shoulders when I mention his brother. "How is he?"

"He's fine!" Ace pushes the prince away from us.

"I-I'm sorry." The prince stutters. "It's just that I haven't seen him in a long time and I am worried about him. As for your question, it is better if you do not know the answer to that. What's more important is that you three need to leave as soon as possible. "

"We already have a plan. All you need to do is shut up." Ace glares at him.

Prince Meruem blinks at Ace's rudeness. "If I may ask, are you her brother Ace—"

"PRINCE." Ace corrects him.

"Yeah, it really is you. I heard about your sharp tongue."

"If you know, then you should start talking."

"Maybe if it is you, then I can consider it." Prince Meruem gives him a resigned nod. "It was a few months ago that my father struck a deal with the kingdom of Tereau. It seems that he is seeking Princess Rose. You know of her, right? The last Tamer."

"I heard that she is very pretty." I insert and got a glare from Ace at my command. "What?" I shrug. Can't a girl have a little bit of fun or start positiverumorss about herself?

"I am sure you are far prettier than she, Princess Mississipi." Prince Meruem says.

I chuckle and point silently at the gullible prince while looking at the Feradin siblings. Ace groans and shakes his head; even Nora gives me a deadpan look. Clearly, I am the only one who is amused by my antics.

"King Ferius offered a high price for her and made a deal with my father. Since my father is already a greedy man, especially when it comes to women, he doubled the order of capturing women. We do not know what Princess Rose looks like, so he simply captured any pretty woman that he sees."

At this, I boastfully glance at Ace. "Hear *that?*" I murmur and point at myself. "They look for *pretty girls* because of *me.*"

Ace and Nora rub their temples and shake their heads.

"Say it again. *Slowly.*" Ace whispers back. "You're the **reason** women are being kidnapped!" He hisses.

I start to sulk at his words.

At least I'm pretty!

"Every night, my father would hand over some of the women that were captured. A general from the kingdom of Tereau would arrive at dinner time and escort them. We do not know what happens to them afterward. But I try to save as many of them as I can." No wonder Prince Meruem looks as tired as he is now. He has to deal with this situation for who knows how long.

"Don't they wonder why the woman went missing?"

"We have a sea witch who's helping us cast an illusion. Some of my father's concubines are still here. I am just looking for the right time to let them escape." He sighs and fishes something out of his pocket. It was a key made out of shells that he hands to me. "This is a disposable key for that door over there. Use this and then break it into pieces when you escape. Once dinner is served, wait for 4 hours before leaving. I will make sure that the guards are distracted. Head east and you will find a darkened path. Look for the blue jellyfish and it will guide you to the nearest port. You have to leave quickly before the others come. Otherwise, it will be difficult." He then hands me a small glass marble. "When you get to the port, be sure to be close to each other when you break it. It has a bit of my magic that will take you to shore. Princess Mississipi, I really wish that I could help you more with your family, but at the moment, all I can do is help you escape. I do hope that one day you will be reunited with your family."

Ah, damn. This Prince Meruem really is a nice guy. Now I seriously feel bad for tricking him with my story.

"Yeah...thanks." is all that I can say.

He bows at us one last time before going out of the door.

"Should we follow his plan?" I turn to Ace since he has better judgment than me.

"I am not so sure." Ace places a hand on his chin like he is deciding whether or not to trust the sea prince.

"Yes, yes!" Nora says gleefully. "His Aura is pink. I think he wikes Wose. We can twist him!"

"No, Nora. He doesn't like me." I shake my head at the little elf girl's words. "He likes *Princess Mississipi Bloom Shakalaka.*"

Calling of the Tamer

Dinner came. Ace, Nora, and I waited patiently for four hours. When the moment of truth came, I used the key to unlock the door. I looked outside to make sure that the coast was clear. When I was certain, I looked back at the Feradin siblings to confirm before breaking the key.

"I can't believe that you trust me with this mission." I tell Ace.

"You are an expert at escaping rooms. Who else is more fitting for the job?" He answers.

"Wow. Thank you so much for that." I place a hand on my chest, feeling proud.

"That was not a compliment." He snaps at me, ruining my moment of bliss.

I let Ace lead the way this time, as he has a more solid sense of direction compared to me. We headed to what I assume is the way to the East. I followed him silently, and I have to say, I was really impressed that Ace moved so quickly despite wearing heels. He was still dressed as LADY Grace.

We were able to slip through the East gate and found the glowing blue jellyfish like the sea prince instructed us. As if the jellyfish sensed us, it started to move.

"Well, that was easy." Like I said before, I attracted a lot of bad juju, which by saying those words, I just jinxed our luck.

A man unexpectedly arrives in front of us while we are sprinting. A guy with grayish hair gives us a smirking glance. His pupils are blood red, and I could see that the whites of his eyes are black.

"Well, well, look at what we have here." We pause and slowly back away when the man carefully stalks us. "Three pretty girls. Two of them ripe for the picking." He lick his lips greedily.

"You're an undead vampire, aren't you?"

"And you're a pretty little elf." The rogue comments before turning his gaze at me. "And you are?"

"A magical unicorn. Princess Mississippi Bloom Shakalaka." The man blinks at my statement as if he is debating whether to believe me or not because of my serious facial expression. "And who are you?"

"My name is Roy Flarick. A general from the kingdom of Tereau." He grins. "I wonder why the king offers us goods of low quality. Now I know. The greedy sea pig hides the best of the women." He chuckles and glances at me. "I have never heard of you, princess Mississippi. Perhaps you want to come with me?"

The fact that Princess Mississipi is popular compared to Rose is kind of bothering me, to be honest. I guess a magical unicorn princess is more valuable than a tamer princess.

"No thanks."

Ace moves and cover me from the vampire's gaze. "This is bad. He's a general." He curse.

Roy looks at Ace and Nora. "How about I offer you a deal?" He tells them. "Leave Princess Mississippi and I will allow you two to leave. You two seem like siblings, so that woman right there must mean nothing to you, right?"

Ace gives me a glance before returning his gaze back at Roy. He hands me Nora, whom I take silently. "Get yourself and Nora to safety." I watch as Ace march towards Roy and punches him hard enough that the vampire falls on the ground. Roy snarls and glares at Ace.

"Woman, how dare you!"

"Dang this stupid wig is getting in my eyes!" Ace screams and throws his cloak and wig aside with a sweep of his fingers, exposing his bulky man muscles . He tears off the dress' constricting sleeves and even went so far as to rip off...no, he just tear off the entire outfit. Now, the elf PRINCE is standing there shirtless and wearing his black trousers that he wore yesterday.

Wait, he was wearing trousers under the dress this whole time!? That's cheating!

Tied to his trousers are a couple of small daggers as well. I have to admit that I am impressed by how he is able to hide them all. Kudos to the elf PRINCE.

Roy's mouth is gaping like a fish, as if he couldn't believe his eyes. That or his brain simply stopped working the moment he saw the beautiful woman turning into another beautiful man.

Ace looks annoyed by the pathetic look on the vampire's face and gritted his teeth. "What? Haven't you seen a man wearing a dress before!?"

At that, Nora claps her hands in delight. "Bwother Aish is so cool."

"Nora, not now." I whisper to her.

"As a mater of fact, I have no." Roy replies to his question with a slow shake of is head. "You are one sick man."

"I do not want to hear that from someone who serves a mad king!" Roy attacked him for speaking out. He tried to claw Ace with his elongated claws that looked like daggers. Ace struck another dagger to Roy's cheek after deflecting one of his nails with one of his blades. Roy fell to the floor, having a big cut on his cheek, which was now healing. The fact that there was no blood gushing from the wound anywhere made me grimace.

"No one insults King Ferius without having his head roll."

"I just did. And as you can see. I am still standing."

"Let's see how long an elf can keep up with my speed." Roy smirks and attacks again. This time he feigns an attack and manages to stab Ace's chest. Luckily, Ace jumps back before Roy's hand goes anywhere deep. Ace grits his teeth, his chest bleeding from the pricks.

"What are you still standing around there for?" Ace gives me a side glance. "MOVE!"

"Aish…" I had to bribe the tiny elf girl to look aside because Nora seemed concerned. I made the decision to follow Ace's instructions since I didn't want to be in his way. Nora and I decided to sprint in the last direction we spotted the blue jellyfish. "Bwother, can't use his powers. *Doesn't work.*" Nora mumbles.

"What do you mean?" I ask Nora as soon as we arrive at the empty port.

"His powers work on earth and not water." She explains. I am just about to break the marble that Prince Meruem gave me when I pause. I know that he is a great fighter and he can easily take on any rogue, but isn't Roy a general? And an undead vampire general at that.

Can Ace really win?

Then I remembered how Roy was able to puncture his chest and my feet grew cold. We still have a few hours before Nate and the others will come to pick us up.

I set Nora on the ground. "Nora, you have to go without me. Nate and Ren will be at the shore. Tell them to come here immediately."

"What about you?"

"I-I don't want to leave your brother. I am currently powerless, but I will find a way to help him survive until the others arrive." I actually have a plan in mind. I just hope that I can make it work.

I give Nora the marble that Prince Meruem gave me and step away. Nora looks like she is ready to cry, but broke the marble anyway. A bubble starts to form around her and carry her off and out of the magical barrier of Atla. As soon as I was certain that the bubble protected her from the water and that it could carry her off to the shore safely, I ran back.

I saw that Ace and Roy were still fighting when I returned.

Ace was able to damage Roy's jaw as it was now hanging on loose veins. The sight of it makes me want to puke. I notice how Ace was only using one hand and realized that his left hand is dislocated. It would seem like Roy want to say something, but his jaw is still healing. I have to look away when I see his nerves wrapping and merging - trying to fix and connect the jaw back to his face.

I learned that in order to kill an undead vampire, we either burn them, cut their heads, or stab their chest with a stake made of oak wood. At this point, the only thing we can do is for Ace to cut Roy's head off. But looking at Roy's jaw, I assume he tried and failed.

Roy lunged at Ace, and though Ace blocked the fatal blow to his neck, he was thrown back by a kick from Roy's foot. To retrieve one of his dropped daggers, Ace spins around and kicks it upward. As he leaps for the vampire, he grabs it in his mouth and kicks the ground. Instantly, upon locking eyes with Roy, Ace hurls the knife at the vampire's eyes. Roy cries out in agony. Ace takes the second knife and stabs Roy in the neck. A terrible crunch can be heard as he hammers the knife into bone before Roy's head hits the floor with a resounding thump.

Finally, it is over.

I run after the fallen Prince. "Ace!"

Ace looked at me weakly and frowns. "Nora." He says and I know what he is asking me.

"She's safe. I sent her out first to get Nate and the others." I crouch and grab the cloak that he wore earlier. I tore it into strips using one of his daggers to bind it to his body until we could fix his arm while using the remainder to stop the bleeding from the other wounds.

"Seems like you…have some use after all." He pants. The side of his lip is turning blue from the bruise.

"Yeah, yeah." I wave his semi insult away and help the royal prince up to his feet. I look at Roy's body and towards the decapitated head on the ground, I grimace. "And here I thought you needed help."

"It wasn't easy. I admit." He cough. "That stubborn bastard scratched me a bit."

I give the elf PRINCE a look. "A *bit* you say?"

"You want to argue with me?" He asks with a raise brow.

"No way! Prince Ace is always right, after all." I say sarcastically with a roll of my eyes. It is a relief to hear that Ace is still his usual self, which means that he would be alright.

"There they are!" Ace and I suddenly turned and see King Virus - I mean - Corona glaring at us. There are a group of rogues and seamen gathering around us in every direction. Ace moves away from me and grabs his fallen dagger on the ground.

"I guess, there's no time to rest until the fang and mutt will arrive."

"Ace-"

"PRINCE!" He corrects me.

"You can't fight them all in your current state," I am almost screaming in his ears because he can barely stand on his own.

"Then who will fight? You?!" He demands. "You stay here and sit!" He pushes me to the ground and starts to take off after our pursuers.

I sit there and watch as Ace fights them. I close my eyes and refuse to watch the exchange. I did say I have a plan to help him, but at the moment I am not sure if I can do it. But if I do succeed, wouldn't it be risky if they find out about me?

I shake my head from the thought and just try to focus on my link with Custard. It isn't easy because of the distance, but I an able to connect to Custard and see through his eyes. From Custard's vision, I see Ren running towards the water to assist Nora, who just emerged from the sea. Nate runs after Ren and wraps a blanket around the little girl. Nora is crying while asking them to go down and help us. Prince Zeraph looks frightened but agrees to help them.

It's too long. They are taking too long. By the time they arrive, it will be too late.

I have to at least try to do something here.

"Kill them! Kill them all." King Corona bellows.

Try to summon Custard. I tell myself.

'Master?' I feel Custard responding through our link.

'Custard, I need you here right now.'

'Master, are you safe?'

'Come here.' I order and temporarily felt drained of energy. No not energy - magic, but then it is gone. I try again and this time, with a very firm thought. I uses every ounce of energy that I can muster. But when I look up and see Ace falling to the ground, I panic and run. I pick up a fallen naginata and plunge it into the shoulder of his attacker. I try to drag Ace into safety but he is too heavy for me to lift.

A beast-man walks up to me and transforms into a bear. It raises it's gigantic paw as it readies itself to attack. Ace tries to push me away, but I stayed put.

There's no way that I am letting this elf prince die today saving me because I know that he will never let me stop hearing about it in the after life.

"***Custard, COME!***"

The air rushes around us, and the fighting stops. When the wind shifts, everyone's attention was drawn to the enormous white wolf that has emerge in the middle of the fight. I am exhausted to the point of fainting. What Ace said to me about calling upon my familiar appears to be true. Custard, who was converted into a massive white wolf, swats the bear out of the path with an enormous claw. Several men were also knock to the ground by the force of the impact. Custard recoils and covers us with his huge body while he deflects numerous incoming arrows and weapons heaing in our direction.

"*She's the Tamer! S-She's the one that King Ferius wants!*"

"*Get her!*"

Custard gives me a glance, as if asking for what's next. I feel ready to puke at the amount of magic that I am using, but I hold my ground, refusing to faint at this very crucial moment.

"Go for it. Knock them all out."

Custard chases after our attackers and strikes everyone who threatens us. He goes on a rampage and knocks back every single person that he lays his eyes upon.

I stumble back and Ace catches me with his good hand. "You're using too much magic all at once."

"If I stop, I am afraid he might morph back."

"Where are those idiots anyway?" He grumbles.

"They…just found Nora. They might probably be still on their way." I tell him what I saw through Custard's eyes earlier.

My eyes widen when water forms around me and I am whisked away from Ace's arms. Before I knew it, I was in the hands of King Corona.

"Either you stop your spirit or I will kill you and cut your eyes out!" He threatens me with a knife aim at one of my eyes.

I glare at the king and laugh. "I have heard a lot of threats from one single person. Yours can't even compare to his threats that I receive on a daily basis." To which, I am PRINCE Ace, of course.

The King sneers. He grabs my neck and starts to squeeze it tightly.

"Father!" It is Prince Meruem. He is panting as if he was running before he came here. He gives his father a pleading look and carefully approaches him. "Let her go. Please. You are siding with the wrong people."

"Shut up! You are becoming weak, Meruem! How can you rule when you don't have the guts!?" He points his dagger at his own son. When Prince Meruem approaches him - still pleading, King Corona finally lost his mind and stabs his own son. Prince Meruem collapsed to the floor, clutching his stomach wound and staring up at his father with pain not just from the injury but from the betrayal he had just experienced.

"I don't need you. I still have another son!" He laughs. His eyes seem like he lost whatever sanity he has left. "Once I deliver this tamer to King Ferius, a new era will rise! I, King Corona, will be known for making it happen!" He let out a maniacal laugh.

"You…you will not lay your hands on Zeraph!" Meruem cries, finally looking angry at his father.

King Corona laughs even louder at his son, who is trying his best to breathe. "What are you going to do? You are no-" There was a sickening jab and I looked at King Corona to see Ace's dagger poking from his head. The king's grip on my neck loosens as he fell to the ground motionlessly.

"You sick fucking King!" Ace staggers until he stands before King Corona's lifeless body and pulls out his dagger.

"Rose! Ace!" I hear Nate and Ren calling for us in the background. I can feel Custard devouring the essence of our enemies. There was so much going right now, but I could only stare at what was in front of me.

King Corona. Dead.

PRINCE Ace had killed him. He killed *Corona*.

Aftermath

"The King is dead!" Someone yells.

It appeared that the fighting had ceased or was at least winding down. Most of the men around us appear to be unconscious. Some of them have dried up and are shaking because Custard ate what looked like smoke. I noticed that the more he ate, the more alert I became. It feels like the essence of them is restoring my depleted magic.

As I continue to wonder, I am suddenly engulfed in an embrace.

"You're okay!" Ren cries. "I was so worried when Nora told us that you were facing a dangerous man and that Ace was hurt." As soon as the words left his mouth, he pauses from hugging me. "Wait, where is Ace?"

"It's PRINCE!" Ace grunts, still kicking the body of the dead king. With his good hand, he points the dagger at Ren. "You better keep that in mind if you want to live."

Ren gulps and nods. Nate comes next and he stands beside Ace. He grimaces at the elf prince's current state. "You look rather…well…?" He says uncertainly. It's like he can't make up his mind on whether to compliment him or tell him the truth.

"And you are LATE!" Ace snaps. "Where's my sister!?"

Nate raises his hands as if in surrender. "She's safe. She's with Prince Zeraph."

Ace's eye twitches. "She's what?!" He yells. Then, with his good arm, he grabs Nate's collar. "You let her hang out with a **boy**?!"

"It's fine. They actually get along pretty great. Prince Zeraph can protect her." Ren says and I feel like I want to punch him for being so dense at times and saying the wrong words. It's like he can't read the atmosphere!

"What did you say?" There's venom in Ace's voice when he looks towards us.

I pray for Ren's soul. Whatever deity they have here, I hope that they would protect my poor idiotic werewolf friend.

"Brother!" It's Prince Zeraph. He is running towards his older brother with Nora following right behind him. The young prince crouches down beside his wounded older brother.

"Zeraph?" Prince Meruem croaks and smiles weakly. "You're well. I'm glad."

Prince Zeraph is crying as he holds his hands to his brother's wound. "I'll...heal you brother. Just you wait." Zeraph gathers water around himself and pours it on his brother's gaping wound. It gives off a bright light, and where the injury was is now marked by a scar that their father gave Meruem.

"Prince Meruem, Prince Zeraph." It's the same man who announces the demise of the king. As soon as Prince Meruem is on his feet, the rest of the conscious soldiers of the Atla kingdom bent down on one knee.

"My father is dead." Prince Meruem confirms. "I, as the crown prince, will serve as the king in acting until I am rightfully crowned."

"King Meruem!" The soldiers all cheer in unison.

Prince Meruem looks at his dead father with understanding. There is a brief look of sadness in his eyes before he looks up at the soldiers. "Arrest the remaining rogues. Bring the injured to the sea witch to get healed and...-" He looks down at the corpse of his father. "Carry my dead father back to the palace. And from now on, we will no longer associate ourselves with the kingdom of Tereau."

Prince Zeraph comes to Ace after that. "Prince, may I heal your wound? I have enough power with me to do that, but I cannot heal your shoulder. I am not that strong yet." The young prince offers.

"I can help with that." Nate grinned and, without Ace's permission, grabs his shoulder and snapped it back into place. There was a sickening crunch as Nate lodged the bone back into its rightful place.

I can't help but wince, not only because of the injury inflicted but out of fear of what's to come to Nate after what he did.

Bless him and his poor ignorant soul.

Ace glares at Nate and uses both hands to grab his collar. "Thank you. Now I can strangle you freely with two hands." Nate could only smile fearfully at him while waiting for his demise.

"Excuse me." Ace quickly drops Nate to the ground when Prince Meruem comes to speak to us. "I cannot thank you enough for freeing us from the reign of my father."

"He killed your dad. The rest of us has nothing to do with it." I point at Ace authomatically. I mean, someone has to take the blame. As far as I know, killing someone with noble or royal blood is a grave offence.

Ace frowns and slaps my hand away.

"And I should have been the one to do it, since it is my responsibility. He also took care of Roy, a difficult man to deal with." Then, the Prince's eyes meets mine. "I guess I should call you Princess Rose and not Mississippi? I mean, that is your spirit, right?" He says, pointing at something behind Ren and I.

We both look back only to see a grown up Custard looking happy. His tail is wagging enthusiastically, and his tongue is hanging out like he's waiting for a pat on the head. Both Ren and I yell out in shock and take a few steps backward.

Ren quickly fixes his posture and points at me with his thumb. "It was her. She screamed." I slap his hand away and lightly elbow his ribs before looking at my spirit animal.

"Custard! Don't scare us like that." At my words, Custard whimpers.

'*Sorry, Master.*' His ears quickly drops.

I kind of felt bad, so I patted his head. "You did a great job. Thank you." At that, Custard licks and nuzzles me with his snout affectionately.

"I want to formally introduce myself again. I am the acting king - Prince Meruem Bastian. This is my brother, Prince Zeraph Bastian." The first prince of the Atla kingdom introduces himself to us.

"Prince Nathaniel Denver from the kingdom of Vertez."

"Prince Renvier Rutledge from the kingdom of Sanver."

"PRINCE Ace Feradin from the kingdom of Tordis." Ace carries Nora in his arms. "This is my sister, PRINCESS Nora Feradin." Then he fixes fix gaze at Prince Zeraph, who is looking at Nora. "She's off limits!" He glowers at the young sea prince in warning.

"I'm Princess Rosalie Amber Stan." I say and gesture at my wolf. "And this is my familiar. Custard."

Prince Meruem nods as he regards Ace and I, who look ready to collapse any minute now. "May I offer you refuge in our palace? I promise that you may leave when you want to. I will ask them to prepare rooms." His eyes dart at Ace's wounds. "We have healers in the palace as well. That or my brother can heal you."

Ace gives the young prince a pointed look. "He may heal me, but it doesn't mean that he can go anywhere near my sister." Ace hands Nora to Nate. "You better not drop her or else." He threatens and returned his gaze back to Zeraph. "Hurry up and heal me!"

Jeez. He can't even say please! And he has the nerve to call me embarrassing sometimes.

As I watched the hapless prince approach the menopausal elf, I couldn't help but feel sorry for him. To divert the prince's attention away from Nora, Ace snapped his fingers in front of him. "Hey! Eyes right here."

I felt Custard returning to his former self. Once he did, my knees felt like jelly and I collapse. Ren catches me as my vision starts to blur.

I could hear their voices - calling me as they did so. But it was no use. I felt so tired and drained that my body couldn't move even if I willed it to.

Not long after, I was finally swallowed in darkness.

***

I dreamed of a man. No. A king.

King Varon Lanis. I am not sure how I know. Maybe it was because we share the same color of our hair – or the fact that he is with a grown white spirit wolf – Nagga.

I saw the pair walking into a strange dark forest with only a bit of glittering light to guide them. King Varon was holding a cup in his hands. The wooden chalice.

There was movement in the forest. A tree nymph suddenly emerged.

"Keep it safe." King Varon said. "It can potentially become a tool for the revival or the destruction of the kingdom." King Varon was speaking to it before handing the cup to the Nymph. The nymph bowed and suddenly vanished into the forest.

King Varon looked at his familiar. "Let's go, Nagga."

***

The dream shifted, and suddenly I saw dead bodies everywhere. Broken buildings and debris were all over the place. Fires continued to burn as they scorched up the rest of the colors of the land.

I saw how King Varon lunged at a man with dark shaggy hair, whom I assume is king Ferius. I saw Nagga in the background pinning the Chimera underneath him. The tamer king gave his familiar a glance; a look of sadness flashed in them. The familiar looked at his partner too, with the same gaze, and whimpered. They knew what had to be done. King Varon will die into sealing his own familiar and the chimera and Ferius.

People screamed in the background as the fighting continued. But all was drowned out when the king spoke to his familiar.

"...no other way." These were the last words that I heard from King Varon before the scene shifted.

***

This time I was watching the Nymph with the Chalice. She was walking down a dark path that suddenly blinded me. Then I saw her giving the chalice to a group of people. They looked like villagers, judging from the way that they were dressed. They were wearing animal skins to cover their bodies.

I watched as they took the chalice from the Nymph and bowed respectfully.

***

Another scene shift.

This time I saw the nymphs gathering around what looked like a birdbath made out of gigantic leaves and vines. They were chanting something in a language that I do not understand. Images of the other kingdoms suddenly flash in my mind. The images of the villagers seem to be being erased from existence.

Suddenly, a nymph locked its gaze into mine while I was watching everything on the sidelines. It was the same nymph that originally held the chalice. The nymph that my ancestor trusts.

"It's your turn to find us, little tamer."

New King of Atla

The next thing I know, I'm lying on a plush bed. Upon taking a good look around, I confirmed in my mind that we were still in Atla; if other kingdoms existed, of course, where shells and seaweed were also utilized as decorative elements. I attempted to rise to my feet, but my limbs simply would not cooperate.

"What the-"

"Had enough rest?"

I turn my head to see PRINCE Ace, who is bound and gagged to a bed like a madman. His injuries have healed and he is now clothed, but the bruises are still visible. As soon as I laid eyes on him, I burst into giggles.

"What the heck happened to you!?" I cannot contain my laughter.

He looks at me with narrowed eyes. "Those worthless princes told me to stay put because I was injured!" He yells and starts struggling to free himself, but to no avail. "Stop laughing! I am merely tied so I cannot move. You, on the other hand, are free but couldn't even lift the finger!"

I stop laughing and urge myself to move in order to prove him wrong. I succeeded but I can only move my arms. I looked back at Ace smugly. "You were saying?"

"Great. If you can move then you better untie me!"

"Aww. But I don't wanna." I say with a lazy groan. "What's in it for me if I untie you?"

"The fact that the two idiots are having a discussion with the son of the dead king."

I give Ace a pointed look. "So? They are simply having a meeting. It's boring to listen to them anyway. Let's just wait and-"

"MY SISTER IS WITH THAT BRAT!" He screams.

Ahh. So that is the real reason. This siscon merely wants to play *keep-away* with his sister. He doesn't like it when children of the opposite sex interact with Nora.

"As you can see, I can only move my arms and not my whole body," I pointed out.

PRINCE Ace rolls his eyes and clicks his tongue. "That's what you get if you abuse magic more than you can handle. You're lucky it didn't kill you."

"It could have killed me!?" My eyes are wide with surprise.

"It would have if your familiar didn't absorb some of the magic from the rogues." He explains. "Now go and wake up your lazy familiar and tell it to untie me!"

"Custard? Where is he?" I actually know where Custard is because of our link. He is sleeping beside me on the bed. I simply want to annoy a certain PRINCE.

"Beside you!"

"Which side?"

"I can snap your head to see him if I could."

"Geez. Just say the magic word."

"The magic word."

I turn to Ace with a suspicious glare. "I know that you know what the magic word is. I'm on to you, *PRINCE*."

Ace pays me no attention and turns his head to the other side.

The door suddenly swings open and Nate, Ren, and Prince Meruem appear. Nate and Ren saw me and immediately grinned. Ren attempted to tackle me in a hug, but Nate grabbed him by his collar.

"She's hurt, mutt."

"Right. I'm sure that's the only reason you're stopping me."

"Good. You both are awake." Prince Meruem says, earning a murderous glare from PRINCE Ace.

"I was already awake when you tied me up! You bastards are lucky that I am not at my full strength." Ace shouts.

"I feel like I am not welcome here." Uncomfortable laughter escaped the mouth of the Sea Prince. "I should get going and have everything ready for you guys."

"Get back here, you son of a virus!" Ace continuous to scream, but the sea prince is now gone behind the doors. Ace diverts his attention to the two other princes in the room. "Well!? You guys had fun. Might as well share what you've discussed!"

Ren and Nate recoil in fear from the elf prince, who can't seem to communicate in any way other than by shouting. "Right. It will we a long talk so get yourselves com-"

Nate was cut off by Ace. "You better not say comfortable!"

"...right. Sorry." Nate mumbled.

Nate and Ren started to tell us what happened after I passed out from the battle field. According to them, the rogues went into an underwater cellar; at least the rogues who still have their essences. Apparently, Custard had taken more than half of the rogue's essence, making them harmless even when they are together. There were a few men from the kingdom of Atla who lost their essence as well, but these were the men who were loyal to the late king and attempted to murder us.

It has been decided that Ace will be forgiven for killing the king because he acted in self-defense to protect Prince Meruem and myself. In addition, the kingdom of Atla has agreed to sever ties with Tereau and to begin trading with the other kingdoms at some unspecified future date. Right now, they want to properly rebuild their place until they are strong enough to open their gates to others.

The women have been safely escorted to their respective families. Prince Meruem also said he would free all the women his father had taken and make sure they got back to their families safely.

I was quite content with the meal that had been prepared for me. Even Custard seems to be enjoying the food. Ace was eating while muttering insults about how the locals are so ungrateful that they even tied him up after saving them. My best guess is that he's already plotting how to eliminate the rest of the royal family.

We were packed and ready to go by lunchtime. Prince Meruem, the unofficial king, and his younger brother, Prince Zeraph, accompanied us to the harbor. Because I still couldn't move, Ren carried me on his back. Nate held Custard as he shook hands with Prince Meruem.

"I look forward to our next meeting," Nate says.

Prince Meruem nods and hands him a conch. "We may contact one another here. Let us know if you ever need help. If it is within our power, then we will come to your aid." Then Prince Meruem moves his gaze towards me. I felt Ren let out a low growl as he starts to approach us.

"Princess Rose, I wish you the best." He says.

"You too!"

"I said she's off-limits!" Our eyes turn towards Ace, who is now carrying his sister and glaring at prince Zeraph. "You can't look at her, you can't speak with her, and you may *not* approach her!"

"Bwother, I wanna say goodbye to my fwend." Nora pouts at Ace while Zeraph is shaking under the elf PRINCE's glare. Nora gently hit her brother with her small fist. "Stop being mean to my fwend! I hate you." The look on Ace's face was so priceless that I had to laugh. Ace gives me an irritated look, making me quickly hide behind Ren.

Soon, we were riding a giant clam that would take us back to shore. We all said our farewells to the two sea princes and waved them goodbye the moment the sea clam carries us up.

I hear someone chewing metal, and I turn to see that Custard has something in his mouth.

"Custard? What's that? Nate, my familiar is chewing something." I tell him. Nate glances down at Custard with a curious stare.

"Hey, little guy, spit that out." He orders and hands the conch to Ace so he could grab what was in Custard's mouth properly. He moves the little wolf so that it is now facing him. "Come on. Drop it."

When the vampire prince tries to grab my familiar's jaw, Custard just grunts and moves his head out of the way. Nate frowns at the stubbornness of Custard.

"Bad boy. Spit it out!" Nate uses his hands to open Custard's mouth. Custard growls, but Nate was too strong, and he finally managed to open the wolf's mouth. The thing in Custard's mouth dropped, and we all looked at the bottom of the clam to see what it was.

It was a pendant made out of gold.

We were still inside the clam, but we all felt the chilling breeze when we realized what was happening.

"OH MY GOODNESS, CUSTARD STOLE FROM THE PRINCES!" I scream in horror. I mean, not only did we-I mean Ace-kill the king, but we also stole from them!

"Should we head back?" Ren suggests.

Custard jump down from Nate's grip and grabs the pendant again. *'Master, I found this in the ground! I never stole it.'*

"Custard, listen. Even if you find it, you simply can't take it."

'I found it on the seafloor! No one owns it.'

Ren opend his palms towards Custard and the little wolf drops the pendant to his open hand.

'Look. It has rust and moss.' My familiar insisted.

Ren brought the pendant up. "It's dirty." He says before handing it to me. "I don't think it comes from their treasury if it's like that."

"Well, I don't want it." I say, pushing the pendant back.

'But, master…I got it for you.'

"Custard, this is not finders keepers you know." I explain to him.

Custard drops his ears and whimpers sadly. At this, the princes and Nora gives me a look that made me feel guilty.

Wow, look at them. They are siding with my familiar now.

Custard's big brown eyes roll around as he looks at me pitifully and he whimpers. I bit my lip as I am too weak to resist that look. I look at the pendant on Ren's hand and snatch it.

"Okay, okay! I'll keep it. Thanks, Custard." I mumble.

At long last, we had reached dry land. We hopped off of the giant clam as we made our way back to shore. The prince's trousers got wet as they walked through the water. A few snorts brought our attention to the 3 horses in front of us. It was Ryde, Garius, and Midnight.

We looked at Ace, and, in return, he raised an eyebrow at us.

"Of course I called them. You think we can walk all the way back to the palace?"

We all shrug and were about to move when Ace stopped Ren. "Take my sister. I need to speak with that." He says and pointed towards me.

"Hey, I have a name." I protested.

Ren appears reluctant to release me into Ace's care. He didn't do anything while he had me on his back besides stand there. I took a look at Ace and concluded that he wouldn't back down unless we agreed to do what he wanted. Nora seemed to be weighing the merits of the two princes by staring at them in a head-to-head comparison. When her attention was briefly drawn away, she flashed her brother an ecstatic grin.

I tap on Ren's shoulder. "It's fine. Meet you with Garius later." Ren gives me one last glance before setting me down. I took my hand and headed over to Ace.

"Be quick." Ren tells Ace a warning before he takes Nora as they make their way to where Nate is with the horses. Soon after they left, Ace took my hand and led me to a comfortable perch on the rocks just above the water. I puzzled over the reason for our meeting as I looked at him.

"Any time now." I told him when a few seconds flew by and he wasn't talking.

"You did good."

I blinked. Did I hear him right? "Pardon?"

"Back at Atla. You did well in using your powers." He wasn't looking at me or even meeting my gaze. "Without you, I wouldn't know if we would have survived." I still look at him, speechless as to what I just heard. Is he complimenting me? There was a slight tint of red on his ears, but I couldn't tell if he was blushing or not since he was facing the other way. "That's why…whatever I said before that upset you…just forget about it."

I tilt my head to the side. "Upset? When?"

"The day we were taken. You were tearing up when I said you mean nothing to me."

I stare at him as I try to remember. "When?"

"When we were taken!" He snaps. "Are you deaf!?"

I remembered him talking at that time, but I wasn't listening. Could he be misinterpreting things?

"Um..." I trail off momentarily. "I don't exactly remember what you were talking about." I laugh nervously and scratch my cheek. "But I didn't cry because I was upset."

"What?"

"I actually couldn't sneeze at that time."

This time, it was Ace who blinks. "You wanted to sneeze?"

"Yeah. But I couldn't because you kept talking about something. Man, you just won't shut up." I chuckle.

"You...!" Ace massages his temples and grits his teeth. His cheeks and ears are beginning to turn red, which surprises me. I couldn't tell if it was from anger or embarrassment.

Either way, I didn't want to miss this opportunity.

I grin teasingly at him and snicker. "Wait. Were you actually worried that you upset me?" My grin grows wider when I see how red his face was right now. "You are!!" I gasp.

"No, I'm not!"

I clap my hands and laugheven more. "Your face! You actually felt bad!" I breathed and started fanning myself. "I should write this in my diary! Imagine. PRINCE Ace. THE PRINCE Ace is worried about hurting my feelings!"

Ace clenches his teeth and ends up giving me the evil eye. Then, with a sneering grin, it appears as though an idea has suddenly occur to him. "Yes. Keep laughing." He smiles evilly and starts to walk away from me. "Keep on enjoying yourself."

I stop laughing. "Ace?" I call for him when I realize what he is doing. "Ace! You do know that I still can't move the rest of my body, right?"

"You can move your arms." He calls out and waves without looking at me. "Crawl if you have to."

This guy! He really is going to leave me!

I try to move my legs but it didn't respond. Damn it. "Ace! Wait. Come on. You can't handle a joke?" I call for him, louder this time. "Ace? ACE!? PRINCE Ace!?"

Knights

I was sitting at the lunch table and listened to their conversation. We didn't have our early morning training today since I don't have a wooden version of the sword that I am supposed to practice with. Plus, I do not have enough magic/mana/power left to even practice my wolf voodoo.

"It's hard to believe that the kingdom of Alta was involved in a trade with Tereau." The Queen, my aunt, said. "It makes me wonder how they were able to reach out to them. The kingdom of Atla never mingles with land-dwellers like us."

"*That's* hard to believe?" I said, with a mouthful of meat. "You should see PRINCE Ace in a dress yesterday. It was very disturbing and fascinating at the same time."

At that moment, everyone stopped eating. Ren, who was seated beside me, handed me another plate of steak while Nate, who was seated on my other side, leaned in.

"Rose? Remember what we talked about yesterday?" He asked me in a very gentle voice as the others watched.

I nod and toke a slice of meat. "Don't mention anything about Ace wearing a dress. If I want to speak, then I should raise my hand." Then I started chewing.

"Can you tell us why?"

"Because I always speak of unimportant matters that lead to bickering or a drastic change of topic."

Then, seemingly satisfied, he placed a hand on top of my head to pat me. "Sorrt, Rose. And stop talking with your mouth full." Looking at one of the servants, he said, "Get her some desserts."

I have a feeling that they were treating me like a child at this point, but I didn't mind. I mean, come on, more dessert? *Yes, please!*

Now that the others were satisfied with my silence, they went back to continue with their boring 'adult talk'.

"Maybe it has something to do with the chalice?" Ren suggested, and I had to give him a look at that point.

Oh, so they let Ren join the conversation and not me!? But all this talk about a chalice is kind of making me remember something. Something important.

"That could be one of the reasons." Ace agreed. "But if that were the case, then why wouldn't that fish prince tell us about this? Did he tell you two about it while I wa resting?" I have to fight the urge to talk and do a correction at his statement. The time that he was resting was actually the time that he was being tied up because he refused to rest.

I sliced up another piece of meat and dipped it in gravy before chewing again. Something tells me that I have to tell them about something, but I can't remember what.

Why do I have the memory of a goldfish?

"He did not. In all appearances, Prince Meruem is a trustworthy individual. All they dealt in was women. They appear to be sending captured women to the rogue king. He has no idea what happens to the women who are transported after that. His father had high hopes for him to carry on the family business after he became king, so he accompanied him on all of their visits. No mention of any chalice." Nate says.

Chalice? Images started flashing into my mind.

A man holding a chalice. An old village. Chantings...

"And I thought that we would finally have some lead on the whereabouts of the Chalice." Ren mumbles.

Didn't I have a dream regarding the Chalice? I raised my hand to talk like how I was instructed. "Excuse me." I speak.

"Dear, not now. We are thinking." My aunt seems like she's in a heavy thought.

"But-"

"Mana, please give Princess Rose some macaroons." Ren calls out in the kitchen doorway.

"Hey! I swear it's important."

"I read the books my brothers gave me. But it would seem that it only gives us a little information about the tamers. Queen, I will write down all the information and I humbly ask that you review it and cross out the false informations."

"Will do. How is her training?"

"Her progress in using her powers is magnificent, even though I hate to admit it." Ace admits.

I fought the urge to boast about what I just heard because I realized that what I was going to say was really urgent. But they were ignoring me.

"Hey...!"

"Her weapon training is on hold until prince Nathaniel can acquire a wooden version of hook swords for practice."

"Can anyone listen to me?"

"Very good. Even though Rose has excellent results in her magic training, please continue to teach her how to fight. A tamer' weakness is their inability to protect themselves when their familiar leaves their side. She needs to protect herself when she is not with her familiar."

"Hey! In case anyone is interested." I slam my hands on the table to get their attention. It seem to work. "I got a prophetic dream about the chalice back in Atla!" I yell.

Finally...FINALLY they stop talking to give me their full attention.

"Back in Atla? Why didn't you say something?" Ren wonders.

"Um..." I scratch my chin as I try to remember. "It's kind of difficult to answer that. I mean, it is a dream, so it comes and goes until something triggers it."

"Rose!" They all yell at me.

"It's the truth. It's the truth!" I say as I sat back down on my seat and cover my face. "I know I make a lot of excuses, but I really didn't remember anything the moment I woke up. I just remembered it when you guys started talking about the chalice!"

Ren gives me an amused look while Nate and Ace were massaging their temples tiredly. The Queen seems like she wants to say something, but purses her lips to stop herself from saying a word. The king simply ducks his head and continues to eat. He obviously doesn't want to be involved in this conversation as much as I do.

"Well?" The queen waits for me.

"Well, what?"

"Your dream, dear. Care to tell us about it?"

"Oh! I dreamt about the late king Varon and Nagga. They were walking somewhere in the woods." I started. "I cannot tell where they are exactly. But suddenly this Ny — thank you, Mana!" I yip in excitement when a plate full of macaroons is place in front of me.

"ROSE!" I jumped at the intensity of their voices when I got distracted with sweets.

"Sorry!" I smile sheepishly and place the macaroon down. I guess I will have to eat it later. "Macaroon?" I offer to lighten up the atmosphere.

"I cannot believe that the fate of this world is in the hands of a girl like her."

"I cannot believe she's related to my sister." The Queen mumbles.

"Now now." It was the king. This was the first time that he had ever spoken since we all sat down. "I want you all to remember that Rosalie is just a young girl from another world. Try to understand her situation. She grew up without knowing about magic."

At the king's words, everyone seemed to finally calm down. Among the others here, the king is the only one who takes my side and treats me like his actual child. The king met my gaze and inconspicuously gave me a thumbs up for encouragement.

Nice to know that someone has my back.

"Where was I? Oh, right. In my dream I saw king Varon and Nagga giving the chalice to this Nymph, saying something like 'it is the only way' or something."

"That's it?" Ace questions.

I shake my head. "No." I furrow my brows as I try to recall the rest of the dream. "In my dream, I was following the Nymph. It showed me the Nymph handing the chalice to a group of people. Like villagers of some sort. It's like another place because the people seemed...um...they were wearing animal skins as clothing. If that makes any sense."

"A village where people wear animal pelts...?" The Queen gives me a questioning look before she turns her gaze to her husband. "Dear, do you know anything about it?"

The king sadly shakes his head. "No, dear, I don't. I have never heard of it. Maybe it's because the dream was already from a long time ago. Maybe the people are modernized in this age."

They all waited for me to somehow confirm it.

"I can't say. But at that time, King Varon doesn't seem to be wearing the same clothing as them. Somehow, I feel like they are cut off from the rest of the kingdom." Then again, it was just a feeling. Custard, who has finally finished eating his meal, jumps on my lap.

"Well, the kingdom of Atla was previously cut off from the rest of the world. I can't see why there won't be others like them." Nate looks at me. "Do you have any more of those dreams? I mean anything that can give us more clues."

I thought about it. "I saw the nymphs gathering in a secluded green area and chanting. They were speaking in a language that I do not understand. And that was it. That was the last of my dreams. Sorry." I look at everyone expectantly as I wait for their reaction. Everyone, except for the king and I seem to have finished our food.

"Well. That was better than nothing." Finally, Ren says as he sags back in his chair.

"I guess, for our situation, it's considered lucky and a blessing. I mean, is it me or does Rose somehow have these specific dreams?"

"It would seem like the spirits are trying to reach out to us through Rose. I mean, I bet she's the only one who can control spirits."

"No need to make it sound like a horror film," I mumble, stroking Custard's fur to distract myself.

"But it did give us a lead." As weird as it sounds, PRINCE Ace sounds genuinely positive. "The Nymphs."

"That is a good suggestion, but how do you suppose we go and look for them?" Nate asks. "It's not like they will magically show up when we ask them to."

"Didn't they appear the night that Rose got lured in the forest? And that time when Rose first bonded with her familiar?" Ren recalls.

I scoff at this. "Yeah. And at first, we thought that the Nymphs were helping me meet Fred. I mean, talk about an awkward conversation there." I chuckle and stop when I see them giving me a look. "Right. Don't speak unless spoken to."

"What the mutt says is right. The last place that the Nymphs showed up was in the forest near the kingdom of Tereau. Price Nate, Prince Ren, and I will go there and check."

"What about me?" I ask at the same time as Custard lets out a whimper. "And Custard?" I added.

"No!" All of them, even the king, disagrees.

Wow. That *one time* where everyone seems to be in agreement is when they disagree with me. I'm glad to be of some use when it comes to unity.

"In case you have forgotten, we are going to the place where we were ambushed by the rogues." Ace points out.

"Dear, you still need to learn how to control - if not master - your powers properly."

"Rose, the rogue king is after you."

"We still have to teach you how to protect yourself."

"Rosalie, my dear, I think it will be safe if you just stay here and let the princes and a few **knights** investigate."

And then there goes my *selective hearing*.

"We have knights?!" I gasp in amazement. My eyes begins to twinkle with interest and excitement. "WHERE!?"

The Queen gives the king a pointed look like she's blaming him for my reaction. "Dear, there is a reason why we keep that information from Rose." At the Queen's gaze, the king immediately slumps in his seat as if it would help him to hide from his wife's glare.

"Where are they? Where are the knights?!" I ask again. I wonder if they are shirtless when they train just like all historical novels that I have read. Do they have abs? I want to know. I NEED TO KNOW!

"Rose. Here. Eat." Nate grabS a macaroon from my plate and place it on my hand. Ren reaches out and slaps his hand away after I start nibbling on the macaroon.

"About going to the area where we last saw the Nymphs? I am afraid that I may not be able to come." Nate speaks shyly, as if he's guilty about missing out.

"Why?" Ace addresses him.

"I have to go back to Denver. My brother may have a wooden version of the hook swords. Plus, I want to come and congratulate him. At least before they held the official engagement party."

I stop nibbling when I look at Nate. As the others sent their congratulations to the young vampire prince's brother, I bit my bottom lip as I noticed the expression in Nate's eyes behind his smile—he's scared to go back.

"Can I come?" I blurt out. "I mean, it is my training equipment. Best to see if I can actually use it."

When I saw that Ace and Ren were about to protest, I added. "Or if not, I can stay with the Queen." I give her a look. "I'm sure she'll enjoy having some *quality time* with me. Right, my *dear aunt?*" I smile sweetly to make sure that my message is received.

The Queen's eyes widens, and she immediately responds. "Prince Nathaniel, I do think that it would be best that she goes with you. I mean, some exposure would do her some good. And maybe she can become friends with another young lady!"

"Your highness, no offense, but won't it be dangerous?" Ren asks in concern. "I mean, there could be the possibility that they might be ambushed."

"I'm right here." I glare at Ren. Since when was he the worrisome type in the group?

"If you guys keep treating me like a kid, then I will never learn." I turn at PRINCE Ace for help. "I mean, ask PRINCE Ace. I helped out a lot. I also learned how to summon Custard." It's a lie. I just got lucky at that time, but it's not like they need to know that. That's for me to know and for them to find out.

Ace gave me a look, and, surprisingly, he nods. "It's good that you admit that you were being spoiled." Leave it to PRINCE Ace to leave out a slight insult before helping out. "And I also think that coming with Prince Nate will do you some good. It's better than you sitting here and doing nothing."

Ouch. At least he's on my side...

"Prince Nathaniel, what do you think?" The queen takes Ace's words into consideration before turning to Nate.

With all the focus on him, Nate appears a little uncomfortable. He then fixed his eyes on mine, and I nodded in support. There is no way that I would let Nate go back to Denver and have his parents berate him again. I know that if Nate does agree then there is a chance that I might disrespect the king and queen, but hey, it is for a good cause.

Just then, Nate leans in to ask. "Is it finally my arc-" Before he could continue, I shoved a macaroon in his mouth.

Damn bastard wants to break the fourth wall again.

"Yes, Nate. We get it. Now, do you agree?"

"I do!" He says it with much enthusiasm than I would have liked. "We can get married in secret on our first date!"

Growling angrily, Ren extended a hand to slap Nate away. Thankfully, I was able to anticipate its arrival and avoid being hit.

Huh. I guess my training is actually paying off.

✳✳✳

Ren, Ace, and a few knights were selected to depart first. Nate and I were told to wait until the area was clear before we could leave. Ren made sure I was hiding my identity by having me put on a hood. He wrapped the hoodie around me and knotted it. He warned Nate several times to make sure the carriage curtains were shut before we set out, saying that he would be held responsible for any mishaps.

Ace finally had enough of the wolf prince's overprotectiveness that he had to drag him out himself. Ace even threatened to cut his tongue to see if werewolf healing could recover a lost tongue.

Thankfully, we never got to know the answer to that.

A carriage was prepared for Nate and I. Since it was a royal visit, we both had to dress appropriately. Nate was wearing a white and gold buttoned coat. A red cape was tied to one of his shoulders that was clasped with golden chains. His now grown red hair was combed back neatly, but bits of stray strands kept falling down over his green eyes.

The restrictive clothes I was wearing made me frown. My dress was a white tube top with a ruffled skirt in white and black. I've put my hair in a half-up style and decorated it with flowers. When Nate took notice of me, he laughed.

"It's been a while since I saw you dressed up nicely." He comments and bent down to scratch Custard's ear when the little wolf runs to greet him.

"Speak for yourself," I start scratching at the spot where my necklace touched. The necklace is the pendant that Custard found when we were in Atla. I was able to clean it up nicely. The pendant was in the shape of a circle with two Viking-like designs of wolves facing opposite directions. The chain hook itself was intact, so I was able to insert a chain to make it usable. I mean, it was either this or some fancy and heavy jewelry. Ever since word got out that I became a princess, my maids have been pretty keen on making me wear one…or a hundred jewelry pieces.

Nate sees me toying with a necklace and grins. "Is that the necklace that Custard found? It's nice."

"Yeah. I just hope I won't get in trouble when Prince Meruem sees this."

"Nah. You won't." He dismissed.

Nate and I soon head for the carriage. Even though there were only two knights protecting us, I couldn't help but sigh in awe at the sight of their gleaming armor. Riding horses, they flanked the carriage on foot. When I peek out the window, laughing, Nate slaps my hand.

"Stop that!" He scolds me. "Don't touch the blinds! We are supposed to keep them close!"

I pout. "But they're knights! I want to stare at them."

"And I am a vampire prince. You can look at me all you want."

If he's a vampire prince then perhaps...

I gasp as my eyes sparkle with an interesting thought. "Are there any vampire knights too!?" I squeal and get my hand slapped again when my hand touches the curtains.

"Rose!"

Ah, right. Curtains are bad. No touchy the curtains...

"But they're knights!" I whine. Suddenly, a slow grin starts to spread on my face, fueled with excitement. "Who could also be **vampire knights**! Hey, would they answer me if I asked them what race they are or is that too rude?"

"And this is why the Queen doesn't want you to know about the knights," Nate grunts and folds his arms across his chest.

Throughout the whole ride, I wasn't able to peek at the knights again. Not with a very grumpy vampire in the carriage, who keeps glaring at me the moment I reach for the curtains.

After a long, painful ride in the pitch black carriage, we made it to Denver. As soon as Nate steps out of the carriage, he turns around to offer his hand. After he had helped me get a footing, I turned around to pick up Custard. I glance back to see that Nate is looking at his old home.

"Home sweet home." He sighs with dread in his eyes.

I place a hand on his shoulder. Nate looks at Custard and I and gives us a smile before offering his hand to me. "Shall we?"

"We shall." I respond by looping my arm with his.

*******Ferius*****

The rogue king, King Ferius, watched as the ice from his glass chalice slowly melts. The trickle of the condensed water diluted his wine. He gritted his teeth and threw the glass away. It hit a nearby wall and shattered into pieces.

He still couldn't believe it. One of his generals, Roy, was defeated by one prince! What a useless man! And imagine that the tamer princess was with him. Leave it to that greedy King Corona Bayrus to keep the good-looking females to himself. He should have known that that greedy pig of a king is useless. Serves him right to die in a brutal way.

"King, the princes and knights have just been spotted walking near our borders." One of his other generals said.

The king raises an eyebrow at him. "Are they attacking?"

"I believe not. It would seem like they are looking for something."

Just then, King Ferius saw a vision of them eating at a dinner table, talking about the wooden chalice and asking the nymphs about it. He grins.

It would seem like *they* are still connected.

"Let them. It seems like they are also looking for the item that I want. It's better that they do all the work for us."

Ghost of the Castle

"Prince Nathaniel." A butler greets us as soon as we enter the palace. Nate, in return, nods his head to acknowledge him.

"Hi, Edward. Is my-" Nate starts off, but I had to gasp loudly at the name of the butler.

"A vampire named Edward!?" When I think of a specific vampire with the same name as Edward in a book I once read, I cover my mouth with my hands.

Edward looks at me suspiciously when he sees my swift response. "Yes...?" He asks while dragging the word out.

Nate put his arm around me to cover my mouth. "Please, Edward. Just ignore her. Where's my brother Adam?"

"Unfortunately, your highness, the king, queen, and Prince Adam are with Lady Gwen's parents. They are finalizing the paper works to make it official." The butler gives Nate an apologetic look. "But I am certain that they will be back anytime soon. Would you and Princess Rose want to have a snack?"

A snack? It's official, Edward is now my favorite butler.

Nate must have felt me talking under his hand because he started to tighten his grip. He turns to Edward and gives him a struggling smile as I try to fight him off of his grip.

"I think I would like to go to our weapon storage and see if we still have Adam's old wooden swords?"

"Which type are you looking for, Prince Nathaniel?"

"Hook swords. Are they still there?"

"Yes. But those are smaller versions. He used those when he was a kid." The look on Edward the vampire's face seemed curious.

"It's not for me." To clear up any misunderstanding, Nate says. "It's for the princess. We are teaching her how to defend herself. Rose and I will head to the room to get it ourselves. And no, Edward, the princess, and I are not a thing." Nate quickly adds when Edward was looking at us as a proud parent. "And least not yet." Nate says, earning a jab from my elbow.

"Well, that is a shame." Edward chuckles and when he notices Custard in my arms, he smiles warmly. "Call me when you need me, your highnesses." He bows, and Nate drags me inside the castle.

Nate still had his hands over my mouth as we kept moving. I was somehow feeling uncomfortable with the situation, so I started to lick his hand — not that kind of lick. Don't be weird. "Gah! Rose." Nate chastises me and finally releases his hold over my mouth. He grimaced at me while I bit my tongue in disgust. "You licked my hand!"

I started spitting. "Pleh! Your hand tastes weird."

I suddenly saw Nate raising an eyebrow and giving me a flirty grin. "Are you trying to *provoke me*?"

"Right now," I show him my fist. "You are trying to *provoke* my **fist**."

Nate laughs and guides me along the never-ending hallway. Rows and rows of painted pictures lined the walls. Empty armor decorations stood as if they were guarding something. I saw a lot of paintings of Adam. Adam with his mother, Adam with his parents, Adam with Nate, and Adam with both of his parents. I rarely see paintings of Nate, or, Nate doesn't have a solo painting of himself unless he is with his big brother. And when he is, he doesn't seem happy at all; just a small smile with a dead look in his eyes. I was so preoccupied with looking for a painting of Nate. At least one painting wouldn't make him seem like an unloved child. I bumped into his back.

"We're here," Nate announces and opens the bronze double doors in front of us. He starts to step in and stops when he sees me following. "Actually, Rose, I want you to stay here. I will be quick."

"Why?" I protest and peek to see all the shiny weapons in the room. They all looked so intriguing that I want to touch them all.

"Look, Rose, I don't want to offend you, but remember the last time that you went inside a room similar to this? It didn't end well." He gives me an apologetic look when he sees me pout. "I promise I won't take long." He utters these words as he slowly enters and closes the door behind him.

Geez. That *one time* I threw a shuriken and they are still holding me responsible for the mess that it caused! Unbelievable.

"It's just you and me, Custard. You and me." I pet my familiar.

Custard suddenly seems interested in one of the paintings. I follow his gaze to see a huge family portrait in front of the room where Nate disappeared. The portrait shows both the king and queen placing a loving hand on a younger version of Adam. The only hand on Nate's shoulder was of his older brother. Adam had wrapped his arms around his younger brother and was cuddling him. Nate simply looked uncomfortable, but the painting captured the small ghost of a smile on his lips. I felt hurt the longer I saw the paintings of the royal family. But something doesn't seem right here.

'*Master. Look.*' Custard speaks through our link.

'*What am I supposed to look at?*'

Instead of answering, my wolf simply gazes at me with his tongue rolled out and wags his tail—some help this guy is. Nonetheless, I look at the portrait again and my vision starts to blur. The only images that were clear to me were of Nate, his mom, and Prince Adam. The king was completely blurred, and I soon realized that I was looking through Custard's eyes. I shook my head, and I am back to seeing with my own eyes.

What was that?

I jump when I hear the door open and quickly turn my back from the family portrait. Nate came out carrying two wooden hook swords. When he sees me, he grins and raises them up for me to see. "Here they are," Nate says. "Kind of dirty but these will do."

He showes me the two wooden weapons. The top part was like a fish hook and the end looked like it was supposed to be sharp. For the hilt, there was a sort of protective guard made out of metal. "Looks like a long fish hook," I observe.

"Hey! These weapons are cool and deadly. They are called hook swords for a reason!" Nate huffs and starts cleaning the dusty pair of swords.

"So basically, they just straightened the body of a fish hook and called it a sword." I point out and enjoy seeing the frustrated look on the vampire prince's face. I see Nate glaring at me and use one of the swords to lightly poke my arm.

I narrow my gaze at him. "Stop that."

Nate grins. "Stop what?" He asks innocently and is now using the other sword to poke me.

"That!" I hiss. When Custard noticed that I was losing patience, he jumped to the ground.

Nate continues to poke my stomach, arm, shoulder, and even use the hook to cover my face with my hair while grinning even wider. I growl and start to retaliate by slapping the wooden swords away whenever they come near me. "Quit it!"

"Look at me. I am Princess Rose. I think hook swords are lame." Nate pokes and prods me with the wooden swords, mockingly.

"I never said that!" I manage to grab one of the swords. I grin and start to pull it away from Nate. Once I did, I felt something prick me. "Ow!" I draw my hand away and see a small wooden splinter. I pluck it out of my hand. "That thing is chipping."

Nate draws the sword close to him to examine it. One of the swords' bodies already has a few chips of broken-down wood. Nate starts touching it and frowns. "I think we can just put some rubber on it. Wait here while I fix it." He says and didn't wait for my response as he disappeared into the room. Again.

I cross my arms over my chest as I glare at the door.

Custard suddenly grabs my dress and starts pulling on it. I turn to him with a raised eyebrow. "Custard, I love you, but you are going to ruin the dress."

'Master! Spirit.'

Custard is looking to his right. I follow his gaze. There, at the corner of the hallway and past the weapons room, stood a man with red hair. I couldn't fully see his face because it was a blur. And his body was transparent enough that I understood what Custard was saying.

I pause, then retreat a few paces. "Nate? Nate!" I quickly ran and started to rattle the door. "There's a ghost! There's a ghost!"

I kick and punch the door at this point. "NATHANIEL!" I scream and stop when someone catches my fist. I looked up to see Nate giving me a look as if I was going crazy. "What are you screaming for? Did you-"

I interrupted him as I pointed down the hall toward where the apparition was standing. "A ghost!"

Nate turns his gaze to where I was pointing. His brow creases in wonder and he turns back to me with his eyebrow raise. "There's nothing there." He says.

"There is. There is!" I insist. The ghost is still standing there.

Custard yips and starts running towards it. "Custard, no! Do not follow it. I will not be like those dumb idiots who follow a ghost and dies first like in the movies!" I yell, but my familiar did not listen. I close my eyes regretfully and sigh. "Oh well. Custard, I will miss you." I whisper sadly.

"Come on." Nate drags me to follow where Custard ran off.

"Nate! We do not follow ghosts. Stop!" I protested, but I couldn't stop walking or I might end up getting dragged across the floor. The little spirit wolf kept following the ghost from corridor to corridor, sometimes stopping to check if we were following.

Soon, we are out of the castle to what looks like the palace's backyard garden.

"How does your familiar know of this place?" Nate asks in wonder once we finally stop. The garden is small, like it was made for only one person. There were a few trees planted near the walls. Varieties of stones and plants decorated the sides. Two fish ponds are to our left and right. I hide behind Nate as I accusingly point at the ghost, that is now standing by the wall.

"I told you that he was following a ghost!"

"Rose, I don't see anyone but you and Custard here." He shakes his head. "But I guess I'll just have to believe you since your familiar led us here."

I look up at Nate. "Where is '*here*'?"

"My mom's garden," Nate whispers. "Hey! Custard, stop." Nate suddenly runs when Custard starts digging at the ground where the ghost is standing. I quickly follow him when I see the ghost disappearing as soon as Nate gets closer. I held Nate's cape for comfort as I looked around us to find the ghost.

I sure do hope it won't reappear in front of us or I will scream bloody murder.

"What's this?"My focus shifted as I look to Nate. He is getting something off of the hole that Custard dug. As soon as it was off of the ground, he dust it clean.

It is an old small wooden chest. Nate hesitates but opens the box anyway. Inside there were dozens of letters and a small torn painting of Nate's mom and... another red-haired man.

"T-The g-ghost." An icy shiver ran down my spine when I recognized the person in the picture. I look closely at the man's portrait. He looks younger than Nate's father. Nate's father has a little rounded facial feature while this man has a strong nose and angular jaw just like...

I swallow my suspicion as I shift my gaze to look at Nate.

...the same features

"Nate I-" The apparition materializes in front of me and seizes my arm before I can finish. I let out a yell as the chill spreads through my body.

"Rose!?" Nate drops the box and grabs. He let out a curse, and I saw him starting to shiver as well when the scene around us began to shift, like our consciousness is getting absorbed somewhere else.

The ghost materializes before us clearly. I could fully see the familiar red hair and green eyes. The man smiled warmly as he gazed at Nate. His eyes brim with tears when he mouths one word that made Nate stumble back in shock. He would have fallen to the ground at that point if I had not kept him steady.

"*Son.*" The words left the ghost's lips.

Hazy Dream

"Nate?" I put my hand on his shoulder and ask out of concern. We stare at the specter. He is still standing before us, looking at him with a mixture of sorrow and pain.

"Rose, he just said son!" Nate breathes out heavily.

"Are you sure he was talking about you and not me?" I didn't know why I said that. All I was thinking about was comforting Nate. It did work, in a stupid sort of way, because Nate looks down at me in a mocking manner.

"Rose, he said 'son'. Not daughter."

"I knew that," I grumble. I love how I can sometime act stupid on purpose and they would think that I am just being my usual self.

The moment that I let go of Nate's hand, he suddenly vanished from my sight. I briefly panic and look around the hazy and foggy area around me.

No Nate. Only the ghost.

I whimper and shakily give a shy wave to the ghost man.

"N-Nate?" I gulp while still keeping an eye on the ghost. It stayed still. It did nothing but stand there and look at me. "NATHANIEL!" I scream with more urgency this time.

"Rose!" Nate suddenly appear behind me with his hand on one of my shoulders.

"Don't just appear behind me and scare me like that!" I snarl as I jerk his hand away. The instant I did, Nate suddenly disappeared again. "Nathaniel!"

"What!?" Nate snaps, his hand is on my arm this time. "Stop yelling!"

"Don't yell at me either!" I retort and yank my arm away in anger. Great. He disappeared again. But this time, he reappeared in an instant while holding my arm firmly.

"No no no! Stop." He immediately said when he saw that I was about to draw my arm back again. "If I lose contact with you then I go back."

"Go back where?"

"The garden. In the real world per say." He explains. "Back there you're…" He hesitates. "You're staring at an empty space."

I cock my head to the side as I fix Nate in my gaze. "I'm what?"

"Nevermind. Look, if you want me to stay, then I have to hold you. Otherwise, you're stuck here. And I do not know how to wake you up either. I mean, I recommend that I stay until we can figure out how to wake you. Do you remember how you got here?"

I thought about it. "The last thing I remembered was seeing the picture and…" I sluggishly move forward while making sure to stay close to Nate and point at the ghost in front of us. "That man touched my arm. And then we're here."

Nate scowls at the man. "Who are you?"

The man only smiles sorrowfully at Nate and makes no reply. Suddenly, the fog starts to lift and the ghost man vanishes from our sight. Nate drew me close as we did a 360 view around us. The mist was beginning to lift, and a recognizable scene was beginning to take shape. Nate and I held hands to keep him with me in this weird dream.

"Nate, this is…" I trail off. I'm not sure if we're where I think we are.

Fortunately, Nate confirms it. "Yeah." He nods. "My home." We were now in front of their castle when he muttered, though I notice that the exterior placement of statues and plants were different. Nate must have noticed it as well, because he appeared equally perplexed as I did.

"This is-" He starts to say but is cut off.

"Terrence, come on!" A young child with red hair who was around 7 years old laughed and began to run *through* us. Nate follows the kid with his gaze, and his eyes widens. "Father?" Now that he's said it, the kid really does resemble the younger Denver king; red hair and a sort of round face.

"Rafael, wait up!" A second kid follows. This one has a darker shade of red hair. He looks younger, and I see his mouth lift up in a beam as he follows the future king of Denver. They run into the woods, tagging and laughing. As soon as they disappeared in the forest, the scenery started to shift.

"What's going on?" Nate spoke in a low voice..

"We're in the past. At least a flashback from the past." I say with certainty. "This is how I saw those dreams back in Atla."

When he looks at me, Nate displays surprise. "Wow. You've started to become helpful." He jokes, making me stomp on his foot since I can't use my hands for fear of breaking contact with him.

We are currently inside the palace, in what I believe to be an office room. The two kids are now teenagers. Rafael slouches on a couch with his head on his fist. The younger one is sitting and reading a book.

A man in his 40s is sitting behind the table. He is wearing a white, fitted coat with gold detailing. His long red hair was tied into a ponytail, with a few strands brushing the sides of his face as he read some files on his table.

"Father, why should I even care about studying!? I will be king someday. We can just hire a smart advisor like Terrence." Rafael points at what I now suspect is his brother.

"Brother, I want to be a knight." Terrence says, briefly looking up from his book.

"Rafael, enough!" The man, the current king in this timeline, and their father bellow in anger. "You are lazy! You are not fit to become king. Maybe I should hand over the throne to Terrence!"

Terrence, gives his father a horrified look as he set down the book. "Father, I-"

"I'm the eldest!" Rafael interrupts him, looking at their father. "You can't just hand over the throne to him!" Rafael was now on his feet. "You're just saying that because you favor Terrence more than me!!" He screams and runs for the door at an incredible speed that reminded me again that they are a family of vampires. The only evidence that Rafael left the room was the loud bang coming from the door.

The scene shifts, and we are now watching a girl with blonde hair walking in the library. She is looking through the books when she happens to bump into Prince Terrence, making him drop a book. They both looked at each other in surprise.

"Sorry!" The blonde-haired girl bent down and picked up the dropped book. "Here." She hands the book to him. When she sees the book cover, her eyes immediately brighten. "Is that Nick Michael's 'Legend of the Faes'?!" She gasps and suddenly stops herself. Her face flushed with embarrassment.

The prince looks baffled at first, but then he starts to respond with a delighted smile. "Yes, it is. I also read 'The Queen's Knight'. Same Author."

The girl's face brightens. Whatever she was embarrassed about earlier seemed to vanish. "I love that! But the ending seems too sad. I would have liked it if the two of them lived happily."

"Well, a knight's duty is to protect their liege. It couldn't be helped." Prince Terrence shrugs and brushes the strands of hair from his eyes. It was getting longer this time—kind of like Nate's hair right now.

The girl pouts. Her green eyes blaze as she readies herself for an argument. "Still, the author could have given them a happy life."

"Maybe the author is just realistic. It did focus on young adults."

"Jeez! Just because you're a knight doesn't mean that you have to be this sour puss!" She huffs angrily. Prince Terrence seems to be so taken aback by the girl's behavior that he looks at her curiously.

"Brother!"

The two were suddenly interrupted when Prince Rafael appeared behind the blonde girl, making her gasp in surprise. She whirls around and comes face to face with Rafael. Her mouth is gaping with embarrassment as she blushes furiously. "P-Prince Rafael." She gasps.

Rafael looks at her with an arched brow and a bored expression. "Who are you?"

The lady did a curtsy as she introduced herself. "Lady Anya Grey, your majesty." Upon realizing that the woman in front of us is Nathaniel's mother, I hear Nathaniel beside me exclaim in shock. We could barely recognize her, as she has a joyful personality in this version.

"Ah, I see. You're one of the ladies my father chose as my potential bride." Rafael rolls his eyes. His tone implied that he didn't care about the arrangement. He turns to his brother instead. "Father wants to see us." After saying that, he immediately left.

Prince Terrence is looking at Anya's dazed look as she stares at the crown prince's back. There was no expression on his face as he follows his brother out of the library.

The scene changes, and we see Anya walking around in the garden with a few maids. In this scene, she and Prince Terrence were facing each other. "I'm sorry!" Anya bows. "I did not know you were the second prince!"

Prince Terrence appears perplexed upon seeing the woman in front of him. "It's fine. I prefer to be a knight more than a prince." He extends his hand to Anya, who accepts it while raising her head to see Terrence smiling at her.

A change of scenery again.

It shows Lady Anya locked in some sort of closet. She is crying and knocking frantically on the door while the other bride candidates laughs, leaving her alone for anyone fortunate enough to find her.

A few moments later, the door burst open to reveal Prince Terrence. His hair was a mess, and he was panting heavily. "Thank goodness, you're alright." Terrence sounds genuinely scared. "I was looking all over for you-" Terrence is cut off when Anya cries into his arms.

"I was scared. I was so scared, Terrence." She lets out a shaky breath.

Terrence can only hug her in return, assuring her that she's now safe. "So was I, Anya. So was I. Starting tomorrow, I will be your escort."

In this scene, it seems like Anya took his words as a worried friend looking out for her, but looking at Terrence's expression, it was already a confession of his feelings to the young noble lady.

The scene kept shifting, showing how Prince Terrence kept glancing at Anya while the lady herself always focused her attention on Rafael. And then we saw how Rafael is seemingly becoming jealous of his younger brother.

"Why can't you be more like Terrence?"

"If only Terrence was the eldest."

"Can our kingdom prosper with Prince Rafael leading?"

The more Prince Rafael hears these words, the more jealous he becomes of his brother. Jealousy transforms into rage, and rage into hatred. One scene shows Rafael sparing with Terrence. The younger prince seemed poised and confident, while the older prince was furrowing his brows in anger.

Terrence would merely block and parry his older brother's attacks, but he slipped the moment something caught his gaze. Rafael took this brief opportunity as he swung his sword and knocked Terrence's sword off of his hands. Terrence crouched down and cast a startled glance at his older brother before turning to look to his right like something is more interesting to him than their match.

Rafael follows his gaze to see Lady Anya looking at him, Prince Rafael, standing over his younger brother with love-struck eyes. The older prince glances at his younger brother and sees a look of hurt in them. Since he now has something that his younger brother Terrence does not, Rafael grins evilly and swears he will never let Terrence have the one thing he desires most—lady Anya.

Another scene shows Prince Rafael standing in front of a crowd with the bride candidates behind him. It appears to be a ball, since all the people were dressed very nicely.

Prince Terrence is wearing a red and white coat as a uniform of the knights and standing beside his older brother.

"I, Prince Rafael, choose Lady Anya as my future queen." He announces as a loud round of applause erupts in the room. Lady Anya is teary-eyed with happiness and delight. Terrence flinched for a bit, but it was immediately gone. Rafael caught it and smirk proudly.

"No offence, but your father is evil." I mumble. "He's marrying your mother for revenge."

"He's a terrible father. I am not surprised by all the things that I'm seeing right now." Nate's gaze is stern and hard like he wants to punch the illusion of Rafael before us.

Fast forward, and we are now seeing Queen Anya carrying a toddler and crying as Terrence cradles her swollen cheek. "This is enough, Anya. Just leave him."

"Adam needs his father. And I love him, Terrence. I can't leave him." She whispers. The child, Adam, simply hugs his mother for comfort.

Terrence furrows his brows. "What do you even see in him? Is he really worth it?" It was a short nod, but it was her answer. Terrence pats Adam's head and gives him a sad smile before turning around. "I love you, Anya. And I mean it. If you ever change your mind about leaving him, I will be waiting." And then he leaves, painfully hiding his sorrowful expression from the woman that he loves and her son.

Something about this is giving me the chills since one could only guess what happens next.

The fog shows us the future of the two, Terrence and Anya, living in a small cot. Adam is jumping on his heels as he tries to see the other baby in Anya's hands. Terrence chuckles and carries the boy to meet his brother. "His name is Nathaniel. He's your brother, Adam."

I knew it.

Still, hearing those words caused me to gasp. Next to me, Nate is shaking so badly that I had to squeeze his hand even tighter to calm him down.

It changes again and again. We saw how happy Terrence and Anya were.

Reading bedtime stories to the kids.

Eating together.

Terrence kissing Nate's forehead...

Then the time came when Rafael and his soldiers burned the cot. Anya and the kids were captured, and Terrence was bloodied and battered as he tried to fight off the other knights. Baby Nathaniel cried, and it became a momentary distraction for Terrence as a knight plunged the blade into his stomach. He coughs out blood and was glaring at his older brother.

"Why do you do this?" He says weakly.

"They are my wife and children! They belong to me." Rafael growls and takes Nate from Anya's arms. "Except for this abomination."

"Rafael, don't! He's just a child!" Anya screams and tries to lunge to get Nate, but the guards stop her. My hands were trembling as I watch Rafael getting a blade as he readied himself to kill the baby. Adam was able to slip through and bite his father's arm. He drops Nate, but Adam was able to catch him.

"Don't hurt my brother!" Adam glares through tear filled eyes as he covers Nate with his small body. "Even though you are my father, I will kill you if you hurt him!"

There was a brief emotion shown in the king's eyes. He suddenly grits his teeth."The child will live." He says darkly. "I will claim him as mine to avoid this scandal, but he will be raised like a bastard. Anya, if I see you dotting on him, I will cut off one of his fingers." Then he turned around to order his men to leave and take his children and wife away. He gave Terrence one last glance. "I will make your child suffer like you made me suffer. If you live, and if I ever see you around, I will kill him." And then they were gone, leaving Terrence to bleed out on the ground as the cot continued to burn.

I was getting dizzy, and when I touched my nose, it was wet. I look at my hand to see blood.

I must be loosing magic just to project this memory. I can only guess that I am already at my limit. Still, I choose to hide it from Nate so we can see what happens next.

Unfortunately, you can't hide blood from a vampire, because the moment that I tried to wipe it off, Nate suddenly grabs my hand and tilts my chin towards him.

His eyes widens for a moment. "Turn it off." He commands with a frown.

"But it's not-"

"Do it now." He says urgently. When I look up at him, his eyes are red. He must have cried earlier and I think that he is about to cry again. "Do it now before I lose you too." His voice cracks.

"I don't know how," I admit. "If I knew, I would have ended it when I saw the ghost in the first place." I laugh dryly.

Nate curses and looks at the scene. "Father," He chokes. "If…if you're there, please release us from this memory. We have seen enough."

No response.

I watch as the cottage is still flickering in flames while Nate is busy calling for the ghost of his father. I see a shadow looming over Terrence's still from the vision. "Nate wait a second. Give it a minute-"

"If you really are my father, then release us now!" This time, he screams loudly.

Before the vision vanishes and we return to the garden, I manage to catch a brief glimpse of the shadow. I blink to shake off the daze from my eyes. I'm feeling pretty light-headed and I can't seem to focus.

I notice Nate wiping away tears as he gazes at the torn-up picture of his father when I turn to face him. He gave one final sniff before turning to face me.

His eyes are red and glinting, but he smiles anyway. "What an adventure, huh?" He chuckles bitterly. Since I couldn't think of the right words to say, I simply nodded and hugged him. I can feel him tensing up, but he returns the gesture.

"Thank you…" He says.

Whatever he was thanking me for, I don't have a clue. I just accepted it and allowed him to cry his heart out.

Drunken Magic

I couldn't help but laugh when Nate and I parted ways. I laughed even harder when I saw how weird and wiggly his face had become.

"What happened? What did I do?" I slur.

"Damn it." Nate curses while trying to hold me steady. My vision morphs making his lips bigger as he talk. Everything around me seems to spin. "You're too drained of magic."

"So what? Not your problem." I snicker and throw my head back as I wheeze.

"Yes, it is. Everyone has a different side effect when they are drained of magic. I guess you're just…a drunken mess." He concludes. Hell, not like it made any sense to me.

I gasp and my head immediately bounces back up. "I'm drunk? What will I tell my mom?" I can feel my face getting pale in nervousness at the sudden realization. "It's my first time to drink and I am underaged!" I grab the vampire prince's collar and start to shake him. "HIDE ME!" I scream.

"No." Nate pries my fingers from his shirt collar with a grunt. "Your mother isn't here, Rose."

Another gasp escapes from my lips when I interpret it in the wrong way. My eyes starts to water. "Y-you don't mean…-"

"No!" He quickly corrects me. "Your mom is alive, Rose. She's alive." I can feel him pulling us both back up to our feet and positions me beside him for us to walk. "Custard, I assume you can walk?" I hear him say it, but I was so focus on a lovely blue rose that I didn't notice my familiar. I did hear him bark in response to Nate. "Good. Let's get out of this place."

I picked up the flower as soon as we started walking and tucked it behind Nate's ear. I start to giggle.

"You're a pretty little thiiing." I drag the words out. Nate did not speak or even try to remove the flower from his head, but I did see his teeth flash in annoyance. I try to poke his fangs, but he moves his head away.

"Cut it out, Rose." He scolds me.

I sulked and stayed put, leaning on him as he led us through the castle. I vaguely remembered Nate cursing and pulling me away from the armor statues in the hallway whenever I tried to touch them. The stingy vampire kept on scolding and nagging me to behave. My hands felt like jelly, and I rolled my head back to avoid hearing his voice.

Nate's hand on my waist trembles as he abruptly stops. When I turned my head again, I could make out three vague figures standing in front of us.

"What are you doing here, Nathaniel?!" Someone scolds him. I was offended by the aggressive tone, so I pushed Nate back, puffed up my chest, and yanked up my tube top, which had begun to slip.

"He lives here!" I yell to the unknown person. "Who are you to yell at him if he goes home or not? YOU LEAVE!!"

Wow. Look at me acting tough in a dress. Ren and Dan would be so proud.

Nate immediately pulls me back and whispers in my ears. "That's the king, Rose. My fath — I mean — uncle." I could vaguely see Nate directing those words to the people in front of us.

My head spins around, and I squint just enough to make out their form. King Rafael, Queen Anya, and Crown Prince Adam were there to greet us. All of their faces mirror each other's in expressions of surprise.

"Nate..." Queen Anya whispers painfully. "How did you...–"

"Does it matter to you?" Nate cut her off. "I didn't come for you anyway. I came here to congratulate the only family I have. Congratulations, Adam." Nate offers his older half sibling a smile.

I grab the blue rose that I place on Nate's head earlier and crush the petals in my hands. Then I approached Adam.

I don't remember why we need to congratulate Adam. My guess is that he has won the lottery or something. Still, I should support him.

"Congrats!" I cheer and make the petals rain around us. I feel Nate pulling me back beside him when I start to trip. I guess he was probably not happy about me littering.

"Are those my blue roses?" I hear the queen wonder when she sees the petals. "Did you.. –"

"Yes, I have. When were you going to tell me that my real father is Terrence? Or were you even gonna tell me at all?" I can hear the hurt in his voice as he says it.

"How dare a bastard like you raise your voice against your mother!" King Rafael's voice booms, making me flinch.

My head is already in pain and hearing this guy yelling only makes it worse.

"How dare a lazy guy like you become the king!?" Hey, it's not my fault if I lost my temper here as I point a finger at the king. For the first time since I got here, I am thankful that I am a princess because what I just "You're so lazy and stupid. Prince Terrence would have been a better king! You simply got rid of your competition. You don't even post pictures of your brother. Why? Are you guilty of killing him? Or are you just too insecure to even see his face knowing that he is that man that you will never be?"

My ears perk up and I squint to see that King Rafael's hand is raised as if he were about to slap me, but Nate has grabbed his hand to prevent it.

"King Rafael." Nate's voice turns deep and threatening. "I would advise you not to raise your hand on the High Queen's blood relative. That is, if you still want to keep this hand of yours." I hear King Rafael yell out in pain, and from the sound of the snap I can only conclude that Nate has done something to his uncle's hand.

And then the scream is followed by a slap. Nate's cheek burns red after the queen had hit him.

"Nathaniel, enough!" The queen orders. There were tears in her eyes as she looks at Nate. Adam quickly pulls his mother back to give Nate his space.

Nate's eyes lacked expression as he reflected on his mother. "You may be my mother, but you lost that role the moment you sided with this man." He says this as he removes his hand from the king's, his expressionless face betraying no emotion. "I am done with this family. I am done being the bastard and the unwanted son. Brother, I will have the servants deliver my gift to you from the carriage. Rose and I will be leaving."

"We are?" I blink.

"Nate, wait." Adam grabs Nate's shoulder. His face etch with pain when he sees the determination in Nate's gaze. "Don't leave this family in turmoil. You can't leave like this."

"I agree." Hell, I don'tremember,r and I do not know what is happening. What I do recall is getting angry at the King, which made me glare and point a finger at him. "APOLOGIZE TO ME! I DEMAND IT!"

Once again, Nate pulls me back to his side the moment I stray away. "Rose, that's a statue!" He hisses.

Now that explains why the King seems to be missing some limbs and suddenly gaining eyesbusts.

"I know!" I lied. "The statue tried to slap me earlier. So ruuude!" I wrinkle my nose and glared at the statue. "So, can you turn me to where the king is?"

"Brother, please." Adam pleads. "You were going to be my best man."

"Can I be the flower girl?" I say dreamily as my head bobs to the side.

Adam stares at me with wide like he is just noticing my current state. "Is she...?"

"She's power drained." Nate confirms and smiles sadly at his brother. "I'll be your best man. But until that day arrives, I don't want to step foot in this house."

While staring intently at Adam, a brilliant idea flashes into my mind, causing me to gasp in surprise. "I have an idea. Why don't we burn their invitation?" I whisper and point at the king and queen. "They seem very rude, like a couple of *K*rens*, if you know what I mean."

"Rose, they're Adam's parents. Of course, they will be invited." I hear Nate sigh beside me, while burying his face in his hands.

"You know where they're not invited? This place!" I glare at the king and Queen and pointed at the door below the flight of stairs to their left. "Get off of my property!"

"How dare a peasant —"

"PRINCESS!" I correct him.

" — like you order me around!? In my own home!?"

"Is it really their home?" I catch Nate's weary nod as I hushedly ask him. I look at the old, cranky vampire again and cross my arms over my chest. "I wanna see the receipt! I want the deed that you own this place. Show me the lawyer and the seller. If not then we will take this to court!"

"Come on, Rose. Let's go home." Nate starts to pull me past them, but I plant my heels on the ground, forcing Nate to bridal carry me instead. We start to head downstairs and towards the door, but I am still glaring at his parents.

"I will post this in social media! You better get ready when the reporters come knocking at your door. I will also file child abuse on your part! Along with murder and homicide. WE WILL MEET AT COURT AND I WILL BE THE JUDGE!!" Just as Nate and I reach the bottom of the stairs, I scream the last part. "Except for you, brother Adam! I will pardon you. I am sure you will be welcomed back to Eden for all your good deeds and right conduct. Congratulations on winning the lottery!"

Adam looks confused, but he smiles anyway. "Thanks…?"

Nate finally set me down so he can talk to Edward, the vampire butler. "Sir Edward, can you get some servants to collect the boxes from the carriage? Those are my gifts for my brother and his fiancé."

I look up at Nate with a pout. "What about my gifts!?"

"Rose, it's –" He immediately stop himself and wipes a hand over his face tiredly. "You know what? Later I will give you some sweets if you behave."

"Yes, sir. I will definitely behave." I nod eagerly and fold the back of my dress and sit on the ground like I used to do back in elementary school.

"Rose, get up. Don't sit on the floor!"

Without a word, I get up. Those desserts had better be worth it.

"As you wish, Prince Nathaniel." Edward bows to Nate.

I sniff and place a hand on Edward the vampire's shoulder. "You may not be THE Edward, the vampire who sparkles, but in a way, I just became a fan of yours. Keep up the good work!"

Nate is pulling me out of the door and towards the carriage. However, before I go inside, I make a beeline for the folks who are wearing shining armor, which I desperately want to touch.

Unfortunately, I had to be dragged into the carriage by some miserly vampire prince. To this day, I still recall the terrifying moment when I was kidnapped and screamed for help. Custard, whom I asked to attack my attacker, was sound asleep in the seat across from me.

Useless wolf…

On the way back, Nate decides to sit next to me after I opened the door when he wasn't looking.

With the lack of anything fun to do in the carriage, my eyes were starting to close because I could not do anything exciting at the moment. I guess it might be because of fatigue or boredom that I finally went to sleep.

***

When I open my eyes, my head is on Nate's shoulder. He's softly prodding me to wake up.

"Rose, we have returned." He says while I rub the sleep from my eyes. "Are you…yourself again?" I look up at Nate to see him giving me a dubious look. I grin and started laughing when his face starts to morph into funny shapes again.

"Nevermind." He mutters and gets off of the carriage to help me down.

The moment I stepped outside, I saw Ace and Ren patiently waiting for us. The sunset hues in the sky made me assume it was growing late. As we were there, I noticed that both princes were looking glum as they waited for us. As soon as we were in striking distance, I made a dash for Ren and seized him by the collar.

"Have you found the treasure?" I asked him quietly and looked around to see if anyone had overheard our conversation.

"What's...wrong with her?" Ren asks while he carefully pries my fingers from his shirt collar.

I see Ace appearing beside Ren. He stares down at me with a raise eyebrow. "You used magic, didn't you? What did you do now?" He speaks in an accusatory tone..

"You know what kind of *magic* your parents didn't use? *Protection*. No wonder you were born." I laugh, and Ren has to move me away from Ace so I won't melt under his glare.

"It's a long story."I can hear Nate talking behind me. "What about your search? Did you find the Nymphs?"

"No." Ren shakes his head. "We didn't, even with PRINCE Ace's magic."

"It appears that the nymphs would only appear when they wanted to." Ace replies. "I don't even know if it is a good thing or a bad thing. If the Nymphs are keeping it safe then maybe it is best that we leave it alone."

"Oh-oh!" I raise my hands excitedly. "I have an idea!"

"Hey, mutt." Ace turns to Ren. "Care to take the princess back to get her some rest? She's more annoying right now than she usually is."

"Come on, Rose. Time to get some sleep." Ren says as he begins to pull me. I put my heel down because I didn't want to move until they heard what I had to say.

"I am trying to help!" I scream.

"Yes, yes. You have been really helpful today, Rose. I mean it." Nate says it with a genuine smile. I have to admit that I was happy that he was feeling well, but I am still pissed that they are ignoring me. *Again*.

"Fine!" I draw my hand back from Ren and wobble a little from the sudden action. "If you won't hear my idea, then ask him instead," I use a portion of what was recovered from my magic to make the ghost of Terrence, who followed us all the way back from Vertez, appear.

The princes follow my gaze, and I could hear a collective gasp of fear and surprise when the ghostly image of Terrence solidified a bit before disappearing because I ran out of magic. I clapped and laughed with my hands like a seal at their reaction before I blacked out.

That's what I get for using too much magic.

Ouija Board

I remember nothing.

The last thing I remembered was accompanying Nate in that horrible dream illusion where I saw Nate's father, the real one, dying.

While pondering over the dreams, I figured out the person that loomed over Terrence just before the dream stopped. It was a Nymph. The same Nymph that my ancestor handed the wooden chalice to, and I know that I have to tell them—the sooner the better.

That was the goal, but when I came to, my body was already dead. What I meant was that I literally could not move a muscle. After using up all of my magic, a doctor came in and told me I would be momentarily incapacitated. Both my aunt and the king appeared concerned, but ultimately glad, that I would be okay in a few days. The majority of my time was spent sleeping. While I had every intention of telling them, all I did while awake was eat. The housekeepers would take care of me 24/7. Even though I was probably out cold, I was still able to hear a few discussions going on around me, though I couldn't make out the speakers.

"…it's been 3 days. You think she'll be fine?"

"Of course she'll be tired. Two straight days exhausting her magic, anyone would feel like their body is made of rock."

"Hopefully we can do something about it."

"What does she mean about asking my father?"

"That's what I want to know too."

I want to go and tell them the truth. To tell them but my body would cooperate. Damn it!

My body feels like it is breaking and burning from the inside. It's agonizing.

One night, I felt someone slipping something on my wrist. Custard made a sound, and I noticed it. There was a loud shushing sound, and I could make out the stranger telling him to go back to sleep. Then the heat stopped, and I could feel my body starting to cool down. When I woke up the next day, I was feeling much better and completely back to my usual arrogant self. There was some type of odd charm on my wrist—a genuine leather wristband.

I was eating breakfast when the princes came to visit. The maids immediately placed a shawl over me before they allowed them inside.

"Hey." I greet them before shoving a mouthful of eggs in my mouth. The yolk drips and drops from my lips and onto the white bedsheets. A petite maid immediately comes to my side and wipes the yolk from my face.

The princes walks with grimace on their faces as they watch me eat.

Can they blame me? For the past few days, all I ate was soup and some porridge. I deserve to splurge a bit with my appetite. I watch as the maids quickly prepares seats for them at the side of my bed. Ren is sitting the closest to me, next to him is Nate, and finally Ace.

"Slow down. No one is going to steal your food." Nate says as he watches me eat.

"Yeah." I nod and point at Ren with my fork. "Except for teen wolf over here, who's eyeing my bacon!" I glare at Ren and move my plate away from him. "Get your own!"

"I-I wasn't looking at the food!" Ren blushes. What a liar.

Nate laughs next to him. "Care to share where you were looking at?" Nate bite his lips to prevent himself from choking. My eyes goes wide when I realize what Nate just said. I immediately pull the shawl back to cover my bare shoulder before I point a glare at Ren.

"And I thought Nate was the pervert!" I yell. This time, Ren was the one who laughs while Nate has a look of disbelief on his face.

"I wasn't the one who looked! It was this mutt right here!"

"Foul! Both of you." I whisper sinisterly at them.

"I swear every time you open your mouth, a fucking argument starts." Ace sighs in his hands. "We came here for a purpose. You mentioned before about Nate's father—"

I gasp loudly. "How do you know about Nate's father?!"

"He told us everything." Ren said.

"What a scandal, right?" I whisper to Ren, who is basically as nosey as me when it comes to scandals.

"I know!" Ren whispers back in agreement.

"Can you both stop talking about me like I am not here?" Nate groans.

"Yeah, right." Ren snickers and turns to me. "You know, this guy tried to leave because of that. He said that since he is basically a bastard son, he is not a prince. What an idiot."

I turn to Nate. "You tried to leave? Are you nuts!?"

"I wasn't gonna. It was more like stepping out of the king's candidate. I am not a prince." He says solemnly and I gesture for him to come close. Nate gets up from his seat and gives Ren a look. Ren nods and hands me something from his pocket. I unfurled the white glove and slap Nate's face.

"Prince Terrence is your father, and the king, even though he has a rotten reason for it, adopted you officially, which still makes you a prince, you dumb*ss." I scold him.

Ren laughs. "She actually got you there."

Nate pouts and returns to his seat while clutching the cheek I slap.

"Are you guys finally done? Can we go back to the main topic?" Ace said while massaging his temples.

As I ask my maids to leave the room, I feel embarrassed for getting sidetracked once more and turn my attention back to Ace.

I told them about the last thing that I saw in the dream. About the Nymph coming to aid Prince Terrence.

"So where is Prince Terrence now?" Ace asks. He made sure that he would be the one talking so that the topic would stay on track.

"Uh..." I look around the room for any sign of a ghostly transparent image of Prince Terrence. Thank God there was none. "No idea. He's not here right now."

"Do you have any idea how to get in contact with him?" Ace asks.

"I'm a tamer and not a spirit whisperer!" I remind him. "If you want to go talk to a ghost, then get an Ouija board or something." I wave my hand in the air in a joking manner.

"What is this Wija board?" Ace suddenly leans forward while showing interest. He must have known that the thing I'm referring to is from my world.

Ah, right. I almost forgot that Ace is the human realm's fanboy.

"Ouija Board. Not wija." I correct him. "It's this rectangular board with a bunch of letters lined up. The material is similar to that of book covers."

"Does it flip and have this triangular shape stone with a circular hole?"

I give Ace a look of both surprise and fear. "How'd you know that?" I ask suspiciously. My gaze zeroes in on him while I study him. "Are you secretly summoning undead spirits to join your demon army so you can become the demon lo–" Before I can finish, Ace is up and on his feet.

"Mutt, carry the princess to the library. Fangster, make sure the mutt doesn't do something funny." He hands out orders as quickly as he is on his feet.

"MY BACON!" I scream and reach out to grab a few bits of bacon before Ren carries me. Ace ties the shawl securely over me before snatching the bacon from my hands.

"We're going to the library! No food is allowed." LIBRARIAN Ace says before we move out of my room with me screaming and yelling about my unfinished breakfast.

***

I can't believe my eyes. Ace actually has a Ouija Board! I knew it. He practices dark magic and summons evil spirits to curse us all! Maybe he is the reason that I have a lot of bad Juju!

"For the last time, I never used this to curse people!" Ace slams his hands on the wooden table. The Ouija board moves and the planchette flipps over. "I don't even know the purpose of it!"

I was sitting on the other side of the table, with the board facing me. "Riiiiight." I nod suspiciously, but my eyes never leaves his.

"Will you show us how to use this or not?! Make your choice before I wrap that shawl and choke you!" Ace screams.

I swear, we don't even need to summon an evil spirit. We have one here right now— one with large and pointed ears.

"Yeah, yeah." I roll my eyes and drag the board closer to me. To be honest, I don't know how to use this, and I could never do it in real life because I am scared as heck when it comes to ghosts. But I do know a thing or two about it from reading. That is, assuming that the sources that I read about them are reliable.

"Grab this triangular thing like this. Make sure not to block the hole. All of you." I give them instructions and demonstrate how to use the planchette. It surprised me how cooperative the princes were, so I can only assume that they are genuinely unaware of the danger posed by this spirit mojo.

"Now what?" Nate asked. Good question! I also want to know what.

"Listen guys." I say in a serious tone. "Before we begin, I want you all to know one rule. Once we start, never let go of this thingy here." I point at the planchette. "If you do, you will be possessed by an evil spirit."

"Nate's father doesn't sound like an evil guy. His real father that is." Ren points out.

"We are not sure if the spirit that answers is Nate's father. That is why when the glass starts moving, we ask the spirit of its name. They cannot lie." I explain.

"Why?" Nate asks.

I gave him a piss-off smile because I know that I will have to invent some b*llsh*ts again. "They respect the board, okay!? The board is magic like the floor is lava. Stop asking questions! Just don't release your hold on the stone. And don't press too hard or the spirit won't be able to move it."Turning to face Nate, I gave instructions. "Nate, you go and call your father's spirit. I bet he will easily answer you."

"How do I do that?"

"I don't know! Think of something. I can't be the only brain around here." I huff.

"Brains? I can't believe you have the *audacity* to say that." Ace replies and gives Nate a pointed look. "Hurry up and call your deceased father before I let you meet him. My way." He whispers the last words as a warning. I guess that his patience is starting to wear thin.

"Father? Hey, dad!" Nate quickly calls out after Ace's warning. "If you are here then, please. We need answers." We waited, and soon the planchette starts to shake. "Father, is that you?"

The stone starts to move.

'YES'

Nate and Ren flinch, while Ace and I remain stoic. I wonder if they know that I was the one who moved the planchette? Nah. They forced me to play this game while I am having my breakfast. This is on them.

"It works!" Ren looks scared, and I have to use my other hand to remind the wolf boy not to remove his hand from the stone.

"Ren, do you want the spirit to haunt us by moving away?! Are you crazy?!" I hiss at him. "This is crucial! If we mess this up, then it is over."

"I can't believe it actually works." Nate mutters in awe while Ace is fixing a look at me. I avoided his gaze as I continue to explain.

"Now we can all ask a question from him. For example." I cleared my throat. "Is it true that a Nymph came to aid you?"

'YES'

"Are you really Prince Terrence?"

'YES'

"Am I really a powerful tamer?'

'YES'

"Is Princess Rose smart?"

'NO'

Huh? Strange. I was trying to move the answer to 'yes', but it seems like someone other than me is controlling the planchette.

I blink and look up at Ace. Seeing the gaze that he's giving me, I gulp.

He knows. He knows that I have been faking it all this time, while Ren and Nate actually believe that we are talking to Prince Terrence. Now Ace is looking at me and urging me to admit the truth.

I look away immediately.

"If I am not smart, then do you consider me a genius?" I ask and force the stone to move. As if I am backing out now.

'YES'

"Give us one word to describe the princess in front of us." Ace ask.

'P-H-O-N-Y' The stone spells out the words on the board. I'm pretty sure that Ace is the one who moved it.

"If PRINCE Ace becomes a creature, what sort of creature would he be?"

'G-R-E-M-L-I-N'

Ace glares at me while Ren and Nate exchange a confused look.

"Are…Are you really prince Terrence?" Ren looks doubtful at the exchange.

'G-E-T-L-O-S-T' Ace spells out.

"Oh my, my my." I say through gritted teeth as I glare at Ace. "It would seem like an evil spirit is fighting with prince Terrence! Don't you agree, PRINCE Ace?" I challenge him.

"Well, maybe the evil spirit is actually trying to stop a certain spirit from fooling around!"

"Hey, spirit," I start. "On a scale of 1 to 10, how much of a d*ck is PRINCE Ace?"

'11'

"Who's the ugliest and stupid looking princess in the whole kingdom?"

'R-O-S-E'

"Who does Nora like more? Me or her brother?" I speak the words out slowly like I am asking him for a challenge. I should have known that this siscon considered it an act of war when I mention his sister, because right now, we are fighting to spell our own name with the stone. Poor Ren and Nate were utterly confused about what was happening, but they were focusing too hard on the board as well.

"WHERE IS ROSE!?" The door to the library suddenly burst open and we all scream.

In shock, our hands flew as the stone fell to the ground right away. Concerned that the spirit's connection had been broken, Ren and Nate begin to panic.

"We're gonna get possessed!!" Ren yells.

"Father, please have mercy. I promise to talk to you every night, just please do not do harm to us!"

"Relax, you dolts!!" Ace glares at me after snapping at them. His gaze sweeps over the others before it settles on me. I wince and turn my head away as I innocently begin to pat my lap. "It was her all along. She's moving the stone." Ren facepalms while Nate gives me a dead look.

"Hey!" I point a finger at Ace. "You moved it too!"

"Only because you moved it first!"

"ENOUGH! How dare you ignore the presence of the queen!" My aunt says as she makes her way towards us. The princes all bow to her while I only look up at my aunt.

"Oh, you're here?" I try to flash her a cute smile, but when I saw her look, I immediately add while spreading my hands in the air. "Sweet aunty! I missed you so muc–"

"Princess Rosalie Amber Stan!" Her voice resembles that of a parent scolding their children, making me flinch. Full name. I must be in trouble.

She slams a piece of paper onto the table. "Why did I receive a letter of complaint from the King of Vertez?! He told me you disrespected him and called him names. Even telling him to show you the deed to his own palace. You even threatened to sue him!?" Ace and Ren share a look of surprise on their faces while I sit there looking confuse.

That son of a rat! How dare he make such lies!

"That's a lie! I didn't even meet them while I was in Vertez. That lying sneaky son of–"

"Actually, it all happened when Rose was drained from using too much magic. I couldn't stop her because I was in emotional turmoil as well. I'm sorry." Nate bows his head to the Queen and apologizes.

"Prince Nathaniel, matters like this you should have told us sooner."

"Sorry, your highness."

I tap on Nate's shoulder. "What else did I....do? I really don't remember anything."

Oh, God. I hope I did not do anything embarrassing again.

Nate taps his chin unfortably like he is recalling something embarrassing. "You littered some blue petals, yelled at the king to apologize to you, told my brother to burn my parent's wedding invitations, and you said you would welcome Adam to Eden?"

My head is spinning as blurred images starts to flood my mind. Some of what Nate is saying starts to take shape in my head like the blue petals raining down and the screaming at the king. I mean, the king is a douche, but I might just have started a conflict or a war with the kingdom of Vertez for what I have done.

"I guess that since Rose didn't do it on purpose then I'll just have to explain it to the king." The queen sighs.

There's a bark at the library door and we all look to see Custard running towards us. *'Master!'* He speaks urgently as he hops on my lap.

"Alright." I scold Custard the moment he is in my arms. "Where have you been, young man?"

Ren comes to my side and lowers his head to Custard's face. "He has something in his mouth." Ren grabs to pick it up. Custard simply drops the item on Ren's hand. It was the pendant that he found in Atla.

'Master, I found the pendant that you lost!' He wags his tail and declares with pride..

"Um...right. Good job." I smile and pat his head. I wasn't even looking for the pendant, but Custard seems to have this idea that it is important to me or something.

Ren screeches out of nowhere and places the pendant on the table. "Ghost!" Ren points behind Ace. We all turn to look but there is no one behind Ace. I stare at the pendant that Ren drops.

Come to think of it, I was wearing the pendant when we came to Vertez and saw Terrence for the first time. Now Ren touched it and claims that he saw a ghost.

I reach out to touch and grab the pendant before looking at the spot where Ren last pointed. There, standing a few feet behind Ace, is Terrence looking amused.

'Master, the pendant allows the holder to fully connect with spirits.' Custard says through our link.

Well, NOW you tell me, Custard. NOW you tell me.

Enchantment

"EEP!" I shiver and throw the pendant towards my aunt. Unconsciously, my aunt catches the pendant. We lock gazes, and I point to where I last saw the ghost of Terrence. My aunt follows where I point with her gaze, and she lets out a horrified gasp.

"Good heavens!" She yells and throws the pendant. It flies in the air before Nate catches it. His mouth drops as he looks back at Ace, and the pendant begins to fall from his grasp. Just as it was about to fall, Ace reached back and grabbed it.

Unlike the rest of us, he dares to approach the spot where Terrence is standing.

"Late Prince Terrence." He bows. I have to slap a hand over my mouth at the ridiculous image of him talking to an empty space. "I am the 3rd prince of the elven kingdom. My name is Prince Ace Feradin." There's a pause until Ace speaks again. "Pardon?" He waits, like he is listening to Terrence talk.

Then, he turned his head to look at me.

Uh oh.

I guess I can consider that my cue to leave.

"Come here." He orders firmly like he reads my mind. I remain seated on the chair and give him a very sweet smile.

I shake my head as I laugh amusedly before I answer him. "No."

"Prince Terrence is asking for you."

"*And I am not asking for him.*" I wheeze because I don't want to see any more spirits or I might start having nightmares.]

Ace begins to walk around the table, so I do the same to keep him on the other side. Ace scowls and makes preparations to move. I move as well, and it appears at this point that we are engaged in a game of "catch the mice."

I smile sheepishly to return his leer.

"What are you doing?"

"What are *you* doing?" I retort.

"Prince Terrence wants to talk to you."

"A conversation needs two willing parties. I am not willing to talk to anyone at the moment."

Ace starts moving again, as do I. "Nate is the son. Let him talk to him. Let them have a father and son moment so he can scold his son for being a pervert." I was just moving around Nate when he suddenly grabbed me. I turn to the empty space where I last saw Nate's father. "See, sir Terrence? Your son is a pervert. Slap him with your ghostly hands, please."

"Keep her there!" Ace jumps over the table to reach us quickly. I squirm and yell when Ace gets closer.

As a means of self-defense, I raise Custard to Ace. When the demonic elf prince looks at him, my familiar lowers his ears and starts to cower.

Some protector he is.

Ace grabs one of my hands making me drop Custard. The small spirit wolf lands on his feet and runs towards Ren, who picks him up comfortingly.

"Can we talk about this?" I offer when I see that he is going to drop the pendant on my open palm.

"An idiot once said that a conversation needs two willing parties. For the record, I am not willing to talk to you." Before I can protest, the cold metal of the pendant is now on my open palm. The image of Prince Terrence suddenly appears beside Ace, making me scream. Terrence just laughs silently at my reaction.

"H-Hi?" I say nervously and swallow the rest of my scream. Prince Terrence still has that amused look on his face as he nods in response. He turns around and starts to head towards one of the walls. The ones with a lot of hand drawn maps of the kingdom. He points at the largest one and looks back at me. I follow his action and point at the same map.

"There." I say. "It would seem like Nate's daddy wants that map."

Nate gives me a look. "Don't say it so weirdly or others might get the wrong idea."

When I point, Ace goes in that direction and checks out the map. He turns to address my aunt. "May I, Your Majesty?"

"Yes." The queen nods. "Whatever Prince Terrence needs."

With the queen's approval, Ace tears the map off of the wall and heads back to the table. He set the large map down and pins the corners with books that were scattered around. We all gather around it along with Terrence. His ghostly image briefly disappears under the light. He looks up and catches my gaze. He starts to point to a spot on the map.

"Here." I place a finger at the area where the prince Terrence seems to be very interested in. The queen and the princes follows to where I point.

To my surprise, Ren pinches my cheek. "I like it when you joke, but I don't think that this is the time for you to be fooling around."

"Ouch! Hey!" I growl and slap Ren's hand from my cheek. "Who says I'm fooling around? I'm serious! Ask him yourself!" I hand him the pendant. Upon setting his gaze on it, Ren slowly retreats.

And I thought he was a wolf, but he is just a pussy.

"Dear, that area is a dead man's grave." The Queen informs me. "There is nothing in that area." She again points towards the direction already specified by. "There is a reason why it is marked as black."

"What are you talking about? It's green. Doesn't that indicate that there's plush vegetation there?" All of a sudden, all eyes are on me. From their gazes, it seems like they are looking at me in a another perspective. "What? Did I do something again?"

"Rose, it's a hollow shape. There's no forest there." Nate says.

"Then why would the map say that there is? I swear I am not making this up!"

"There is nothing there. I don't feel anything either." PRINCE Ace confirms. Then he leans in towards me curiously. "Are you really telling the truth? Because in the map, all we see is this vast gapping space here. No indication of a forest or anything alive."

"I know I fool around a lot, but I know what I am seeing. And I clearly am not color blind." I give Ace a convincing look as I turn around. Fortunately, it appears that he has grasped something, or at least has a general concept as to why we are not seeing the same thing.

"Perhaps there is a reason why Prince Terrence asked to communicate with you. Tell me, what is he doing now?" Ace crosses him arms and focusing his attention on me.

I bring my attention back to Prince Terrence to see that he is already standing beside me. He starts to move his lips like he is trying to convey something to me.

"Dude, increase the volume, please?" I know that it is futile, but at this point, we won't be going anywhere if I can't understand him.

"What's going on?" Nate asks upon noticing my distress.

"How should I know?" I whine. "Someone pressed the mute button on him. UNMUTE HIM!" I scream to no one in particular.

"Stop screaming and focus on reading his lips!" Ace suggests.

"Stop telling me to do what I can't do!"

"Then give it to me!" Ace snatches the pendant from me, and I instinctively move it away. With an eyebrow raised, Ace looks at me, and I smile sheepishly as I hand him the pedant.

"Sorry. Old habits."

Once the pendant is with Ace, the ghost of prince Terrence disappears, to my relief.

We all watch as Ace stares at an empty space, where I assume is where Prince Terrence is standing. It took a while before PRINCE Ace speaks again.

"Those who lived and those who are born in this realm shall be blinded." He translates and turns his gaze back on us. "He says those are the enchantments of the Nymphs."

"Totally understand you." I clap my hands unenthusiastically. Here we go again with the mythic riddles. I sure am getting tired of them.

I mean, what is this? A fantasy novel?!

"It means that even though you are originally from this world, you were not born here. Therefore, the enchantment of the nymphs doesn't work on you." Ace explains.

"Oh, I see." I nod and smirk arrogantly at everyone for being special. "In other words, it makes me precious!" I boast and tilt my chin up proudly, cackling like loon.

"Yes, and if we are to find the Chalice then you are going to have to come along with us." Ace deadpans. "You are the key that can lead us towards it."

"Of course!" I pause as I realize what I just agreed to. My smile diminishes, and I turn to him with a look of horror, hoping that I heard him wrong. "Wait, what?"

"We have the location. We waited long enough." The queen adds while I am just standing there dumbfounded. "Hurry along, dear." My aunt tells me. "Make sure to pack lightly."

"Hold on. Don't I get to say something?" It seems like I, the special one, is getting ignored, now that they have found a lead to the chalice.

"When are we going to leave?" Ren asks while brushing Custard's fur with his hands.

"Tomorrow. We leave tomorrow." Ace, who is always the acting leader of the group, says.

"Oh, come on!" I whine and slump on a chair while the others are already planning our departure for tomorrow.

No one even considered that I had just recovered! I still want to go to sleep. I want to enjoy some real food in the palace. I want to enjoy my warm and comfy bed and not go traveling again!

I can already feel my introverted self crying from the inside.

I hate the sun. Most importantly, I hate waking up early!

I glance at the Ouija board one last time before their planning comes to an end. Maybe this thing really is cursed after all.

I'll burn it,t and I will make sure to bury the ashes is Ace's room.

About the author

Kiraran is a writer who works on a variety of online platforms. She currently has six works published online and two novels published by Ukiyoto Publishing. Wattpad has a list of her works available as previews.

www.ingramcontent.com/pod-product-compliance
Lightning Source LLC
LaVergne TN
LVHW091631070526
838199LV00044B/1015